Levees Break

a novel

by

Vince Moore

Bayou Noir Press

Levees Break

by Vince Moore

Copyright, 2007

All Rights Reserved

ISBN: 9798550401439

Bayou Noir Press

Prologue
August, 2005
New Orleans

The industrial music in the Dungeon, a goth club in the French Quarter, was still pounding, but Dirk had a temp job in the morning. It was time to head home and get some sleep before answering phones as a receptionist for some part of corporate America that could care less about him or any other individual.

Dirk waved to some of his friends. They were his people; some he knew well, and some were new to him. He made it downstairs and past the beefy bouncer who always wore Hawaiian shirts and always looked at Dirk and the rest of his dark friends with contempt.

"Nice shirt," Dirk said scornfully as he walked by. The guy didn't hear him. His orange earplugs were always in place.

By the time Dirk had walked a few blocks, the ringing in his ears had let up. Then he saw one of them. It was muscular, wearing old clothes and a face with no features—its forehead sloped down to its low cheekbones and the mouth was just a shadow. The rest of it looked like a person. It turned its head and, despite not having eyes, it looked at Dirk.

"Oh no," he said. "Not again." He started hurrying along Royal to get out of the French Quarter and home in Faubourg Marigny. It was following him, floating along behind him.

Before he got through the next block, he felt the ghost's icy claws on his shoulder. It pulled him back, lifting him off the ground.

"No!" he shouted and, from somewhere inside him, he pushed back...no, he *pushed*. Solid flesh was under his hands. He could feel bunched muscles, and he slipped loose.

Dirk ran. Full speed. It wasn't until he got home that he noticed the blood on his shoulder. It was still seeping through his Type O Negative—a band he followed-t-shirt and down his skinny arm, making his spiked bracelet slip against his wrist when he moved.

The small wound was nothing compared to his excitement. He got away from the ghost. More importantly, he touched it. He pushed the ghost and made it solid. Breathing heavily, he thought about what he had done. He was still high when the ghost grabbed him, but all his life he'd been seeing them, sober, high, drunk. At first they just watched him. Then they started pushing him, but when he'd try to push away, his hands went right through them. This was the first time he had touched them.

Thinking about it as he showered and dressed his wounds, he remembered what his mind was doing when he *pushed*. If one of them got close again, he'd try pushing, but he wasn't going to go look for them. Maybe this was a fluke. He was no hero. He wouldn't go looking for them to test his newfound ability.

"Don't you have a job in the morning?"

His roommate Lex had come back from the club to find Dirk sitting in the small kitchen with a cup of hot chocolate. Dirk's makeup was all washed off and he sat in sweat pants and a white t-shirt.

"Yeah, I just can't sleep," Dirk said.

"Mind if I turn on the TV?"

Dirk nodded. Lex always had the TV on. It stopped bothering Dirk a long time before.

A half hour later, while Dirk sat staring at a cold cup of chocolate, his roommate called to him.

"You should see this," he called.

Like a ghost himself, Dirk moved into the cramped living room. On the twenty-seven-inch screen, the Channel 6 news was on. Some hurricane expert was saying that the coiled mass of greens, yellows, and reds on the screen was heading right toward New Orleans.

"They're saying we should evacuate."

Dirk nodded. "You going to?"

"I don't know. That looks pretty bad."

"If you go, can I catch a ride with you?" Dirk didn't have a car.

Lex nodded. "Let's decide in the morning. But we should pack up our bags just in case."

Chapter 1

When the skinny little Emo kid came by asking about Karate lessons and how much I'd charge for private instruction, I was tempted to tell him to keep walking. I live in New Orleans and have seen lots of Emo and Goth kids all over the French Quarter, but that doesn't mean I like them. To me, they're like the homeless guys who come up and bet me they know where I gots my shoes. I'm no tourist, I know I gots my shoes on my feet. As for the Emo kids: I suppose they'd be OK, if it weren't for the whiny attitude; it doesn't work in the martial arts.

Since Katrina and her bitch-sister Rita, I've been reestablishing my business, so I wasn't about to send a paying customer away. I didn't have the hundred or so regular students required to stay in the black, so every little emo bit counted. As it was, I was teaching part-time at Tulane and Loyola Universities, as well as Delgado Community College to tide me over until things picked up. I had been displaced, but the cold climes of Ohio were just a memory again. From the sour beer and sewer smell of Bourbon Street to the zydeco pouring out of every souvenir shop to the street musicians and fortune tellers to the blistering summer heat, I was glad to be back.

"I mean, I really have to know how to defend myself quickly. Can you do that?" he asked desperately, his mascara-rimmed eyes wide and full of hurt. I immediately regretted my first impression of him. My heart went out to him like it would to a hurt puppy. Maybe the poor boy was being beaten up in a relationship or at school. He might have been out of school and in college or of college age. Damn college kids keep getting younger and younger while I stay the same. And Emo, the emotional, nerdy goth fashion, with its tight-fitting black shirts, pale faces, and mascara, makes kids look younger. He wasn't a pretty boy, but the make-up and fashion was probably enough to turn him from unattractive to attractive to some.

"We can do that. It'll take a lot of work, though. And if you want to be good in all situations, it'll take much more time." It was pretty much the party line. People often came to me for quick results. A week later, they were a dim memory to me and their Karate training was even dimmer to them. On the other hand, I established my reputation by being able to teach people very quickly. But for that, people had to really apply themselves.

"Why do you want to learn?"

"I don't think you'd believe me if I told you," he said.

"What's your name?"

"Dirk Hemlock."

I almost went with my first impulse, but I didn't kick him out. Instead I laughed a little.

"Of course, I should have known."

He didn't bat an eye at my sarcasm. He had probably heard worse. He wasn't going to leave, though.

I told him the costs and we arranged times for practice. We arranged for two private lessons per week and one group lesson with other beginners. If he did well, he'd move up to intermediates. While we were doing the paperwork, five of my senior students came in for their advanced class of brown and black belts. Joe, who was one of the black belts, looked at the boy and then at me, pointing to his own face.

"You'll have to take out all that, uh, jewelry when you practice. I don't want your nose or lip rings pulled out, or any of the other things," I told the kid.

He nodded. "Is that a class starting? Can I watch?"

"Sure."

After a quick explanation of our protocols—bowing, shoes off, and holding tempers—we went into the open space.

"Gentlemen," I announced—the two women in the class hadn't arrived yet, "this is Dirk Hemlock. He's going to be joining us, mostly in the beginner classes, but he wanted to watch us today."

The guys nodded, grinned at his name, shrugged, and continued their warming up. The girls arrived within minutes and warmed up as well.

My school isn't as formal as the traditional martial arts school. I teach the appropriate bows and traditional stuff, but that's only because when we go to tournaments those things are required. When I was beginning in Karate, if I was late, I had to do ten push-ups for each minute I was late. I wouldn't make Heather and Diamond do any push-ups, but I didn't explain the presence of the observer.

After half an hour of going over the basics, we got to the serious stuff. For young Dirk's edification, we did some self-defense that he would be able to learn pretty easily. We were hitting pretty hard, which the kid would work his way up to, but the moves were basic. If he stuck with it, he'd be able to buckle the bag in the spine-jarring way my students were doing. I knew, from his registration forms, that two of my advanced students in that class were younger than the boy, but my people were proven quantities. And although we joked around a lot, I knew they were maturing…most of them had been training with me for five years now.

Out of the corner of my eye, I saw the kid practicing what we were doing. He experimentally elbowed one of the bags with a water-filled base that the children and the aerobic kickboxing students used.

He wasn't getting much power, and Joe wandered over and gave him some advice. "What you wanna do is *extend* through the bag," he said. "Your energy is coming from the ground. Think of it as holding a fire hose. You brace yourself against the ground, then hit through, like the water coming out of the hose. Does that make any sense?"

Hemlock nodded nervously at Joe. Joe was a formidable-looking guy and his unsolicited advice probably scared the kid as much as it helped him.

Still, I noticed he bit his lower lip and tried again. Joe watched him, nodded, and went back to his own training.

After a few tries, Hemlock was going at it like the black belt students were doing to the much harder and heavier hanging bag. His hits were weak and not coordinated very well, but he was hitting in earnest. He definitely needed to hit something or someone. I decided to invite him to join us toward the end of class. I would also ask again why he needed to learn to defend himself. Not only was I curious, and telling me I wouldn't believe him was the sort of thing that would only add to my interest, but by knowing about his tormentor, I could better design his self-defense program.

"Not scared away yet?" I asked after the class was finished. The rest of the senior level students were hanging around practicing.

He shook his head.

"Would you like a lesson now?"

"Yeah."

I started showing him what to do if someone grabs him from the front. There has got to be a hundred different responses to this, but I didn't burden him with that fact. It's better to know one move well than to know a hundred moves without being able to use them.

After he got a handle on one move, I had him add the elbow strike he had been practicing when the class had been working out.

"What do you think of Mister Hemlock?" I asked the students who were still around after Dirk left.

"Nice name," Joe said. "Dirk Hemlock. Yeah, right."

"Like we should talk, Spider," I said. Almost all of us had nicknames acquired at the dojo. Some of the names stuck better than others, though. Joe was Spiderman, because he was a former skateboard competitor and still went for extreme sports. He was a shodan, a first degree black belt, in two styles, Ju-Jitsu and Shotokan. Lowell, another shodan in Shotokan, was sometimes Frood, which came from the movie *Bill and Ted's Excellent Adventure* and was a mispronunciation of "Freud". Lowell was a graduate student in Psychology. His younger brother Connor didn't have a nickname. He was a brown belt and our youngest senior student. Bob, another brown belt, was Mouse because he was huge, and Rufus Lamont, a second degree black belt in American Kempo, refused all nicknames, although he didn't like his name. Sometimes we called him Lamont—pretending it was his first name, Lamont Lamont—but not too often; he was a big guy and very tough. Heather was new to the dojo. We called her Bruiser because although she was so tiny, she hit so hard. She was a third degree black belt in Tae Kwon Do and the highest ranking person in the group. And Diamond was already a nickname, since her Chinese name was Damyeng or Diamyen or something like that. Diamond was a black sash in Wu Shu. Lowell, Connor, and Bob had started with me and worked their ways up to their present ranks. The other students had high or fairly high ranking belts from other schools and had continued with me.

I was a fourth degree black belt and unlikely to be in a situation in which I could test for my next belt for a very long time. Like my students, I had a nickname. They called me sensei, of course, and sometimes Mr. P., since my name was Paul.

"He seems eager. Troubled, too. I wonder what his story is," I said.

"Awww, that's so cute," Joe said, he was putting his own lip ring back in. "You think he's cute."

"Watch it Homeo," I countered. I teased and threatened him often, but he wasn't afraid. He was an MMA competitor and nothing seemed to faze him.

He held up a finger, as if to scold me. "Remember, Karate is for beautiful people," he said.

*   *   *

Four years before Katrina, in the summer of 2001, I took a chance. I had been an English professor—Dr. G. Paul Layton—which had been my dream for years. Being a professor was nice, but I was getting sick of the bullshit. Most of my students were business or criminal justice majors who would rather plagiarize from the Internet than think. My academic writing had dried up and most of my time was spent working on various committees. I went to the occasional conference, but my main focus outside of school was the next Mardi Gras, or the next Jazz Fest, or Halloween, conference, or any excuse to go to New Orleans. I often said that if I ever won the lottery, I'd retire to New Orleans.

In addition to English, I also taught a mixed style of martial arts in the university's Karate club. That was often my favorite part of my job as a professor. I had friends who had opened their own dojos. I envied them and often thought of following in their paths.

Other things happened in my life, too. There was a woman, as there often is, and a failed novel I was writing, as there also often is. And when it came to teaching, like I said, I was spinning my wheels. So, surprising everyone, myself most of all, I chucked it all—from my TIAA-CREF retirement money to my savings to my tenured position—and moved to New Orleans to start my dojo, Crescent Dragon Karate. I had a good amount saved and did pretty well when I sold my house. While there are no guarantees for a small business, I figured that I could do some adjunct teaching or cook at one of the many restaurants in the area if money got tight.

Things went pretty well with the school. I taught part-time while I established myself. After a year, I had stopped working as a cook. I had enough students to keep the business going and to pay myself a little more than half of what I made back when I was a professor, so I counted that as a success. I was also scrambling around and challenging myself. I thrived on that. I even published two academic articles over the years, just in case I needed to go back to teaching.

I was starting to put some money into the bank for a rainy day, and then the rainy day came. That rain was propelled by hundred and ten mile per hour winds and storm surges that showed how poorly built some of the levees were, and the city flooded. The dojo didn't flood—most of the neighborhoods right along the river didn't flood—until the Industrial Canal and then everything poured into the Lower Ninth Ward. Some of the roof came off in the back and there was water damage. I had to replace the mats because of the mold and throw out most of the equipment.

The house I shared was flooded. I came back three weeks after Katrina and went through all my belongings. I was forced to throw away over ninety percent of everything I owned. My three hundred dollar set of chef's knives had disappeared. They didn't float away; they were looted—the only thing in my place that had been taken. On my own initiative, I duct taped the refrigerator and hauled it to the curb to join the many that had their contents rotting in the heat

Things at the dojo were better, but the place wasn't going to be ready for business. I met with the landlord and he promised he'd keep the lease in my name.

Back in Ohio, where I had evacuated to, I taught. People were great—even the students I had despaired of were helpful. I went back to the school where I had previously been an associate professor and taught as an adjunct for the first semester. I lived in campus housing for a few weeks, then found a small apartment. Second semester came along and I stayed on, working as a full-time temporary with my associate professor's pay for second semester. The president of the college and the Dean of Faculty told me I was welcome to return on a permanent contract. I was tempted, but I knew I couldn't. The martial arts club, which had continued without me, helped by holding a Break-athon to raise money to help re-establish my school.

That's what I was doing now—reestablishing. I had forty students, which was less than half of what I needed. The dojo was about to go into a slow period, since it was a week after Thanksgiving and the holidays would cut the enrollment for a bit. There really wasn't a question about letting Dirk Hemlock join. Especially since he was paying extra for private lessons. To make ends meet, I still taught at three different colleges. I had lived there four years, was away most of a year, and was now rebuilding.

The city was rebuilding, although not as quickly as I needed. Only two hundred thousand people had returned so far, and there had been over half a million in the city itself, plus another half million in the connected cities. We need those people back to get the economy going—I needed them back to get my business going.

I was coming back as someone who was transplanted to New Orleans, not a native, but I knew it was different for people who had lived there and lost everything. I was able to pack most of my important things when I evacuated, but I was an academic. I was used to moving from job to job when looking for a permanent job and from school to school when I was getting my degrees. In New Orleans, I was still living like a student.

I had faith that New Orleans would come back eventually; I just hoped it recovered some time before I starved.

Chapter 2

A couple days before Katrina hit, my friends from up north started calling me. I'd been keeping an eye on the Weather Channel and the local news. Earlier that summer we had weathered a couple hurricanes that had come close, but Hurricanes Dennis and Emily, and Ivan before that, weren't enough to scare most people out of town, despite being serious storms. Dennis made it up to a category 4 before it hit the Florida Panhandle and Emily briefly reached category 5 before heading to the Yucatan Peninsula. Katrina didn't look like she would miss New Orleans and was making people nervous. The talk of evacuation had started early.

Katrina was up and down. Category three, tropical storm, category four, then five. The winds were as low as 70 miles per hour at one point, but the Gulf waters energized the system and the sustained winds hit 170 with gusts at 215. It looked like it was heading directly towards the Crescent City.

The world knew something was happening. Experts had been predicting the failure of the levees for years. Mayor Ray Nagin called for an evacuation. Some friends of mine in Hattiesburg, Mississippi invited me to stay for a week or so if necessary. An old girlfriend who was now in Nashville gave me a call. Another girlfriend in Connecticut invited me up. So did one in Seattle and a few in Ohio. Most of my friends back in Ohio were telling me to get out. The warnings weren't something I could blow off.

On Saturday night I got an e-mail.

> *Dear Professor Layton,*
>
> *I don't know if you remember me I was in your Freshman English class and later your Modern Lit. class. You left for New Orleans when I was a junior but I remembered you. When I saw the news about the hurricane I thought I'd try to find you and see if you're okay.*
>
> *Last year my older brother Tony was on vacation in Thailand when the tsunami hit. He was one of the lucky ones but he was missing for three days and it was another day before we heard of him.*
>
> *I'm worried about you in New Orleans. I saw a documentary about how the levees could break. You were a great influence in my life my freshman year and you reminded me of my brother since he's also really into Karate. I thought I'd write you an e-mail to tell you to be careful and if you can please evacuate.*
>
> *--Angel Klumm*

I wrote her back an e-mail saying I did remember her (I think I did, a tall girl with dark kinky hair), and thanked her for her concern. I asked what she was up to, told her I had every intention of evacuating, and wished her and her brother a successful life. I didn't say anything about how she forgot everything

I taught her about commas. Instead, I packed up my little Saturn and resolved to leave the next morning.

I was from Ohio, after all. I was used to tornadoes, which were quick cuts from the heavens. Hurricanes were a different story. Meteorologists sometimes compared them to atomic bombs, saying this hurricane or that was a hundred thousand times the power of the bomb that was dropped on Hiroshima or Nagasaki. Hurricanes were that powerful, but the bomb was one quick blast. A hurricane went on and on. And New Orleans was mostly below sea level, a fact that I knew, but didn't pay much attention to when I moved there.

That evening I made a bunch of phone calls. I called as many parents of my students as I could to tell them the dojo was closed for a while—most of them were smart enough to have already left. I called my older students and left messages saying I was evacuating. I called my landlord at the dojo, who told me he had already boarded up the windows there. I called a few friends, both in New Orleans and in Ohio, then caught a few hours of sleep.

I left at four-thirty in the morning. My housemates, a grad student couple —he was getting his M.A. in English and she was all-but-dissertation for her Ph.D. in Ethnomusicology—had left a couple hours before I had received that e-mail. But they were leaving just to hang out with some friends in Little Rock. The way they explained it, evacuating was just an excuse to go to a big party.

My drive was beautiful. The skies were bright and blue with plump white clouds. I hadn't listened to the radio too much. When I drove I listened to books on CD. I found they kept me more alert. I listened to *A Confederacy of Dunces* and *Midnight in the Garden of Good and Evil* on that trip because I had my own copy of the former and had just signed out the latter from the library. It would be months before they got their book back.

I was in a hotel near Louisville, Kentucky when I learned that Katrina had shifted. I thought I'd head back, but I was close to Ohio so I decided to continue on my way just in case. I would see my friends there who had generously offered me refuge from the storm.

I was safe in Ohio by the time Katrina hit. Then there was a day when everyone thought it had blown over. The next morning, though, I was with the rest of the world watching the flooding when the levees broke. The city was drowning and I wasn't there to help. I knew I couldn't help, and that feeling was, at times, stronger than I was. A week later, I went through the same hell when Rita pummeled the coast into submission again.

*   *   *

After a week of classes for the mysterious Dirk Hemlock, he was picking up a couple things. He had drive, since he came in every day and practiced, whether he was having a lesson that day or not. He had potential, and with a couple years of practice he could be good, but as it was, he had far to go. He was too weak and had no coordination to speak of.

"Dirk, I need more information," I said, before his private lesson. He'd had two private lessons and one group lesson, as well as four other solo practices during which I helped him a bit.

He looked worried and a bit sullen, like a teenager who was getting grounded for a good reason, but who was desperately trying to show he didn't care.

"You can become a good martial artist, but it'll take a year or two until you can really handle yourself. You have to build up some strength, and you have to learn all of this reflexively. If I know why you need to protect yourself, I can help you with more customized training. Then you won't have to wait so long."

"I—I really can't say."

"Are you in an abusive relationship?" I persisted.

He shook his head.

"You can tell me anything. I'll keep it confidential, and it can only help you."

"You won't believe me," he muttered.

"Try me."

He took a deep breath. He was wearing a sleeveless t-shirt and showed off skinny, tattoo-free arms. He had lots of scars on his forearms, though.

"If I tell you, will you still keep teaching me?"

I was almost shocked by the question. Of course I would…I was asking in order to help teach him better, after all. I told him that, and added that I was willing to believe anything.

He smiled. For the first time he seemed confident. He knew something that made him have something over me. Then he started on his story.

"Do you believe in ghosts?"

I shook my head.

"Well, I believe in ghosts. I've been seeing them for years." He sighed heavily, probably waiting for me to say something skeptical. I kept silent. "Then they started crossing over."

"Crossing over?"

"Yeah, now they can touch me. There's, like, a barrier between the worlds. Most ghosts, when they come over, they can't touch you. But they started being able to touch me. They could be solid for a bit."

I nodded. Already I had decided that his story probably reflected some sort of childhood abuse. Aliens probing kids, ghosts slipping into children's rooms, all that was most likely the child mind rationalizing the abuse they were receiving from parents and other adults. Dad or Mom or Uncle Norman couldn't be doing these horrible things, therefore it must be something supernatural. The supernatural choices depended on the mythos, too. Before extraterrestrials were part of popular culture, the abuse was done by devils, witches, fairies, and ghosts. Nowadays, devils, Satan worshiping cults, extraterrestrials, and ghosts were still the evildoers, since the abuse was just too horrible be accepted as real in the victim's minds.

Dirk held up his arms and showed the many scars and bruises. The newer bruises could have been from our training, but many of the scars had been there for a while. Those could be signs of defensive wounds, or he could just be a cutter. One hears about young girls cutting themselves, but it wasn't uncommon with boys. Maybe he was a cutter whose conscious mind denied that he was doing it to himself, so he invented this fantasy.

"They grab me, like they were trying to pull me in after them. I fight back, but they can hurt me.

"When I moved here, I thought I could find someone who could help me. There are so many ghosts here, and there's all that voodoo and stuff."

I nodded. I had been on ghost and cemetery tours of the French Quarter a few times. It was a good thing to do on a date if a lady friend was visiting from out of town. Ghosts, voodoo, vampires, and all manner of the supernatural were part of the city's incredible cultural diversity and history, but to me it was just folklore.

"I couldn't find anyone, though," he continued. "People here are mostly just talk. Then I found this one old man just shuffling along the road begging for money."

He paused, looking embarrassed again.

"I thought he was just some homeless guy. But he asked me if they could touch me too. He didn't say how he knew, he just said, 'They touch you too?' and he rolled up his sleeve. He had scars like mine. Then he said, 'They trying to take you with them.' I think that was the first time someone had believed me, even though he didn't even know me. I asked him what to do, and he said I should fight them."

I said nothing. I didn't want to say the obvious. Here was a kid with delusions—possibly hallucinations—and he had put his trust in a wandering schizophrenic with a similar pathology. It was sad.

"I worked on it, and now when I see them, I can make them solid if I want. I don't have to wait for them to touch me. I can touch them first." He looked triumphant. Then his smile faded. "But I don't know how to hurt them. They still hurt me, and now it's sometimes easier for them. But I'm sick of it, so I want to take the fight to them, like that old guy said." He looked intently at me.

Now I was on the spot. Saying nothing and nodding my head had worked for a while, but he wanted a response from me.

"Uhhh, well, I don't know what to say. I'm not sure how one would fight a ghost, even if he could make it corporeal."

"I told you you wouldn't believe me."

I shrugged. "It is a pretty hard to believe tale…."

"I can show you. We're in New Orleans, there are ghosts all over. Especially after Katrina. They're close to the surface."

I felt a chill. I didn't believe him, but his statement was so final. He believed it. Besides, it was growing dark outside and New Orleans can be a town that inspires chills.

"C'mon, let's go," he said and started for the door.

"I'll have to lock up," I said, kicking myself for saying it. I had given in when I should have begged off. I should have come up with an excuse to not go, instead of weakly saying I had to lock up the dojo. That was committing to go on some silly ghost hunt with a disturbed and possibly schizo-affective student. I couldn't see any good coming from this.

I had to follow through, though. I made sure the back door was locked, turned off the lights, and locked the front door before pulling down the grate and locking that.

My dojo is just off Tchoupitoulas Street, closer to the Warehouse and Arts District than the Garden District, but the area was called the Lower Garden District anyway. I can walk from my front door to the Convention Center, which had been in the news so much after Katrina, in less than five minutes. I figured there would be ghosts there.

We didn't go in that direction, though. Hemlock led me in a winding path. At Coliseum Square he stopped.

"Do you see them?" he asked.

I shook my head. I didn't see anyone. This neighborhood hadn't been the worst, but now that gangs were reestablishing themselves, it was hard to know if we'd suddenly become victims of a drive-by. I can have any belt in any style of martial arts, but that doesn't do much against a gun.

"Four of them," he pointed. I looked. In the growing darkness, I strained my eyes. I saw nothing. The little park's fountain was lit and jetting water into the air. I looked past it, for people dressed in dark clothes, and, although it doesn't sound politically correct, I was looking for dark-skinned people, since I figured I wasn't seeing anyone because it was getting dark out. All I saw was a young couple with a puppy that looked like it was a young Chocolate Lab. They were responsible dog owners. When the puppy did his business, the woman pulled out a plastic bag and scooped up the poop.

"I'm going to make one solid," he said, nervously. He stepped forward. I followed, hoping that my eyes weren't failing me as I got older and that I wasn't going to have to protect the boy from walking in on some drug deal.

He stopped. Took a deep breath and looked serene. And grabbed something.

Immediately he was struggling with something that seemed solid. I've heard how people can throw themselves around when in a religious ecstasy or when they think they are possessed and it looks like they are actually being manhandled by someone who isn't there. Still, I think I could tell, since I know how someone would have to balance and push against the ground to get leverage to throw oneself around as if attacked. Dirk looked like he was really off balance. He even seemed to be lifted off the ground a few inches at one point, and I hadn't seen him jump.

I did nothing until I saw a spot of red on the back of Dirk's shoulder. Indentations formed and then a puncture wound opened, then a second dot of blood started growing. He seemed to be pulled toward something. That's when he called for help.

Not knowing what to do, I put my hand on his shoulder to steady him. I felt it. An arm I couldn't see. Someone, an invisible someone with a muscular arm, had grabbed Dirk and was squeezing him hard enough to break the skin.

I reacted.

One principle of Jui-Jitsu, Aikido, Judo, and most other styles is body awareness. If my attacker grabs me, that just makes it easier for me. I know where the rest of that person's anatomy would be just by touching any body part of the opponent. We practice for hours wearing blindfolds so we can make it reflexive.

With my right arm I pulled the claw-like hand off Dirk's shoulder, while simultaneously slamming my left forearm into the outside of the elbow of the arm. I felt it dislocate, but that didn't stop me. Still holding tightly to the wrist in my right hand, I continued the movement of my left hand into a hammer fist to the throat, opened my hand, grabbed its neck, and pulled the head into my knee. I felt the back of the invisible neck break against my knee strike. Then I was holding nothing.

"What the hell?" I said. I felt I should be breathing hard. Dirk was. I hadn't done anything unusual for me, except I usually practice on throwing dummies and not invisible ghosts. For a second I couldn't process what happened.

"Did you see him?" Dirk asked.

"What just happened?"

"You saw him, right?"

I shook my head. "I didn't see anything. But, but I felt an arm and throat. I...I don't know."

"I made him solid," he said satisfied. "Let's go...the other ones look like they might try to get us."

The other ones. I couldn't see anything, but I had just encountered something invisible. It was a person—I could tell that when I hit it. And there were others.

"Yeah. We should go."

Chapter 3

For years when learning martial arts, I was never sure if I could use those skills in a real fight. Most martial artists I knew had those reservations—it was understandable. Classroom drills and sparring was structured and controlled. Street fighting was without rules and it could be lethal. I knew the theory that all the self-defense techniques I learned would become reflexive and I'd gain the confidence to use them, but I was unsure. The first time I had to use my martial arts skills on the street was after more than fifteen years of training, and that time it was against a drunk frat-boy, who I very much out-classed in every department.

Instead of a twenty-something loser, this was a ghost. And instead of controlling the fight, I had killed it, or something like that. It was unreal.

I was justifiably freaked out. I didn't believe in ghosts—at least not as spirits of the dead. I think that when one died, that was it. No heaven, no hell, no wandering in a chain forged from our sins in life, no gods, no angels, no devils—none of that. I was a skeptic. My skepticism wasn't shaken, even in the face of what had just happened,

We didn't go back to the dojo. We found a bar not far away and we ordered beers. The cute redheaded waitress didn't ask him for an ID, although I still wondered if he was over 21. I almost got a coffee, since that was my comfort food. Thick, bitter New Orleans coffee made with chicory. That was still on my mind as I sipped my beer, but I knew the caffeine would keep me up all night, which I probably would be anyway, considering what had just happened.

"What just happened?" I asked.

"Welcome to my life," he said. Instead of sounding triumphant, he sounded like he was about to cry.

I put my disbelief on hold. That was about me, and Dirk had to deal with this all his life. I told myself to be supportive.

"Well, now I know what to recommend for self-defense," I said. I was falling back on familiar ground, which was often my way of dealing with anything that disturbed or confused me. I'd wax didactic about something I knew.

He perked up.

"Just use a weapon. Weapons are the great equalizers. Hit them with a hammer; that should do for now. Cops recommend keeping one by the bed in case of home invasion. They're easy to use and cheap. One end is a rubberized grip while the other one is pure destruction—hammers break whatever's in its way, from hands to heads to any other body part. Baseball bats and golf clubs can be taken away pretty easily; guns could jam, kids could get to them and kill themselves; knives are too dangerous for the non-expert to use; pepper spray, especially in a small room, can blind everyone."

He shook his head. "I tried that, but they don't work. They just go right through."

I sighed. "You've tried things like silver, cold iron, different woods?"

"And crosses, rocks from graveyards, different herbal things on weapons, and everything that every medium, Voodoo priest, and mystic has recommended." This seemed to cheer him up. "I tried holy water and even had a saint bless a baseball bat."

"A saint?"

He nodded. "His followers think he is. Some cult that tried to get me to join."

"So much for traditional things, and then some." A thought hit me. "Have you ever damaged any of them?"

"Not really. I just kept them away at the most. When I learned that elbow strike I used it the next day when one of them grabbed me. I hit its arm and it let go."

"It let go? Then what did it do?"

"It watched me for a bit, then went away. It was starting to get light out and they leave by then."

"Have you ever made one disappear like I did?"

"No, they just wander off a little before it gets light.

"Do you think I killed it?"

"I don't know. I've never seen one just vanish like that. You really hit it hard."

"I didn't see anything, but it just suddenly wasn't there. But I think it was enough force to kill a person, so maybe I killed it." I took a sip of beer. I should have gotten the coffee. "So I was able to do what all those mystical weapons couldn't...maybe I'm holier than that saint."

He looked at me like I was crazy, then he caught the joke and snorted. "Yeah, right."

"You couldn't see them, though?" he asked.

"No. I felt the arm and reacted. That's something you'll learn in with us in time."

"I don't know—I can see them, after all."

"You should have an easier time with something you can see."

"Why can I see the ghosts when you can't? But you can touch them, too."

"I don't believe in ghosts. I still don't, even after tonight."

"But they are ghosts...I see them."

"And I felt one, but I don't know..."

"I've been seeing lots more since Katrina," he said.

"That's interesting. Could you describe them?"

"Like people, but not right away. They start as just a bit of light. Then they take shape. Sometimes they change their shape, though. They're usually like people, not totally, though."

"Like people?"

"Sometimes they're like caricatures. Like they can be missing things or be lopsided. I think that's how they died."

"Hmmm, maybe."

"What do you think they are, then?"

"Do you ever see anyone you know?"

"No."

"What color are they?"

"Huh?"

"White? African American? Other races?"

"White, I guess." He paused. "That's weird, I've never thought about it, but all white."

Despite what had just happened, I still didn't believe in ghost. I wasn't going to argue. He could have been right and I could be wrong. It was one of those debates that was impossible to win until it was too late and one was dead.

"Can you teach me?" I surprised myself by saying.

That stopped him for a second. "I don't know, especially if you can't see them."

"Maybe I can learn to see them. How do you do it?"

"I've always been able to see them."

"When did they start touching you?" I asked.

"I don't know. I was about sixteen. And I figured out how to touch them last year right before Katrina. And afterwards, I saw lots of ghosts."

"You said you figured out how to touch them. How did you do that?"

"Y'know, it was kind of easy. It just happened when I thought I could do it. Once I had the idea that if they could touch me, I could touch them, I started trying to figure out how they did it. I remembered how it felt, then kind of thought that, but without the getting hurt. At some point I sort of *pushed*, and I was able to get through to them."

At that point the waitress came back. "Need anything else, hon?"

"You could save my life and my sanity, Love, if you could get me some coffee and, oh, some cheddar fries," I said. "And a cup of your red beans and rice." I felt an immediate sense of well-being knowing that the food was coming.

It's hard to visit New Orleans without gaining weight. Even the air seems full of calories; at least that's the excuse we have while we munch everything from beignets to alligator. Why all the food? For some, I'm sure, it's just something to eat when on vacation. But for the real Nawlins lover, it's a way to become part of the city, or, more accurately, it's a way for the city to become part of ourselves. We eat, and when we eat the local delicacies their magic becomes part of us. Our metabolisms become suffused with the spices. We wake and sleep to the rhythms of thick, strong coffee and beer and hurricanes in go-cups. The butter in the roux slows our systems down to the Nawlins pace of life, while hot sauces and spices keep us in time with the jazz that beats around us. Our cells start speaking with a Cajun accent, and we, temporarily, are part of the city. I made that jump to living here—the food spoke to me too strongly.

"It'll take a few minutes to make a new pot." She smiled, her eyes twinkled flirtatiously. "Heyyy, I know you." Dirk looked up, as if she had said it to him, but she was looking at me.

"Really? Sorry, you'll have to remind me from where." She was in her mid to late twenties, so maybe she had been a student at Tulane or Loyola when I was teaching there part time during the first couple years of establishing my dojo. I knew she wasn't a current student; I had two classes and would recognize any of the students in them. I also knew she hadn't ever been a Karate student of mine.

"Didn't you work in the kitchen at the Bluebird Café?"

"On Prytania, yeah—for about three months when I first came to town."

"Right. I worked there. We talked about Karate."

I didn't remember her from there, but it had been six years and I had been super busy then.

"I had green and purple hair, I think," she added.

"But not at the same time. And you had your labret pierced. I remember." It had come back to me. She wore a black metal collar and sometimes a chain from her labret to the collar and lots of black. She looked quite different. In addition to a change in hair, she was wearing jeans and a white t-shirt under her server's apron. She wore a minimum of make-up and her hair looked naturally red.

"That's right." She dimpled. We chatted for another minute, and then she went off to place the order and start some coffee. Dirk was looking impatient. When the girl left, we got back to the discussion.

He kept describing what he did and it reminded me of some principles in different martial arts. In Aikido, extension was a technique we use. It gave strength to one's moves, even if it didn't look like one was using a lot of power. In board breaking, which we did in Karate, we aimed through the target to focus our energy. Some called it *chi*, although I always looked for a more scientific explanation. In our dojo, we did a lot of what I called *time dilation*, but that was merely a perceptual trick. By calming down, slowing down, and seeing beyond target, we could react to faster attacks as if they were slow motion. It sounded like Dirk was describing something akin to those techniques. I made mental notes, trying to figure this out.

The food and coffee came. I doused everything with Krystal Hot Sauce and sprinkled some Tony Chachere's Creole Seasoning on the fries. By then I'd remembered the girl's name—Brianne, but she went by Bri. The coffee was perfect, strong and aromatic, and soothed my troubled sense of reality much more than the beer had. The food wasn't the best, but it fit with my surroundings.

After an hour of Dirk's explanations and my questioning, I had an idea of what he was doing. I didn't know if I could do it, but I thought I would try next time he found me a ghost.

"Now for the hard part. I need to see them."

He pointed to the front window of the restaurant. "See out there? There's one right in front of the window there, by the No Parking sign."

I looked, snapping my head quickly since it was so unexpected. I saw a light. It wasn't a bright light, or a coherent one, but more like a flaw in a piece of glass. The light wasn't a flaw in the front window of the restaurant; it was past the window, in the air. It wasn't coherent, just a gleam; then it was gone. I would have assumed it was just a trick of the light—we often see things that are optical illusions or what the perceptual psychologists call visual icons. In this context, however, I thought it was something else. I told Dirk what I saw.

"I see a man. He's wearing a suit, but no shirt. He also doesn't have a nose…it's more like a smudge on his face."

"Wow. All I saw was a little light."

"He's still there."

I looked back and saw the flaw again for a second. Again it disappeared. I looked away again, emptied my mind and though about some of the things he said…not about making them solid, but about how he was able to see them. I snapped my eyes to the front window; a bigger flaw floated there, vanishing after ten seconds.

This time when it disappeared, it didn't look like some sensory icon left on the optic nerve because of reflected light. It was floating there.

"There it is," I said. I pointed to where it had just disappeared. "Just in front of the window."

"About three feet back from it, but he's there."

I was already trying again to look, using the same method. I saw it for three seconds or so. I tried extending, to see past the light, maybe that would help. I had no luck—just the flaw, floating there. I kept trying but couldn't see past the flaw, and I couldn't hold the image for too long. After some discussion, I decided that what I saw was about a foot from the window.

"Maybe I'm just seeing the opening—the, um, rift between realities," I said.

He paused and considered it. "I guess."

I could tell from his tone that he had no idea. He saw one thing, but I saw something different. He could see past where I could, and I couldn't see that point for very long. Also, he was used to seeing past the rift, so he didn't really know there was a difference.

We tried a few more times—me working on just seeing the flaw in the air, and him directing me to see what he saw. As time went by, though, I was only able to see the rift for fractions of a second again. I was losing it. While that was going on, Dirk grew more impatient. Finally, I said it was time to end it.

"Are you going to be able to make it home safely?" I asked.

He looked at me like I was patronizing him. "I know how to get home," he said, petulantly.

"Yeah, but since you've never struck back to these ghosts, they may be lying in wait. One is watching you already."

"I can take care of myself," he whined.

"Hey, just remember who you're talking to. I'm the guy who believes you. I can't see these things, but I've touched one. Besides, you came to me to learn to defend yourself from them. OK?" Although I never had kids, I felt I was being a parent there. I was using a tone I rarely had to use as a professor, but even in college we have spoiled brats to deal with.

He hung his head. "I guess."

"I'll at least get you past the one outside."

A look of relief passed over his face. I almost changed my mind about escorting him. The kid was schizo…then I reminded myself that I originally thought he was schizophrenic because of his hallucinations. Maybe he still was. I should still treat him with care.

I paid the check and we left. The ghost wasn't outside of the restaurant, according to Dirk. I didn't see the flaw, but by that time, I wasn't seeing anything. I guess I was worn out. I walked him two blocks but the way looked clear.

"You'll be OK to go home?"

He looked around. "No ghosts."

"OK. Keep an eye out, though."

He nodded. I shook his hand at the end of the block. He went his way and I went back to the bar. Bri was still there. I sat at the bar, she joined me.

"It's so weird to see you back," she said.

"Yeah, so many people are gone. I'm always surprised to see people, myself."

She nodded. "And I never knew what to make of you. You were cooking and talking about your Karate school. I never thought you'd make it here. And now to see you back after Katrina."

"I'm full of surprises." I smiled and she did, too. "So you're still here. Did you evacuate?"

"I got out the day before it hit. It took ten hours to get up to Jackson, Mississippi. I was gone for about three months." She paused, getting her thoughts past that time. "Let's see, I graduated from college in '02. Y'know, I was surprised you were teaching there while also working at the Bluebird. I mean, here was this cook, and he was a professor, and he had a Karate school. That was weird."

I shrugged. We were getting into my story and I was more interested in hers.

After she graduated, she went home, which was in New York, and worked for a while, but came back to New Orleans for a guy. She wasn't with him anymore, and had some hard times after Katrina.

"What happened?"

"My landlady evicted me. I wasn't allowed to have my daughter. I mean, I started living there when it was just me, but I was pregnant. I signed the lease for one person. So when Katrina hit, and Annie was two years old, we went to a friend's place near Jackson, but came back right away. Our place wasn't flooded, so I thought everything would be OK, but after a few weeks, that woman kicked me out for violating the lease. Then she rented the place to some FEMA people for twice what I was paying."

"That's awful," I said. I had heard similar stories, some were worse, but after Katrina, stories like that were almost common. Disaster brought out the worst in some people. I also now knew why she was looking so much more normal—she was a mom.

We talked some more; only a few times she had to get up and serve a customer. It was the same kind of catching up I did with neighbors and former customers during Mardi Gras of '06, right after Katrina. During the smaller crowds at the few parades, neighbors and acquaintances would find each other and exchange evacuation stories.

We were both New Orleans residents but not natives. We had come from elsewhere and were now devout lovers of the city. We had chosen to return after the city was nearly destroyed, so that made us locals. In some areas of the city, almost all the residents were from out of town. Even the families who had been there for generations were eager to talk about how their ancestors came from France or Spain or some other place. Everyone was a transplant.

We talked for a while, and I flirted a little. Like food and coffee, women were another thing that made me feel better when I was upset.

My history with women had been varied over the years. I was forty-six and had never been married. When I was young, I couldn't get a date. I was the typical nerd when growing up, and had no dates until college. Then I started dating, but irregularly; I never had a serious girlfriend until I was in my late twenties. That lasted for three years and then we went our separate ways. When I started on-line dating and things got a lot better. I started making up for my lean years. I had a few relationships that I thought could lead to more, but something always happened. Then I moved to New Orleans. I was too busy to date at first, but eventually I started having a rich social life. Serious relationships still seemed to be beyond me, but I kept trying.

I got her number and gave her my card. She was a cutie. She had given me some signals, and we had a bit of a history as acquaintances and we were getting along. After the year we'd all had, it was good to see people, even if they weren't close to us. Brianne and I were among that number of people who found relief when we'd see someone or something familiar that had survived. Too much had been lost. We promised to get together and eventually I headed home.

As I walked home I stopped thinking about Brianne and the small connection we had made. I grew paranoid about ghosts and kept darting my gaze around, looking for that rift. I hoped Dirk had made it home safely.

Chapter 4

The adrenaline and caffeine kept me up pretty late, and I didn't sleep very well. I thought about ghosts all night.

Were they ghosts? If they were, could I have killed them? If not, what were they?

I hadn't been to war, nor had I ever been a police officer or in any life-threatening situation. I had never killed a man. But that night I had fought something that had limbs like a person and a neck that could snap. I had killed something, or someone.

Can ghosts die? Weren't they already dead?

That right there convinced me that they weren't ghosts. Whatever they were, ghosts can't die. I killed something. Did it deserve to die?

When I was young, I was like Dirk Hemlock. I was skinny and bullied—not by ghosts, of course, but by everyone else it seemed. Until college, I was the punching bag of most of my classmates.

I was a science geek back then. I devoured science fiction—Heinlein, Asimov, Clarke, LeGuin, Lewis, and many more—which was what probably led to me becoming an English professor. I was always with a book. Even in gym class, I sat on the sidelines and read. It didn't make me popular, and I lived as a victim. In college, I started lifting weights in order to be more attractive to girls. I started Karate a couple years later. In college I didn't have any bullies. I was lifting and learning to fight in order to improve myself and probably to compensate for a lifetime of being picked on.

Those kids who thought it was funny to make the scrawny nerd cry probably never knew what they were doing with their taunts, pokes, shoves, and punches. What they had done, in my case, was to put fifty pounds of muscle on the little nerd and give him an attitude.

I could never get into the mind of a bully. I never understood why they felt the need to torture those weaker than themselves. And that's what the ghosts were doing. They were picking on Hemlock for no reason. He could see them, but was that a reason to injure him? They had drawn blood and were lifting him off the ground when I intervened. If that had been a human doing such a thing to someone who was just walking along, we'd call that a mugging. He had been stalked for years and now was getting attacked. According to the boy, the attacks were getting worse. If I hadn't stepped in, there was a good chance that attack would have been fatal.

Did I feel guilty for killing the thing? No, I decided. It was a reflexive response to an attack on someone under my protection.

My conscience was clear. Until I fell asleep, I thought about what the ghosts could be instead of feeling bad for killing the one that was attaching the poor boy in my charge.

All I had that morning was some grading, then to go to the dojo. I made breakfast at home, but went out for more coffee afterwards, lingering over a cup at CC's Coffee. I graded there, then went to the dojo and worked out. I also did some more cleaning and repairs. I'd been at that for months, but it was a never-ending process.

My back room, The Pit, had been destroyed from the mold sludge. Over the months I had fixed up the front room, but not the back. The Pit was where we did our Judo, Aikido, and Jujitsu. The floor was a foot lower than that of the front room, and I had built it up to the same level by lining it with used tires I got from a junk yard, putting a layer of 3/8" plywood over it, then putting a layer of padding over that and throwing mats over that. It was as springy and shock absorbing as a pro-wrestling ring; "was" being the key word. After Katrina I had to throw out all the mats, padding, plywood, and tires. Although I had shoveled out the mold sludge, the room still smelled foul, and black mold kept returning. I had bought mats with the insurance money I got, but it was slow going, especially since I was expanding The Pit to fill the entire back room. Before Katrina, I used half the room for storage.

At about one, the bell rang as someone entered the dojo.

It wasn't a soccer mom coming to register her already overworked child into one of my classes. The man who entered was about my age, mid-forties, overweight, and in a lightweight sports coat. He looked pissed off.

Back when I was a professor full time I thought I had some street sense, but I was only fooling myself. After living in New Orleans and working with such a variety of people and seeing a lot more on the street, I was getting a little more. I also now had enough to know that I wasn't streetwise and never would be. Nevertheless, I could tell right away he was a cop.

"Hi; can I help you?" I asked, all smiles.

"Are you the owner here?"

I was wearing shorts and a bleach-spotted t-shirt while I cleaned the back room, and I was a little light-headed from the chlorine fumes. It was understandable that he'd wonder if I were the proprietor, since when most people come into a martial arts school, they expect to be met by someone in a traditional gi. Black mold waits for no man.

"Yes. What can I do for you?"

"Joel Bouchard, New Orleans Police. You're Gillian Laycock?"

"That's Guillaume," I stressed the French pronunciation. In Ohio, my family had pronounced it "Gilliam", but I was in New Orleans, after all. "And I go by Paul. Professionally, I'm G. Paul Laycock."

"Professionally, huh?"

"For publications and when I sign my name, yes."

"Publications—uh huh. Do you know of someone who called himself Dirk Hemlock or Eugene Helman?"

I nodded. "Yes, Dirk Hemlock. He's a recent student here."

"Were you with him last night?"

"Yeah. We talked a little while after his workout."

"Where was this?"

"We were at the Half Moon; I walked him a block towards the Quarter, then went back to the bar. Why, what's going on?"

"Helman—Hemlock's real name—was killed last night. He was stabbed and beaten to death."

"Jesus." I knew it was the ghosts. That puncture wound I saw was the beginning. I didn't have to ask, I knew that most of the wounds were shallow, but they added up. I didn't know what to say, since even I still didn't believe they were actually ghosts. And I certainly didn't want to talk about ghosts to a cop. I've seen enough television and had read enough detective fiction. He was probably establishing whether I was a suspect or not.

"When did you leave him?"

"About ten."

"And you went back to the Half Moon?"

"For an hour, maybe a little more."

"Why did you go back?"

I shrugged. "To flirt with the waitress. She and I worked together a few years ago and we were catching up."

"Will she verify that?"

"I would think so. I gave her my card, and we're going to get together sometime."

He nodded, not looking like he trusted me. "Did Mr. Helman say anything about enemies?"

I almost laughed out loud. The story I could spin for him. Of course he wouldn't believe it.

"No."

"Did he say why he wanted to take Karate classes?"

"No. I asked, but he said I wouldn't believe him. I asked him again and he said the same thing."

"What did you talk about?"

I shrugged. "Ghosts. He seemed to be really into the supernatural."

"Are you?"

"No. I'm not into that. I just talked to him about it to humor him. I was hoping he'd open up about why he needed to learn self-defense so I could customize his training."

"Customize his training?"

"Sure. If he was being abused in a relationship, if I knew the types of abuse, the size of the person, the situations, then I can advise him better. It may just be that he was worried about living in the big city—maybe some dangerous looking people have started hanging out on his street. I've been at this for a while, so I've seen a lot. Sometimes it's an abusive spouse or boyfriend or girlfriend or other family member or whatever, and sometimes it's paranoia. Sometimes I tell them to call the police, sometimes I show them specific self-defense tricks."

"I see," he said in that skeptical way that so many people have about the martial arts. I could tell he thought, deep inside, that he thought it was bogus and the God-given ability that he was born with was better than anything I could possibly teach. He believed in the right cross and his physical presence. He had probably been a jock in school and a bit of a bully. His sarcastic "I see" had put him in a specific category—in with the bullies that had driven me to study Karate. I didn't like him because he obviously didn't like me.

"You do that kind of training a lot?"

"Sometimes."

"You do it back in Ohio?"

"On occasion. I didn't have a dojo there; it was just a college club."

"What college?"

"Griswold College."

"Never heard of it."

I shrugged. There were a lot of colleges, I wasn't offended that he hadn't heard of one.

"What did you do at this Griswold College?"

"I was an English professor. I retired young and opened a Karate school."

He looked around the lobby of the dojo. He glanced above the reception desk to the poster of the dragon superimposed over the Crescent City and following the river with its tail—the Crescent Dragon Karate School's logo. He peered into one of the display cases where I sell various martial arts weapons. "Could I see one of those?" He pointed at a shuriken. I unlocked the case and gave him the one he pointed at.

Bouchard looked at the shuriken for a bit. "These are throwing stars, right?"

"Right."

"Can you use these to stab?"

"Not if you don't want to puncture your own hand—there's no way to grip it for stabbing. Besides, the ones I sell are dull."

He nodded, putting it down on the counter. "That's what I figured."

"What was he stabbed with?"

"We're not sure. The coroner's report will take a while."

He asked a few more things, then asked Brianne's name and number and said he'd be in touch.

Dirk had been killed by the ghosts, or whatever they were. That was obvious to me, but it certainly wasn't something I wanted to tell the police. I also didn't believe they were ghosts, or how could I have killed one? But the thought that bothered me the most was that I caused his death. If I hadn't fought and killed that invisible being, Dirk would probably still be alive.

I tried to tell myself that once Dirk learned more self-defense skills, he'd have fought with those ghosts and then they would have killed him. That rationalization didn't help me at all. Even if Dirk had learned to defend himself well enough to fight them by himself, it would have been months or even years before he was good enough to successfully fight them off. By killing one of those beings, I had pissed them off. I had denied the boy of several months of life.

That day passed, slowly and full of mistakes. My mind was elsewhere, and when Brianne called to ask what the deal was with the police, I wasn't at my best. I wasn't insulting or anything, but I was awkward and thought I sounded like an idiot.

I continued like that through the next day, Friday, which was my busiest day. I had my two classes at Tulane and tried to get some work done on my on-line class in Literary Theory. At the dojo, I had one children's beginner class, one children's intermediate class, the adult beginners/intermediates, and the adult advanced class. My day started at six, when I woke up and read of Dirk's murder in the *Times-Picayune*. Helman had died from blood loss from an unspecified number of puncture wounds. That's about all they had.

By nine at night, I was still on the go. The adult advanced class went well, despite me being practically asleep at the wheel a couple times.

It was after class, with two of my black belts helping me lock up, that I was attacked from beyond.

As I turned around from locking the front door, the flaw was right in front of me. It didn't disappear. I reached out and extended like Dirk had told me. I thought maybe I could make it visible. Instead, I felt the punch in my throat. I had made it tangible. I grabbed the arm, found the wrist, and broke it. I was unable to breath for a second, but I let that panic fuel me as I pulled the wrist down and forward, kneeing something hard—probably its head—and as it went down, I stomped. It disappeared—turned into nothing—then.

"What the hell?" Joe asked. I clutched my throat and gagged.

Heather reached up and put a hand on either side of my neck. "Can you breathe?"

My answer was a deep, ragged gasp.

"What happened?" she asked. Heather was tiny, barely four foot ten, yet in this situation, she seemed to be in control. She was the only one who knew what she was doing, and that was tending to my throat.

"I'm OK, Bruiser," I said, with a forced grin. I was about to try to spin a lie of some sort, but nothing came to me.

"Something hit me in the throat, and I fought back," I said.

She nodded. Joe looked confused.

"It was invisible," I added weakly.

We went to Dino's, which was in a better lit area. I was being cautious, hoping they wouldn't attack in the light.

Over more comfort food, this time an alligator appetizer, fried olives, coffee for me, beer for Joe, and a daiquiri for Bruiser, I told them the long version of the story, starting with Eugene Helman's death. They had both heard about it but didn't recognize the unfamiliar name as the school's new student. I told them the cause of the death, then backtracked to my part in the adventure. My explanation was a bit scattered, but they seemed to follow it and show concern. Joe showed more disbelief than Bruiser did, but the welt on my neck seemed to be convincing them as it turned yellow and looked like it would become a real bruise soon. I had gotten a bag of ice from the waiter, and that was helping.

"You're sure you're not hallucinating it all?" Joe asked.

"Get real."

"No, seriously, maybe he drugged you." "He" was Dirk/Eugene. We had run into a roadblock when saying his name, so we started using pronouns.

"I don't think I'd be hallucinating two days later. And there wouldn't be bruising."

"It's probably your Alzheimer's, old man," he said.

"I'll show you old," I snarled, and it hurt my throat.

"You and what army?" He paused. "I know...the Army of Darkness, right?"

I shook my head. "Cute. How about if I try to teach you how to see them and touch them?"

"You can do that?" Joe asked, wide-eyed.

"I don't know. I can tell you what he told me, and we can see if it works at all."

"Sounds like the scientific method," Bruiser added. She was smiling, so I didn't know if she was joking and humoring me or serious. She was a scientist, after all. Thirty-three years old, a Ph.D. in Geology, she worked for an oil company but at the moment was on a special project to help figure out the future of New Orleans, the Gulf, and the oil drilling there. She was my highest ranking student and was a serious workaholic. If our belief systems weren't so different, I would have been wild about her. She's a conservative Republican and Christian, and I'm a liberal and an atheist—so it goes.

I explained to them how to see the ghosts, reminding them of the extension exercise we used in Aikido, time dilation, and our in-class discussions of chi, and told them how Hemlock had told me how to apply those things to the ghosts when we saw them. I told them of Hemlock's history with them, how at first they were just something he saw, then they started attacking him. I told them how he was getting afraid for his life and how, on advice of a homeless guy who also saw them, he tried to fight them back. I even told them about the baseball bat blessed by the supposed saint. They nodded instead of laughed, so I felt they were humoring me instead of believing me. I would have to show them.

When we left the restaurant, I looked around. There were flaws in the light not far down the block.

"There, look there. Extend your chi, or your perceptions or whatever."

I bit my lip...I was hoping they'd see the irregular lights floating in the air, although the flaws soon disappeared on me.

"Where, by those guys?" Joe asked.

"What guys?"

Bruiser seconded my question.

Joe pointed.

"Did you extend your chi?" I asked. He nodded. I had an idea. "Look away from them and divide sixty-seven by thirteen."

"Huh?"

"Do it."

He looked at me and I could see his eyes roll up to the side as he tried the math.

"Look now." I pointed to the ghosts.

He looked and shook his head. "They left."

"Now, extend your chi."

There was a pause. "Fuck," he said.

"Did they just appear?"

"Yeah."

"Heather, did you see anything?"

"No. But that's really interesting." She considered it. "Although maybe this is some sort of hypnosis."

"I'm not hypnotizing Joe."

"Why can he see it and not me?"

"I don't know."

"Then how can I know they're real?"

"How do we know any of our perceptions are real? They could all be manufactured and external. With the exception of smell, all of our senses are electrochemical translations of external stimuli. And the sense of smell can be artificially fooled. We could be all plugged into some sort of mega computer that is controlling our senses for experimental purposes."

"Like in the *Matrix* movies?" Joe asked.

"Yep."

"Fuck, they disappeared again," he said.

"Your mind isn't extending."

"Weird."

"That wasn't what I was asking," Bruiser said.

"I've been thinking about these things for days now. It would be nice if the ghosts were some sort of hallucination or trick. Remember, I'm a skeptic."

"I'm not. I have faith," Bruiser said.

"Me neither," added Joe. "I'm not a skeptic, either." He had that hopeful look in his eye that maybe she'd notice him as more than a younger guy. She looked at me and I continued.

"You're the scientist," I said. "You should be more skeptical. I'm working on a theory for this, but we'll have to see."

She shook her head. "I believe in God and in heaven. But I don't know about these ghosts you're seeing."

"If it helps, I don't think they are ghosts."

"What are they then?" Joe asked.

"I don't know. I really don't. Tell me, what did the people you saw look like?"

"I don't know…Goths, sort of. I didn't see much of the faces. Um, they were dressed in layers—mostly gray and black. They all had hats. Fedoras."

"Did they have all their features?"

"What?"

"They all had noses, eyes, mouths?"

"Of course. It was hard to see their eyes 'cause of their hats, but it looked like they have them."

"Hmmm," I said. What he said and what Dirk had seen were different.

"'Hmmm', what?" Joe asked.

"Dirk saw them differently."

"Yeah," Joe said slowly. "Maybe I'm just seeing different ghosts.

"Still see them?" I asked Joe and Heather. Joe nodded. Heather shrugged.

"Are you trying?" I asked her. She shook her head. "So much for the scientific method."

"I just don't think this is something we should mess with," she said. She looked frightened.

I glanced again—the lights were moving slowly, as if they were intending to surround us.

"Joe, what are they doing?"

"Uhh, they're moving in our direction…two of them look like they've split from the other one, but they're still heading in our direction."

"They're trying to flank us. They may attack. Dirk said they can touch us if they want to. At least some of them can. That's why he figured out how to make them solid, so he could touch them back."

"We may have to bring the fight to them," Joe said.

"You're kidding," Heather said. Joe said nothing, but his eyes gleamed with excitement.

I started to tell them again how to touch the ghosts. I was focusing on how they felt when I touched them—solid, yet not there visually—and not to panic, but to react.

Before I had finished, someone or something grabbed a handful of my hair from behind. I clamped my hand over the claw-like hand, dropped into a crouch, and spun in the direction against the outside of its wrist. I could feel the hand go limp as the bones in the wrist crunched and broke. I punched to where the groin should be and missed. Rising, I did a sweeping hook kick, but no target. It was intangible. I calmed myself down and extended again. The flaw was in front of me and I kicked, hard.

I made contact, but I couldn't tell if what I did was lethal or not. I looked over and saw Joe taking a beating. One of the lights were hovering by him and he was being pummeled and not hitting anything with his wild swings. He kept his arms up for defense, but something—a sweep or a kick or even a tackle—brought him down. I jumped over, with a jumping front snap kick and felt the collision jar my entire body as I hit something that was invisible. Landing like a cat, I sprung at Joe's attacker and got what felt like a forearm across my face. It hurt—my face went numb and my nose started bleeding, but it also gave me a better idea of where the ghost was. I hooked the arm, broke it at the elbow, and broke its neck.

The one I had first made contact with was still up. Two ghosts. One connected with Joe and he sailed into the street, rolling awkwardly. The other grabbed Bruiser. She kicked out and missed as her foot went through the thing. She jerked forward, still struggling, and was lifted up, her flailing feet almost four feet above the ground.

I don't think I've ever kicked that hard. Whatever my side kick made contact with dropped Bruiser. She tumbled and I kicked again with a front kick, causing the thing to twist to face me. Something, probably a backhand, caught me in the middle, just below the solar plexus. I felt the wind leave me.

As I staggered backwards, the one that had so easily knocked Joe into the street caught my arms in a powerful bear hug. I still couldn't breathe, but as it pulled tighter I saw the other one approaching and I knew what would happen. I lifted both legs and kicked it. The one holding me fell over backwards and I was freed. I thought for a second that I had lost it—that I had not been able to keep it tangible, but it was gone. Maybe it had hit its head on the road and that had killed it. I pulled myself upright with a painful gulp of air. I didn't see it, but that didn't mean too much. Maybe I had killed it with the kick, but maybe it had just gone where it had come from.

From the street I heard Joe stir.

"I'm OK," he said. He held his head, as if he was severely hung over, and stumbled to a low stone fence. He retched over it, out of sight from us, thankfully.

"Bruiser? Heather? Are you OK?"

"I'm OK." She kneaded her arms where she had been grabbed. "It was strong and I couldn't hit it."

I patted her on the shoulder. "Put some ice on your bruises when you get home. Did you see them?"

"No, nothing."

Joe sat upright, spitting once before speaking. "I didn't see them at all. They were just hitting me."

"Do you see them now?" I asked.

He took his hands down from his head and scanned the area. "No."

"Did you see them when they were attacking?"

Joe screwed up his face in an annoyed and confused expression. "Yeah, at first, but when I punched at one, my hand went right through. Then he disappeared. Then I was down on the ground and it was kicking my head, so I covered up."

His hand went to his temple and rubbed gently. His other hand massaged his knee. I could see that hand was scraped and swollen.

"Are you alright?" Heather said. She sat next to Joe and with one hand started massaging the back of his neck. Joe's eyes grew wide.

"Yeah, I'm OK."

"I couldn't touch them either. Oh my dear lord Jesus, it was terrifying."

"We're going to have to learn to make them solid. I want to hurt them the next time."

She took her hand down from Joe's neck. "I don't want to fight them. I think we should stop and try to avoid them."

I nodded. "I just hope we have that choice."

"You had to say that, didn't you?" Joe asked.

Chapter 5

Joe Graves felt awful the next morning. He was as sore as after any of the no-holds-barred contests he had fought in. He hurt almost as much as he did after his accident the time he took a spill when street luge-ing in San Francisco. That time, though, he had scraped off half his skin on one leg and actually broke his elbow.

He got out of bed, a double mattress on the floor that he sometimes shared with his roommate Diane. She was at her girlfriend's house, so he had the apartment to himself. This was a good thing, since she'd try to mother him and he just wanted to forget the injuries.

Diane was two years older than he was, but had an attitude of being world-weary and mature. She described herself as ninety percent lesbian, except for when she was between relationships when she and Joe sometimes slept together. They didn't do anything more than cuddle, she said that was all of the remaining ten percent. She was a large woman—not fat, just large—and she preferred tiny women, just like Joe did. He liked Bruiser, but knew he had no chance with her. She was tiny, like Leah, who had been his true love in ninth grade. She was back in Baton Rouge and married now, so it was over. Still, maybe Bruiser would be interested in a younger guy....

He lurched to the bathroom and inspected the damage in the mirror. Blood was smeared on the side of his face, but it must have come from his hands, since he wasn't cut anywhere in the head. He had some swelling and probably bruises, but they were under his hair. His ribs and shoulders were scraped. They throbbed and his knee was sore and clicked when he moved it. His neck hurt. He had a headache.

A shower did nothing to make him feel better. The water pressure in the city was still low in some places, and his Bywater apartment was one of those spots. At least the water wasn't ice-cold, which it often was unless someone hit the reset button on the water heater. It was up to the tenants to take care of that detail, since the landlord still hadn't replaced the ancient water heater.

He put frozen gel packs on some of his wounds and filled a plastic bag with ice, which he wrapped around his knee. He always had lots of ice and gel packs in the freezer. He didn't want to go to work, but he'd missed a couple days recently due to a trip home. He worked construction, although he didn't have any skills. Since Katrina, there were tons of jobs for unskilled guys with muscles and endurance, and Joe was learning a lot. Joe's money went home to where his mother was having troubles since she got laid off.

Over his Granola, he thought about the attack. About the whole thing. He was embarrassed that he was beaten, even though he couldn't touch the two ghosts who were beating him. He had to learn to strike back.

The cereal tasted like wood. It hurt to chew. He put the half-finished bowl in the sink and grabbed his cell phone.

"Hey Sensei, wanna get some coffee?" he said. To his face, Joe called him Sensei, but the students had their own nickname for him they sometimes used behind his back—Mr. P. It was short for Mr. Peabody, the time traveling dog in the old cartoon. They called him that because he knew fuckin' everything—or thought he did—and he made bad jokes too often.

"Hey Spiderman—how ya feeling?"

"Eh, I've been worse."

Half an hour later they met at the Market Café on Decatur. A jazz band was setting up outside, but Mr. P. was indoors at the buffet.

In the restaurant there were a few tourists, some locals, and two National Guard. Although he wasn't the tallest person there, Layton still dominated the room. He was vain as hell, wearing a fitted Crescent Dragon Karate t-shirt. He often complained about having a few extra pounds, even though he was built like a young George Foreman. When he entered a room, people gave him space.

As if he sensed Joe's arrival, he turned, smiled, and pointed to a table that already had two place settings and two steaming cups of coffee.

Joe nodded and walked to the buffet tables. He put some eggs, grits, and Jell-O on his plate. Layton, whose plate was loaded, shook his head, and headed to the table.

"Not eating much?" he asked, when Joe sat.

"Soft foods," Joe said, and rubbed his jaw. He had a pretty impressive bruise under his chin and his upper lip was swollen on the right side. Layton had a welt across his face and a bruise on his throat, but his injuries didn't seem to stop his appetite.

"I hope you don't mind if I pig out. I won't have many chances to eat today," Layton said. "I also can't go to a buffet and not stuff myself. It's a law of nature."

Joe shrugged. He wasn't there for the food.

"I want to fight back," he said. "I could see them, but not touch them. I think I lost my cool."

"You have to have your mind in the right space." He shoveled some andouille sausage and rice in his mouth.

"You have to extend in the same way you did to see them."

"I could do that. It was pretty easy."

"Not for me, actually. I can't really see them. I can touch them, though."

"And they can touch you."

"That was Hemlock's problem, but they were never as aggressive as they were to you."

"Until the very end."

Layton nodded. "It feels like it was my fault."

They sat in silence for a moment. Joe wanted to agree, but didn't want to sound like he was accusing him of anything.

"They're panicking because they're threatened...because they've been hurt."

"And you're the only one who as hurt them."

Layton nodded. He pushed his food around a little with his fork. It looked like he was swallowing with a little difficulty. He drank down his coffee and that seemed to give him some relief. The waiter was there in seconds with a refill.

"Regular, right?" the waiter asked. He was a skinny bald man with a red mustache.

"Of course."

"That's my man. Coffee without caffeine is like sex without being handcuffed."

The sensei grinned and slapped the man's palm. Joe laughed and they looked at the waiter as he went to the National Guardsmen and offered them coffee. He poured for them and repeated his joke.

Layton thought for a moment, the grin leaving his face. "I don't know if we should just try to avoid them or work on getting you to be able to fight back. Maybe if we leave them alone, they'll stop bothering us."

"I don't know...Dirk was attacked a lot, you said. I think we should be able to defend ourselves."

"Good point, but we don't know what Dirk did over the years. Maybe, as he could touch them more and more, they were threatened."

"Or maybe they found they could pick on him and he was afraid for his life and came to us for help."

"I guess that's how it was," Layton conceded.

"I'm going to touch them. I'm going to touch them hard."

Layton considered it. "It's getting dark early these days, so we can try tonight. I've been looking to see them during the day and haven't had any luck. I don't know if it's because of the light, if they're nocturnal, or if it's just me. Still, I don't know if we should. You're pretty beat up. Maybe another night."

"I'll be OK. I just want to learn to make them solid. I won't take a bunch of them on. I don't want them to have the advantage." Joe rubbed his shoulder. "I should get going. I'm already late for work."

Layton sipped his coffee dreamily—the man loved his caffeine. He put his cup down. "You're working on Saturday?"

"It's Saturday? Shit. I forgot. I can sleep in." He could work on Saturdays, there was work on the site seven days a week, but Joe took most weekends off so he could train.

"And recover. And if you don't want to come to class today, it's no problem"

He thought about it. "I'll be in late. Then we can go look for them."

"Maybe," Layton said. "I think we're in way over our heads with this."

*   * *

Joe made it to the dojo as the sun was touching the horizon. It was also time for the last drop-in class of the day. All students, from the five year olds up to the black belts were allowed to work out at the same time, concentrating on their own goals. Layton would often do paperwork at this time and let Joe or one of the other advanced students supervise so the younger kids didn't get rowdy and hurt themselves.

In one group, Lowell supervised two teenage boys who were wrestling on the new mats, fruitlessly trying to throw arm-bars and missing other possible holds. A listless girl looked on, probably waiting for her ride home. In the other group, Connor, Mouse, and Bruiser were practicing some punching drills. Layton was nowhere to be found.

"Hey guys," Joe said. "What's up?"

Bruiser looked at him with concern. "Are you OK?"

"Yeah, a little sore, but that happens."

"What happened?" Mouse said. His name was Bobby, but no one called him that since he admitted to being called Danger Mouse in high school. He was 6'3" and weighed around 280 or so. He looked fat, but he was fast and good at katas when he concentrated. He didn't make it to class often enough, though, and that was why he was a brown belt when he should have been a first degree black belt by now.

"You didn't tell?" Joe asked Bruiser.

"I'm not sure I believe it happened," she said.

Joe nodded. "Oh it happened." He turned to the guys, "We were fighting ghosts."

Quickly, with Bruiser supporting him and filling in blanks, he told them about the previous night's experience. Midway through the discussion, Lowell joined them as the kids left. Then he started the explanation all over again when Lamont came along. The only black belt who didn't show up was Diamond, who was probably working.

They were skeptical, not believing Joe, but trusting Bruiser's authority. Eventually, they were all curious. With the exception of Mouse and Rufus Lamont Lamont, they all responded like he expected. Mouse, who was into vampires and fantasy and stuff like that, was totally skeptical. Rufus, who Joe expected to be skeptical, right away stated how they were dealing with evil forces. Everyone else was still not believing, but they were curious.

He wasn't sure he could do it, but he told them everything Layton had told them, instructing them on extending their chi and looking away, then trying to see with their peripheral vision. Eventually, when he could see that their sensei wasn't coming back, they closed up and he took the group, with the exception of Lamont, to look for ghosts.

"Man, you're messing with things you really shouldn't," Lamont said. "My grandmother always told me stories about things like that. You should just say no."

"What was she, some old voodoo momma?" Mouse asked.

Lamont turned so they were face to face. "Yes Bob, she was. You got a problem with that?" He and Mouse were the two tallest students in the school, but while Mouse was plump, Lamont was hard muscle and had a deep, dry voice, like a crypt door being forced open. Mouse backed down, grinning and blushing.

"Hey, I didn't mean anything. Just wanted to know," he squeaked.

Lamont didn't move. Then he nodded.

"This is dangerous stuff here. I'm not kidding. Think twice before you try to deal with the other world."

"Guys, let's focus," Joe said. "Bruiser, where's Mr. P.?"

"He got called away," she said. "He asked us to close."

"Who called him?"

"No idea."

"Why not?"

"Probably because I'm not his secretary or yours," she said.

"Oh." He paused. "Well, want to go out and see if we can find some ghosts? I think I can do it now. I've been thinking about it all day and it's stuff we do all the time. I'm not going to be freaked this time."

Lamont shook his head. "I can't be any part of this." He walked to the changing room.

"He's right," Bruiser said. "You shouldn't do this."

"Are you going to walk off, too?"

"I don't know. Someone should watch so you don't get hurt."

Joe turned to the rest of the group. "What about you guys? Are you all in?"

"Yeah," Connor said. "Let me change first."

"I don't know," his brother said. "Mom would kill me if you got hurt."

"Hey, I'm nineteen. And we just won't tell her."

Lowell looked concerned, but shrugged.

"Mouse?" Joe asked.

"Hells yeah. I'm in." He tried to look tough after backing down from Lamont.

"OK, let's change and go fight ghosts."

Chapter 6

Two things happened that I hadn't expected that afternoon. The first was a call on my cell phone from Brianne. She had the night off. Her daughter's paternal grandparents were in town from Florida, so the girl was spending the weekend with them. Apparently, Bri had moved back to New Orleans to be closer to Annie's father, who was now in Slidell. She wanted the girl to grow up with a father, and living in New York for grad school was too far.

The second odd thing was a call from Detective Bouchard. He wanted to talk to me about something and asked if it was OK to stop by the dojo. I thought it would be better to meet elsewhere instead of in front of my students, so I named a coffee shop. I would meet with him before going out with Bri. I hoped I had time for a shower between the two engagements.

Bouchard was at the coffee shop as I entered. It was a warm December night, and I had a light jacket over the T-shirt I had worn all day. He was in a light suit that strained against his paunch.

I got a coffee and sat down at his table.

"What can I do for you, Detective?"

"Well Gillian, you come right to the point."

I didn't like that. He knew the right pronunciation and that I didn't use the name. He was trying to intimidate me or get me riled.

"Yes Joey, I do."

"That's Joel. And I prefer Detective Bouchard," he said.

"And my name is Guillaume, not Gillian. Guillaume Paul Layton. And prefer Dr. Layton. OK?"

He shrugged. "Whatever."

I took a sip of coffee and waited until he spoke. He said nothing. It was good coffee and I took another sip, smiling in enjoyment. I was going to out wait him. He called me, after all.

When I was a boy, I would get teased with the name "Gillian". Those who could pronounce it, would use my name properly, but with scorn. I stopped using it when I was about twelve. Guillaume came from the French side of the family, but they had come from Massachusetts and before that, Quebec, not New Orleans. It was a long way back to actual French ancestors. Before I had ever been to the city, probably from the first time I had heard of it, I always felt the pull of New Orleans. I could use my first name in this city; everything was French, but I couldn't get past the childhood taunting. And now some fat local cop was trying that juvenile tactic in order to get me riled. I refused to rise to the bait. I blew on the coffee, took a sip, and smiled again.

It sipped about a quarter of the cup before he finally gave in. I think it was my expression as I drank the coffee. I was giving myself to the pleasure of the perfectly brewed drink. Sometimes a cup of coffee could be the best part of the day.

"I made some calls about you," he started.

I said nothing, just had another sip. It was cooling down and I was able to drink it faster.

"Don't you want to know what I found?"

I shrugged. "I can guess."

"What would you guess?"

"That I have no record, except for taking out two different restraining orders against a police officer in Ohio."

"And why'd you do that?"

"Because he was harassing me."

"Why was he harassing you?"

I knew it. He was a cop and cops stuck together. It didn't matter how dirty the cop was, there was a loyalty, and *us versus them* mentality. I was *them*, so I was the enemy.

"It was over a girl. They were dating, then she broke up with him. We started dating and he went nuts."

"Nuts?"

"I know. I'm a Ph.D., I should use more elevated terminology."

"What did he do?"

"He tried picking fights with me. He pulled me over when I was driving and ticketed me for having a broken taillight, which he broke with his night stick after pulling me over. He staked out my house. He gave me a ticket for parking in my own driveway and one for the grass on my lawn being too high. Both were ridiculous charges. He pulled me from class over nothing. Finally, he supposedly *accidentally* discharged his weapon in my presence—he shot over my head. All in all, he was put under investigation, was suspended for six months under psychiatric counseling and anger management, and then he came back to work. The first restraining order kept him three hundred feet away—that was while he was suspended. The second restraining order was when he was back on the force. Because he was back in good standing as an officer of the law, it was a limited restraining order. He had to keep a minimum of one hundred feet from me unless in the case of extraordinary circumstances. Then he could only approach if he was with another police officer or rescue worker. And by judicial order, all of the tickets he gave me were expunged from official records." That was the short explanation of why I didn't trust cops anymore. I had the feeling that Bouchard was going to make me trust them even less.

"Basically, he was a bully with a badge. I don't like bullies." I glared at Bouchard.

"And that's your story?"

I scowled. "It's a matter of public record. If you called anyone about me, that's the story you would have gotten. If you talked to Officer Forrest, you might have heard something different, but consider the source."

"That was his name?"

"Rance Forrest. If you called about me, you would have heard the name."

"What about a Beatrice Smith?"

"Who?"

"A hooker. She also went by the name Bibi Love. Ring any bell?"

I shook my head. As far as I knew, I had never had any dealings with prostitutes. I had been solicited by many, mostly in New Orleans, though. I just ignored them or made a joke and went on my way.

"I don't know who that is."

"According to the Cleveland police, you do." He pulled a sheet of paper from his jacket pocket. "Says here, you were in Cleveland's Coventry section and you came to Miss Smith's rescue."

That came back to me. Three young men were pushing around a young lady. I stepped in and stopped them. One of the guys took a swing at me. I did an irimi, which is an Aikido move, spun him around, then dumped him on his face. The police came along minutes later, while the other two guys were working up their courage to take me on. They were being urged by the guy who was still on the ground with scraped knees and a bloody lip. He could have gotten up at any point, but I think he wanted the others to fight for him after he saw what I could do.

"That girl I helped out? She was a prostitute?

"Don't tell me you didn't know."

"I didn't."

"Says here, Cleveland cops think you might have been her pimp, coming to her aid so's the johns didn't damage the merchandise."

"You've got to be kidding. I'd never met her before and never saw her again. Where the hell did they get that idea?"

"Doesn't say. Probably because you were her pimp?"

"Get real."

"So you're just walking along and you see a girl in trouble and you step in, right?"

I looked at him with disdain. My coffee was cold and had lost its ability to please me. "What would you do in the same situation?"

"This isn't about me."

"It's not about me, either. It's some story you or someone else imagined. If you see some girl getting slapped around, you'd step in. It's the right thing to do. If I do that, you call me a pimp." I paused. "Someone isn't thinking very clearly."

He said nothing.

"Jesus. I bet Forrest planted that seed in the Cleveland P.D.'s mind. I wouldn't put it past him."

"Why do you say that?"

"I was a hero that night. I made it all over the news. There's even a video. The whole encounter was filmed by a local artist who had a video camera. He was there for his friend's art gallery opening. That gallery was where we were going, in fact. And if you look at the video, I'm with my date. I tell her to go inside the gallery, then I went to the guys who were roughing up the girl."

"Yeah?"

"And it happened during the time Forrest was under suspension for harassing me and discharging his gun in public."

Bouchard pulled at his lower lip. I could see his mind working.

"Sounds awfully convenient."

"What does?"

"Being taped. You just happened to be a Karate expert and there was someone with a camera."

I shrugged. "So was that why you called me? You thought I was a pimp because I helped some girl out?"

"What do you think?"

I wasn't going to tell him what I thought. "You tell me. That's why I was asking."

"I think you're a pimp and you got involved with something with that Helman kid. Then you or someone else killed him for it."

I shook my head. He was fishing.

"No, you don't think that," I said, dismissively. "If you really thought that, you'd have taken me in. I'd be needing a lawyer by now. As it is, you just wanted to ask me about that stupid accusation." I paused, seeing that I was right. "And you don't even believe it. I bet you saw the video by now. You probably found it on Youtube."

He said nothing, but I could see some red in his cheeks.

"Yeah, and I know there's something going on with you." He looked at me with a firm set to his face. "What about your students?"

"My students?"

"You ever sleep with them?"

"What are you talking about?"

"That why you left that school? You sleeping with your students? You pimpin' them out? I bet some of those hot young college broads would do anything for a grade. Was that Bibi girl a student of yours?"

"No, of course not. And I never slept with any students."

"Don't make sense to me. You professors have a pretty nice life. You got summers off, you get tenure and they can't fire you. Don't make sense that you up and quit to open some Karate school that's barely making ends meet."

I was about to argue, to say how far off the mark he was, but he had made up his one-track mind.

I was right. He was making me trust cops even less.

I looked at my watch. I had less than an hour to get home, shower and change, and meet Bri. I was riding my bicycle, so I'd have to hurry.

"I've got to go." I was going to tell him to contact my lawyer if he had any more questions, but the only lawyers I knew were friends from my undergraduate days, and none were in Louisiana. With no lawyer to advise me to act maturely, I took another dig at him. "I had a lovely time, let's do this again," I said in an overly sweet, almost effeminate voice.

"This ain't over."

"Let me know when it is. I'll send the fat lady some flowers."

I biked home, showered, changed, and drove to meet her. I made it to Frenchman Street barely in time. I was lucky in finding parking.

Frenchman Street is just past the French Quarter in Faubourg Marigny and is where the local bands play. There are some excellent clubs there and some incredible restaurants. It's where the locals go because it hasn't really been discovered. The serious New Orleans regulars go there, but they still spend their time in the regular places. The people who work in the Quarter go to Frenchman Street to have their fun.

Brianne was walking down the street as I got out of my car.

"Bri," I called. She was wearing a green summer dress and had a big purse, which I later found held a jacket in case it got chilly. December temperatures in New Orleans could be in the eighties, but they could also drop to the forties by the time one finished dinner. She wasn't dressed entirely for the warm weather; black leather boots covered her legs to the tops of her knees, two inches below where the dress stopped.

"Hey you," she said, grinning to show perfect teeth.

"Perfect timing. I just got here." She surprised me with a kiss on my cheek. Immediately I forgot about about Bouchard and his ridiculous line of questioning.

"I didn't think you'd make it. It was such a last minute idea when I called."

"I'm glad you did."

She smiled again. "Where's this restaurant?"

I pointed to Adolfo's, which is upstairs from the Apple Barrel. The Apple Barrel is a little bar and jazz club that has some good regular bands.

"I've been to the bar there, doesn't Coco Robicheaux play there?" she said, naming a local musician.

I pointed to a small sign in the open door that said he would be playing there the next weekend.

"Oops." She blushed as red as her hair. "I didn't know there was a restaurant. Is it new?"

"It's been here for quite a while. I remember it from way before I moved here. It's just a small place, but really good."

We went up and I had the chicken with penne and she had their fish special. We talked about nothing for a while, just more things to get to know each other. Like most New Orleans tourists and long-time residents, we talked about food. It was a distinctly New Orleans tradition, talking about restaurants while eating at one that was also excellent. We found we had similar opinions on many restaurants: we liked the burgers and potatoes at Yo' Mama's; we couldn't agree on the best gumbo on town; we both liked the red beans and rice at Mena's Palace, but preferred that and the fried chicken at Dunbar's and we hoped that they'd rebuild; and we'd only been to a few of the really high end places, such as Emeril's or K-Paul's or the Court of the Two Sisters. We were both too poor to frequent the expensive restaurants. She asked if I knew if a couple places were open. I was happy to tell her I knew one place was and saddened to tell her that another wasn't.

That killed the time before the food arrived, and during the meal we went to different, getting-to-know-one-another topics. It took until we were finished and waiting for the check before I mentioned Bouchard and Dirk Hemlock.

"Wait, you can't just stop here. You've got to tell me all about that."

"Which part? This crazy detective thinks I was a pimp in Cleveland and he wants to connect me to some poor kid who was one of my Karate students."

"I want to hear it all."

I thought about it. I didn't want to tell her about the ghosts, but I was willing to tell her everything else.

"Let's get something to drink. I had some coffee while I was talking with the detective, but it sort of went bad."

"I could drink," she said.

We went into the Quarter, talking as we went. Bri had questions that Bouchard had never thought of. She wanted to know about Janice, the woman who the Griswold cop's ex. She hadn't started it all, but she was a bad choice for me.

"Shortly after we stopped dating, she started seeing another professor I worked with. He was a good friend of mine, but the cop, Forrest, didn't ever hassle him. Still, he and I stopped talking. I don't think they're still together, but I don't know."

"Do you miss her?"

"I miss Steve more. He and I would sit around and complain about students and the administration. He was kind of funny, thick glasses, wild hair, a laugh like a donkey braying. It was weird that she went for him, but I guess she wanted someone who was different from Forrest or me."

"Was Forrest like you?"

"Physically, I guess. He was taller than me, but muscular. He didn't ever try anything with me, but he made threats. He kept saying that he wasn't afraid of my bullshit Karate."

"Would you like to have fought him?"

I grinned. "Oh yeah—he needed it. He needed to be put in his place, but I knew if I tried anything, it would be a disaster."

"Did you move to get away from him?"

I shook my head. "I moved to follow my dream."

"How about to get away from her?"

I shrugged.

"I bet that was part of it," she said. A moment later, her arm was in mine. I continued with my story, getting to Dirk Hemlock's mysterious death.

"That's it?" she asked when I had finished.

"That's it," I lied. I wasn't going to go into the ghost angle. I still had a hard time believing it—I wanted rational explanations. "Real life ends with questions, not answers."

"You'll keep me posted?"

"If I hear anything, I will." Soon we were at Ryan's Irish Pub on Decatur. Before entering, I saw a familiar sight—a flaw in the air. We went in and I kept my eye on the floating light. It didn't follow us in, though.

"You should tell me all about your life," I said, when we got our drinks. "I feel like I've been monopolizing the conversation since we left Adolfo's."

"You have," she giggled. "But I don't have any cool stories about cops bothering me."

Over a Celtic singer and three back up musicians, I heard about her on again/off again relationship with her daughter's father and her dreams of becoming an art teacher. She was thinking of going back to grad school, but couldn't commit to the idea when things with her finances and her time with her daughter took priority. I nodded and said encouraging things at the right times. I'm like every guy—women are a mystery to me. But I did know one thing. When out with a woman, pay attention to her. Focus on her. Don't look at the other hot women who walk by. She needed validation and a friendly ear to listen to her, so I focused on her and her alone. It wasn't an act, though. I was genuinely interested. I just had to keep my eyes from wandering.

"I'd love to see some of your art some time," I said.

"I haven't done much in a couple years. I was working on one piece before Katrina, but when I came back, it was destroyed."

"What was it?"

"A sculpture. Sort of a free-form wood and fiber thing. It was in the car port of the apartment I was at. When I got back, though, it was all mold. I tried to clean it, but nothing could save it."

"That's too bad."

"Sculpture really isn't my thing. I do more collages. I thought I'd do something that was more conventional, though. I haven't really done anything since then."

"I hope you get back to your art some time."

She was quiet for a moment. "I think this is when I should invite you back to my place to see my etchings."

"Sounds like a plan to me," I said. She finished her Bass ale and I had the last of my Guinness. "My car is on Frenchman."

"Mine too."

"Hmmm, so we run into the logistical problem of how to get back. Want to walk to the cars? I can follow you then, or we can take only one car." I was kicking myself for taking her all the way across the Quarter for drinks. Now we'd have to walk back.

Outside, Bri and I walked along Decatur. She pulled her jacket from her over-sized bag and I helped her put it on. Out of the corner of my eye I saw something. A man was there, which isn't uncommon in any big city. But when my eye caught the same spot again, he wasn't there. There was a flaw hovering in the air, hovering fifteen feet behind us. I stayed a step behind her, in case it got closer.

"I have an idea," I said, my eyes flicking back to the flaw. It was keeping its distance, but for how long I didn't know. I didn't want to fight an invisible opponent in front of her.

"Hm?"

"Let's take a cab to Frenchman."

"Good plan." We cut through two groups of tourists, one was speaking in German, and hurried across the street to be on the right side of traffic. It wasn't hard to wave a cab down in front of the Hard Rock Café. I couldn't see the flaw anymore, so I was hoping we were safe. Although with my record at seeing the damn things, maybe I had just lost my concentration and it was climbing in the cab with us. Nothing happened, though, except the cabbie tried to rip us off.

"Frenchman Street," I said, and he made a U-turn and started taking us away from our destination, toward Canal.

"Whoa," I said, rapping the back of his seat. "Where the hell do you think you're going? Frenchman is the other direction."

"Oh," he said, with some accent I couldn't place, "I thought you meant something else." He took another U-turn and we were on our way back. Bri laughed and I looked angry.

In three minutes we had reached Frenchman Street and were getting out of the old Caddie that stank strongly of cigarettes and incense.

"Seven dollars, man," he said.

"Seven?" I dug into my pocket and found a five and two ones. "Don't ask for a tip."

He grumbled, but not aloud enough for me to hear anything specific. I wasn't being a tightwad—he was trying to pad the bill, then he overcharged me. A minute later I felt guilty for stiffing him. It was post-Katrina. People needed the money, some took shortcuts.

Chapter 7

Heather knew it was a bad idea. She lagged behind the guys as they excitedly exited the dojo. She checked the door to make sure it was locked and hurried up after the testosterone gang. Joe was telling them again how to extend to see the ghosts and to keep a cool head if they wanted to touch them. Heather took a breath and tried to extend her chi. She saw nothing.

She was new to the dojo and to New Orleans. She had been there a year, coming along four months after Katrina. At first she drove to a Tae Kwon Do school in Hammond, but when Layton's school reopened the summer of '06, just a few blocks from her rental, she joined right up. She liked the workouts and the camaraderie of the school. Layton taught an eclectic, aggressive style, but was able to tailor techniques to her size. She'd often fight against Lamont or Mouse, who were each somewhere between two and three times her size, and she did well. In the school in Hammond, she got paired with kids. And there, like in every dojo and gym she had worked out in, she got nicknamed Tinker Bell, since she was small, blond, and her last name was Bell. Here, the first time she sparred with Layton, he started calling her Bruiser, and he wasn't being sarcastic.

New Orleans was a scary town. When she first got there, military, police, and emergency workers from all over roamed the streets. As the months passed, the police presence dwindled a bit, but some parts of the city were still under martial law. The population was growing, and gangs were establishing new territories. Heather was tiny, and even her years of Karate didn't help. A big city was scary. New Orleans was more so.

Raddeville, in southern Virginia, was the type of town she was used to. The neighborhoods were small, the people were mostly the same as each other —she, in fact, stood out because she had stopped growing at eleven. There she knew her place in her family, her church, and situation. She went to the University of Rochester, way up in New York, for her bachelor's through her doctorate. And now Heather, who was raised a Christian, and born again when she was thirteen, was living in the city that God forgot. Vegas may have been nicknamed Sin City, but New Orleans was all sinners. People walked around with alcoholic drinks in their hands, strippers and prostitutes were all over the French Quarter, where tourists and locals exchanged money for putting their souls in danger.

They were heading out at random, but the gravity of the French Quarter seeed to be pulling at them. The path wound through the Central Business District, which was usually safe. It was night, though, and the whole city wasn't as safe as it used to be. Before Katrina, it had been the murder capital of the United States. Since then, it was worse.

Joe walked ahead of the group. He had a cocky strut that showed he was looking for a fight. Mouse plodded, his weight obviously slowing him down. Lowell walked stealthily. He didn't confront, but avoided obstacles. Connor's walk was slow, as if he was often distracted and then catching up. She wondered how she walked to an outsider. Maybe she should ask someone to tell her how she walked. Maybe, she thought, she'd ask Layton. She couldn't remember how he walked...like Joe, maybe.

The guys were getting away from her, so she hurried up.

"You know what would be hilarious?" Connor asked the group at large. "If someone tried to mug us."

"Yeah," his brother said, "some gang banger pulls out a gun. That would be hilarious."

They almost looked like a gang themselves, Heather thought. The guys were wearing jeans, t-shirts with the school's emblem, and the school jackets. The only exception was Mouse. He was wearing a sweatshirt and shorts. It was cool out, but not overly so for December, and Mouse never seemed to mind the cold. She was wearing jeans, a sweater, and a belted black leather coat that went down to mid-thigh.

"No, no guns. I was just thinking that if someone tried to jump one of us, we've got all these black belts. I mean, imagine his surprise, you know."

"We'd just let you defend us," Joe said. "We'll stand back and see how you do. If you beat up a whole gang of muggers, you get your black belt."

"How about if I beat up one of these ghosts?"

"Yeah, let's just see if we can touch them first."

Canal Street was bright, but still not nearly as crowded as a usual Saturday night. Small knots of people filled some of the void, some were tourists, most were locals waiting for the buses, since the streetcars weren't running their full routes. There wasn't the pre-Katrina energy, and a lot of people didn't know if the spirit would come back.

They crossed into the Quarter, Heather still lagging. For all their martial arts expertise, they weren't paying much attention to their surroundings. Typical male attitude. Totally goal oriented. They were a large enough group and in a well-patrolled area, but she looked around for possible attack anyway. As she did, she saw that Lowell was also looking around. She breathed a little more easily knowing she wasn't the only one keeping an eye out for more than just the supernatural.

Chartres runs horizontal to the Mississippi. It leads to the St. Louis Cathedral and Jackson Square. Along the way there are many cross streets, and Heather didn't know all their names. The passed Iberville, Bienville, Conti, and kept going deeper into the Quarter. They took a left at some point, toward Royal, then wove around a bit until Joe stopped, his arms outstretched, stopping the group.

"There they are," he said. "In front of that bakery. Two shapes. See them?"

A few seconds passed. "I see something," Connor said. "Lowell?"

"Hang on. It's like those 3-D illusions. I gotta keep looking; it's like something is there, but I can't see it."

They were quiet for a second. Heather looked at all of them. Connor was rapt, looking at things that weren't there. Lowell was squinting in that direction. Mouse was also looking in the direction, but he was looking scared.

He saw something. She looked back at the ghosts. Nothing was there. She took a deep breath through her mouth and let it out slowly through her nose. Nothing. They were all looking, even Lowell wasn't squinting anymore—his eyes were wide in shock. She tried again, extending her chi. She cleared her mind. And there they were. Her eyes went wide as she took in what she was seeing. She started to pray.

"I'm going in," Joe said.

"Don't," Heather said, but he couldn't hear her. Her voice was stifled by the appearance of the two creatures.

Rocking his neck from side to side, rolling his shoulders, Joe approached. Heather and the group watched as he got to the first of the specters. It moved and Joe gave it a shove.

A shove in everyday life is never efficient. People stand up straight and push as if they were doing a bench press. They are off balance, and their opponents are too. Shihan Layton taught them how to drop into a low front stance, get under the target's center of gravity, and push by extending through the target.

Joe must have figured that the move would maximize his extension. Extension was the key to touching these things. One of the keys, that is. Heather held her breath and hoped that he remembered the other techniques.

The thing went flying backwards, through the store window a few feet behind it. The window didn't break, the thing just phased through it. The second one started for Joe, but he was ready for it. He held his hands up to block its grab, then he lashed out, a swift kick to the leg, and a palm heel strike to the thing's face. It backed off a step, possibly surprised. Then it lunged again.

Joe blocked a swinging slash toward his throat. He struck out, making contact again. The thing sped up its attack and Joe blocked furiously. Heather gasped as a punch got through to Joe's face, then she saw a movement behind him.

"Joe! The other one!"

She hardly had the words out when two shapes rushed by her, Lowell's five feet ten and Mouse's six-three. Lowell's jumping side kick hit the creature in its side, and as it fell, Mouse was there with a powerful fumi-komi—a stomp—crushing the thing's head. It disappeared. Joe was on the ground by then. From the ground he aimed a kick up to its groin. It went down. Joe scooted forward and ax-kicked it over and over, until his heel met no resistance and hit the sidewalk.

"Damn," Connor said softly, still standing next to her.

*   * *

Ten minutes later the group was sitting around a table at the most popular coffee shop in the city, perhaps any city, Cafe du Monde. Cafe du Monde is a mostly open-air establishment with a small inside area and one of the more disgusting restrooms in the Quarter. In the morning, the place is choked with tourists; the lines were long then, and the wait staff took their own sweet time. In the evening, Heather had learned from Layton, service was much better and there usually wasn't a line. They served two things, their signature coffee and beignets—small rectangular pieces of dough, fried like doughnuts, then covered with tons of powdered sugar. Everyone ordered cafe au lait and beignets, Mouse ordered two servings.

"That was awesome!" Connor said. He directed his question to Lowell, "What did it feel like?"

"I don't know, like kicking a person." He shrugged.

"Yeah, like a person," Mouse added. He was breathing heavily, but it had been long enough since the encounter that he shouldn't be winded.

They all looked at Joe. He chewed a beignet, swallowed, chased it down with some coffee. "It was like a person. It hit pretty hard, and those fingers are like claws. They're fast and they seem to just be in attack mode. They don't have any style, though."

"Do you think you killed it?" Connor asked.

"I don't know." Joe paused, then asked the question that was on everyone's mind. "Can you kill a ghost? Aren't they dead already?"

"That's what I figure," Mouse said.

"So what happens when we kill them?"

"Maybe we just banish them," Mouse said. "Send 'em back to the other realms."

"Other realms?" Lowell asked.

"To wherever it came from. Or maybe where it should have gone originally. Maybe it's stuck here before going to whatever happens after death? We're just helping them along."

"Like heaven or hell?"

"Or purgatory. Or another dimension. Or even to final rest. We don't know."

The guys started talking at once. The conversation was discordant for a moment. Then they stopped. Joe spoke up.

"I'm not really sure what we're doing. I know they attacked me, and they killed that guy, that Hemlock."

There was some nodding. "Whatever they are, they're bad."

"I still wonder. Can a ghost die? Isn't it a soul?" Connor asked. All eyes turned to Heather. They all knew she was religious, she was a scientist, and she was the oldest one there.

"I'm not sure. I don't know if they were ghosts. Or souls. I think they were demons."

"Demons?" Lowell asked. Mouse sputtered some powdered sugar and supplied a laugh.

"C'mon. They weren't demons," Mouse said. "If they were demons, they'd be, I don't know, different. We wouldn't have such an easy time kicking their asses if they were."

That brought out some high fives and a chorus of macho self-congratulation. Heather sat through it, sipping her coffee. She wanted to get back to the discussion of souls, but the guys had other ideas.

"Their weakest spots are their throats and heads. Those seem lethal."

"The joints, too. Those can be broken."

"What about the groin?"

"I don't know. They seem male, maybe they have 'nads."

"Why?"

"Why what?"

"Why would they have them? Ghosts can't reproduce, can they?"

"It doesn't seem likely."

"Yeah, but when I'm dead, I want all my equipment still with me."

"If there was one part they could keep intangible. It would have to be the groin."

"Next time, try kicking the groin. It would be good to know if they can be taken down that way."

"Yeah, I can just see that, Casper the Friendly Ghost getting a swift kick in the yarbles."

"Yeah, Casper packs a pretty package."

"Hey, he satisfies Wendy the Witch."

"Who?"

"Never mind."

"We are awesome, though," Connor said.

"It's like we're superheroes," Mouse said.

"Yeah," Joe said. "Too bad we can't tell anyone."

"That's just like it is with superheroes," Mouse said. "Secret identities and all that."

"Except those are so the villains won't track them down and kill them and their families. We can't tell anyone because no one would believe us," Joe said.

"We could leak the story around," Mouse said.

"Yeah, but who would believe in ghosts? Would you believe a story about some guys who are fighting bad guys that no one can see?" Joe countered.

"Good point."

"So we're secret superheroes. That's cool. Yesterday I was just some guy taking a year off before college," Connor said.

"You haven't killed any of them, though, so you're not a superhero yet," Joe said.

"He's part of the team, though," Lowell said.

"And I can see them. That's more than most people."

Eventually, the coffee was gone and the beignets just piles of powdered sugar that Mouse was dipping his finger in and licking off. The conversation returned to the ghosts.

"Do you think they're people who died in Katrina?"

"I don't know. I don't think those people would be so aggressive," Lowell said.

"The city has a ton of ghost stories. Maybe it's some of them. Ghosts of murderers and things like that," Connor suggested.

"You never know," Mouse said.

"Y'know, we should see what Mr. Peabody has to say about it," Joe said.

"Yeah," Lowell agreed. "Dr. Layton seems to have a theory."

They looked at him. "When did he become Dr. Layton?" Joe asked.

"Somewhere around nineteen ninety..." Mouse supplied.

"Not that way," Joe said. "I know he has a doctorate; when did he become Doctor Layton to us?"

"Since I want us to take this seriously," Lowell said. "We should be afraid. And we shouldn't do anything until we know what we're doing."

"You're pretty close to a doctorate too, Frood, and Bruiser has one. And hers is in a science, not English, like Mr. P.," Joe said. He turned to Heather, "What do you think, Doctor?"

For a second she felt her mouth go dry, but she spoke anyway. "I think we should pray."

At her apartment she prayed. It was an hour later, but they had all walked back to the dojo, got in their cars, and drove Heather back to her building in a convoy. Joe in his pick-up truck, Lowell and Connor behind him in the SUV they both used, and Mouse followed in his big old Cadillac.

Heather Bell, third child of six of Reverend and Mrs. Eli Bell, prayed several times each day. She prayed for her family, for guidance, for the city she was stuck in, for the nonbelievers at the dojo who she really did like, and for her sins. She had the sin of vanity, the sin of impatience, of judging people, and of lust. It was the last one she couldn't live with. She didn't lust after any of the guys in the dojo; not Joe, although he was the lady's man, or Lowell, who was close to her age and more on her intellectual level, or even Layton, who was smart and attractive for an older guy. She was sure lots of women were interested in him, but to his credit, he never made any suggestions or hints, like most of the others had. No, she wasn't interested in him.

She lusted after women. It was wrong, but no matter how much she prayed, she would still wake up at night with dreams of things she had never done with a man, much less a woman. Her gaze would linger on Maria, the receptionist at work, on Diamond, when she'd stretch, and at the numbers of women not wearing much in the Louisiana heat. She'd even walked up and down Bourbon Street on weekend nights, seeing the college girls flash for beads, even though it wasn't Mardi Gras. It had been like that since high school. She'd tried dating, she'd had boyfriends, she'd lost her virginity—it was a sin, but it seemed the lesser of two evils at the time. It all left her cold. Now she was thirty-three and the only unmarried one in her family. She needed to find a good Christian man and marry and have children.

Hers was a sin of the flesh. The Bible was clear, women should be with men, not other women. Genesis, Leviticus, and so many other part of the Good Book called her evil lusts an abomination. From the beginning, the Garden of

Eden, God's plan was man and woman, as shown by Adam and Eve. Like her father said, it was never Adam and Steve. And it was never Heather and Eve, either, but he didn't say that because he'd never know.

The Lord was perfect and Man was created in God's image. By sinning, she was rejecting God's glory and His plan for her. She prayed for Jesus to help her get over the temptation. She knew if she kept up the lusting in her heart, or if she ever acted upon it, she'd wind up in hell. She hated herself for her weakness and hated the despair she felt.

The demons she saw were a warning; it was that simple. The guys were calling them ghosts, but hadn't they seen them? Didn't they see the horns, the cloven hooves, the enormous bat wings on the one Joe fought, the flames? They were devils.

Chapter 8

I didn't go to Bri's house to see her etchings—or anything else, sadly. Bri and I had taken the cab back Frenchman, and there was a little tension then. I suggested we stop in at the Praline Connection, which we did. We listened to a jazz trio, had a couple more beers, and went our separate ways with just a kiss on the cheek.

I would have liked to do more—I think she would have liked to do more. That comment about seeing her etchings was a good come-on, and I wanted to take her back to my place, or go to hers, but I had a change of heart. I was fighting ghosts and the one that followed us had spooked me. Bri had nothing to do with them, and I wanted to keep it that way. I didn't want her to get hurt. I made a half-assed excuse and promised we'd get together another time, then I drove home swearing at myself and the ghosts.

When I got home, I had a beer. It had been a long day and I was wound up. I needed something to calm myself down. It wasn't too late. I watched *Saturday Night Live* and had a couple more beers. I wasn't sleeping and I knew what was bugging me. It wasn't that I probably blew it with Bri.

Detective Bouchard was going to be a pain in my side. I had an idea of what he wanted, but nothing specific. He'd be on me until he got something. He was probably in contact with Officer Forrest back up in Ohio. I couldn't think of anything I could say or do to get myself off the hook with him.

I'm not a heavy drinker. Being a health nut, I never got into it in college. It wasn't until grad school that I suddenly became a big fan of stouts, porters, and bock beer. Later I learned to like lagers and ales. But while I was learning to like alcohol, I wasn't building up a strong tolerance.

A few beers and I felt light headed. I was still wired from the evening, though, so I had one more. I switched the TV to the Weather Channel

I woke with a start. I nodded again, then turned off the television. I switched off the lamp that stood next to the sofa. Carrying my bottle and the ounce or two of beer that was in it, I walked to the kitchen.

The house was a duplex, two shotgun layouts side by side. It wasn't quite a shotgun. If one opened the front door and shot a gun straight back, it would hit the sink, which is next to the back door. The living room leads to the dining room and that to the kitchen. The stairs to the upper two floors comes out in the dining room, right across the fireplace with the big cracked mirror above it.

As I passed the mirror, I thought I saw something. I spun around. Nothing was there. I took the seven or eight more steps, rinsed out the bottle and put it in the recycling bin. Done with my mission, I considered the mirror again. What I had I just seen? Some glint of light, but maybe it was one of the ghosts. I entered the dining room again, my hands up to defend myself.

Nothing was there. A look around the room convinced me I was alone. I let my breath out, a self-conscious grin on my face. In the dark room there was no glint of light floating around. I turned to the mirror. He stood behind me.

I spun. Nothing was there.

I had seen someone. It was one of the bullies who used to pick on me in junior high. Johnny Bailey. He was a big guy, a year ahead of me, with red hair that had started thinning by high school. What I had just seen was an older version, with red and white hair in a weak comb-over. He had the same sneer he'd always had, though. It was a trick of the light and my memory must have filled in the blanks.

I prowled around the room again. I was alone.

I laughed nervously. I had looked around the room, but not in the mirror. Standing by the mirror, I turned my head toward it. It just reflected me in the dim light from the streetlight that reflected between the houses and through the open blinds of the dining room window. I faced the mirror fully. Nothing. I leaned on the mantle and closed my eyes. It was time for bed.

The first attack was a punch to my lower back. I fell forward in pain. My eyes shot open and Johnny Bailey was behind me, his face in the same smirk it had been in when he was beating me up over thirty years before. I turned, a chop aimed at his throat. My hand went through it. He was there, though; he wasn't just visible in the reflection. He hit me again. I missed him with my elbow and fell forward, crashing on the small table we used as our dining room table and desk.

He pulled me off the table and slammed me against the mantle. I rolled toward the living room. He followed, kicking me as I moved along the floor. I tried kicking up and almost dislocated my knee as my forceful kick met no resistance.

I tried guarding myself, but his punches went wherever he wanted them too. Drunkenly, from too much beer but also from the pain, I rose and stumbled to the front door. I had to get away. At the door, he rushed me, a vicious kidney punch and a knee into my hamstring almost made me collapse.

I twisted the knob and pulled. Another hit to my kidney and I felt him grab my hair. He pushed my face into the door, grinding it against the pitted paint of the door. The deadbolt. I reached up and flipped the deadbolt. Finally, I fell out of the front door.

He towered above me in the doorway. I pushed back as he raised his foot to stomp on me. He missed and I pivoted. I rose and ran. He followed. In seconds, though, I couldn't see him anymore.

I stopped at a shop on Magazine. There were restaurants and coffee shops still open and the street was well lit.

"Jesus, what happened to you?" a skinny boy with blond dreadlocks asked from behind the counter.

"Can I use your restroom?" I asked. Right behind him a sign said, "Restrooms are for Customers ONLY."

"Yeah, sure." He gave me a key chained to a bent Bourbon Street souvenir mini street sign. "You're that Karate guy, right? I saw you at some festival, didn't I?"

Of course he did. Our little demo team performed at neighborhood street festivals, at the openings of movies, and at schools. It was a way to recruit students. And me, wearing a t-shirt that proclaimed the name of my dojo, I was recognizable.

In the restroom I rinsed blood off my scraped face. My shirt was spotted with red. I was bruised. What a great advertisement.

I had no money. My wallet and my keys were on my coffee table and the door was wide open. I realized I was wearing slippers. They were a dark brown suede with rubber soles, so at least they looked like shoes. I drank a couple handfuls of water from the faucet in the dingy bathroom. I needed to sober up.

"Thanks," I said to the guy at the counter.

"Hey, what happened to you?"

"I'm going to go with fell down a flight of stairs," I grinned. "Does it look like I fell down a flight of stairs?"

"No," he said. "It looks like you got the shit beat out of you."

"Thanks for the use of your restroom," I said.

I made it home without being attacked. At home, I looked all over for ghosts. Nothing. I was pretty sure I was safe. I was sober. I sat up until false dawn with ice packs on my bruises, thinking about why I could see the ghost but not touch it, while at other times I could touch them, but not see them.

*   * *

The next day was Sunday. Since there were fewer students, and since it was Sunday and the town was mostly Catholic and other Christian religions, I only had the dojo open for one session. From two to four we had an open session. Sometimes I wouldn't even show up and one of the upper levels would run things, but usually I was there. In the morning, I'd take my laptop somewhere, Royal Blend Coffee in the Quarter, Coffee Mojo, or a CC's and grade papers. More and more places were getting WiFi, which made my work easier. Before Katrina, Nagin talked about turning the whole city wireless. Surprisingly, he followed through despite the disaster. Mouse had been part of the team to institute the change.

I woke up shortly before noon. The smell of coffee crept into my dreams. The dream wasn't very mysterious. It wasn't some deep subconscious message, as far as I could tell. I was sitting in a dark restaurant or bar and Johnny Bailey was sitting across from me. He reached over to my cup of coffee and drank it. When he put it down, I pulled it to my side of the table. But he pulled it back and drank from it again. The smell was too much to resist. I woke up. Lying in my bed I wondered why I hadn't kicked him under the table and taken the coffee. It smelled soooo good. Then I wondered who made the coffee. My housemate was a tea drinker. I got out of bed, groaning with my aches and pains.

In the living room of the shotgun-style duplex sat Joe, Mouse, and Lowell, all holding steaming cups. The living room was chilly. It was supposed to warm up later in the day, but it was a cool morning.

"'Morning, Sensei," Joe said.

"Your roommate let us in," Lowell said.

I nodded. Samir, a graduate student from Turkey spent most of his time with his girlfriend, Ozlem. The rest of the time he was in his office working on his dissertation project. Since I was always at work, I only saw him a few times a week. We were virtual strangers, but we got along OK. He was good about replacing things he used in the kitchen, and we both kept the place clean. He wasn't there the night before, but must have come in to shower and change clothes that morning before going to campus.

"Who made the coffee?" I asked as I walked gingerly back to the kitchen.

"Joe and Lowell," Mouse said.

"It's a two-person job?"

"Lowell made it. I helped him find the filters and the coffee."

I kept the coffee in the freezer. I bought the beans I liked, ground a few days' worth at a time, mixed in some chicory, and kept it all frozen to keep the flavor longer.

I poured a mug and added some skim milk. It hadn't been in the pot long enough to burn, so I was pleased.

"Lowell, you're promoted to nidan," I said holding up my coffee. Nidan is second degree black belt.

"Don't I get anything?" Joe asked pretending to pout.

"You found the filters, so you can help Lowell find his belt if he ever loses it."

Lowell shrugged. "Sounds fair to me."

I grinned. The coffee was good.

"Bastard," Joe said.

"OK, you're both nidan." I turned to Mouse. "See what you missed out on for not making coffee?"

He shrugged. "Is there any more?"

"About half a cup."

"Fine," he lumbered to his feet. "I'll get the next pot going. That should be worth a measly little shodan."

"Dream on."

"What happened to you?" Joe asked. "Damn, you got seriously stomped."

"A ghost did this. But I saw him. I actually saw one."

"Wait, what happened?" Mouse came back from the kitchen, holding the coffee carafe.

I told the story and my conjecture that I had only seen the ghost because I was drunk. When I had done, Mouse shrugged.

"You saw it in the mirror? That's such a cliché." He went back to the kitchen.

"You know the weird thing? The guy I saw is still alive."

"Huh?" Joe asked.

"I went on line when I got home. The person who I saw the ghost as is alive and well."

"So unless he died last night, and that didn't make it to the news, you just imagined the face," Lowell suggested.

I nodded. "What are you guys doing here anyway?"

"Uhhh, we went ghost hunting last night."

"What happened?"

"We went into the Quarter, found two ghosts, and fought with them."

"We kicked their asses," Mouse said. He was back, standing in the doorway to the living room and holding the filter basket. "Lowell and I killed one. Joe got the other."

"More coffee, less boasting," Joe said.

"A pox upon thee," Mouse said. He returned to the kitchen.

"That's basically it," Lowell said. "We fought two of the things and fought with them. Joe started fighting the two of them, and when one got behind him, Mouse and I got that one."

"It was the three of you?"

"It was all of us, except Lamont. He didn't like the idea of messing with ghosts. But it was us three and Bruiser and Connor," said Joe.

"I want you to tell me exactly what you saw," I said to Lowell. He was the grad student in Psychology. I wanted his point of view, then I changed my mind.

"Wait. I have a better idea. Mouse, get back here." I went to the dining room table. It was really a Formica kitchen table but we didn't use the dining room for dining anyway. Samir and I kept our bikes in the room and we threw random things on the table—keys, papers, books, pens. I found a pad of paper and two pens and a mechanical pencil.

"Write down exactly what you saw. Describe the ghosts in as much detail as you can. Don't discuss it with each other." I paused. "Did you talk about what they looked like last night?"

"No."

"Good. I'll finish the coffee."

"Oh man, I'm never going to get my black belt," Mouse rolled his eyes in mock frustration. Nevertheless, he sat on the sofa and started writing.

"Face it Mouse, I'll always make better coffee that you ever could."

"Philistine."

A few minutes later I returned with a full cup of coffee. Coffee was still dripping into the carafe, but I had bogarted a cup with only one drop hissing on the heating plate of the machine.

"OK, let's hear what you have." I sat in my recliner but didn't recline. I leaned forward, eager to hear their observations.

Joe started, but he had seen the same thing he described before. They were men in trench coats and fedoras. Black and gray with pale skin.

"That's not what I saw," Lowell said, looking surprised. Being a good grad student, he looked at his sheet of paper. "Two ghosts, misty white, the heads and upper bodies were clear, although their lower portions were wispy. They looked desiccated, with their skin very close to the bone. The eyes were wide open and so were the mouths."

Mouse was shaking his head through it all. "You both missed it. They were tall, about six, six, and had big pointed ears and were really thin. They were wearing these cassock-like things."

"What color were they?"

"Oh yeah, they got it right there; they were really pale."

"You know what I just realized?" Joe said. "They were like they were in black and white. Like an old movie."

"That's unusual. Did it seem that way with you two?"

"Not really," Mouse said.

"There was color. Not bright, but some in the clothing," Lowell said.

"You should call Connor and see what he saw."

He shook his head. "He went to church with Mom."

"Is it a holiday?"

"No, she just asked him and he said OK."

"And Bruiser's probably at church, too."

"Yeah, she wanted us to pray," Joe said.

"And she thought they were demons," Mouse supplied.

"And I only saw them as a little glare floating in the air like a flaw in a piece of glass. But last night, the thing looked like an older version of this guy who used to bully me when I was in high school. I looked him up on the Internet, though. The guy the ghost looked like is still alive. It wasn't a ghost. Those things are something else."

"Weird," Mouse said.

"Let's find out what the others saw without telling them what you saw."

"Sure," Joe said.

"You see where I'm going with this, right?"

I expected Joe to answer, but Mouse spoke up. I sometimes forgot how smart he was. He never finished his B.A., but he was a specialist of some sort for some computer company before Katrina, but was working at a computer retailer right now. He was also working on a novel that I'd read part of. It wasn't too good, but it was about the supernatural.

"We're each seeing different things. Maybe they don't have a real form, but we supply it from our subconscious."

"Right. What did you see again?"

"You know. Tall, thin, pointy ears."

I got up and went to the bookshelf. I found one of my books on German Expressionism. It was one of the academic books I had a chance to replace since Katrina, and the only reason I had a copy was that I saw it at a garage sale in Ohio when I was evacuated there.

"And they wore these cassocks that emphasized how skinny they were?" I asked. "And their fingers were long, with claw-like nails?"

"Yeah, I hadn't mentioned the fingers, though."

I found the photo I was looking for. "Max Shrek. Starring as Count Orlock in Murnau's 1922 classic of German Expressionism, *Nosferatu*."

Mouse smacked his forehead. "Oh! I should have known that! I've seen that film a hundred times. Oh man!"

"It was the cassock that made me think of *Nosferatu*."

I showed the other guys the still from the movie. "I used to have a copy of the DVD I could lend you, but it's long gone."

"I've got one if you want to borrow it," Mouse said. His novel had vampires in it. New Orleans was a good place for vampire lovers.

"I'm starting to think your theory is right," Lowell said.

"There's more to it. We haven't seen many of them, but Joe, you saw them the night before last. And Dirk told me a few things."

"OK...."

"In every sighting, the ghosts were white. Now, we're in New Orleans, a mostly black town. When Dirk and I were talking, he said he thought they might be people who died after Katrina. Most of the people who died from Katrina were also African American. When he described them, none of them were black. Would the ghosts all be white? Statistically, that's unlikely."

"Or maybe those ghosts just went to heaven?" Mouse asked.

I rolled my eyes. "Remember, I don't believe in heaven or spirits or any of that. If I did though, I'd still wonder at the odds of all those ghosts being exempted from roaming the earth.

"But I saw them—and will probably keep seeing them this way if I kep from drinking too much—as flaws in the air. Like a break in a pane of glass. I think that they're different from person to person, and you seem to prove that.

"Now, I'm not against the idea that black spirits go to heaven while white spirits roam the earth, but the odds are against it. If I were a believer, I'd be more inclined to assume that the afterlife is based on individual merit instead of color of skin. But I'm an atheist, so what do I know?"

"OK, I get it," Mouse said.

"Tonight I'll look to see if any are black," Joe said.

I shook my head. "I don't like the idea of getting them riled up. We should be careful."

"Careful?" said Mouse. "It's too late for that. They're riled."

*　　　　　　　　　　　　　*　　*

The guys went their separate ways and I stayed home to have something to eat and to try to get some work done before going to the dojo. I thought grading would keep me from distractions, but my mind was elsewhere. I only got through four papers instead of the twelve I was hoping to.

I arrived a little early, which was my habit most days so I could get in my own workout and see to anything that needed doing. My morning coffee companions and Connor were all there. The place was open for business, and everyone wore their gis, but no one was practicing.

I hung up my jacket and went to the heavy bag, where I started my warm-up. I hit and kicked it for a few minutes until I decided to finally let their eager gazes catch my attention.

"Looks like everyone is ready to work out, but I'm the only one doing anything."

"We figured we should talk before the kids start arriving," Joe said. They stepped in closer, making an oval around the bag.

"And Connor has his story to tell," Lowell added.

"OK, let's start there." I gave the bag a roundhouse kick and Joe put hand out, stopping it from swinging too far.

Connor stepped forward, looking a little nervous as all eyes were on him. "Lowell told me you wanted to know what I saw last night."

"The ghosts."

"Yeah, I don't know. It was like these shadows, you know? They were like shadows."

"Like a shadow? Black you mean?" I asked. There went my idea that we were all seeing what we wanted to—that we were seeing white ghosts since we were all white.

"No, not really. No color or anything. Just a blank space, kinda shaped like a person, but I couldn't really tell. I don't know, instead of a shadow, it was like a hole where they stood. Like I was looking into something. Maybe a tunnel. A dark tunnel, but with no light coming from it, so it's all in shadow, you know?"

I nodded. "I get the picture."

"What do you think of that one?" Lowell asked.

"I wonder." Ideas were coming together in my head. Connor's observation, although the so-called ghosts were human-sized tunnels of darkness, was more like how I saw the things. We weren't seeing them as any specific creatures, but as some oddity of perception. For me, it was a flaw and for Connor it was a tunnel. Poor Dirk had described the person he saw as standing a few feet behind what I saw.

"Here's what I think," I said. I punched the bag a couple times. "The creatures aren't ghosts. But you already knew that I don't believe in ghosts." I slammed the bag harder, feeling its resistance up through my shoulder as it tried its best to stop my punch. "I think we're dealing with something from another dimension. What Connor and I are seeing is the rift between the realities. We're seeing the rift in different ways, just like the rest of you are seeing the creatures in a different way."

"The rift is what, like a wormhole?" Mouse asked. He stepped up to the bag and gave it a good, solid front punch.

"Exactly."

"And why do we have wormholes here in New Orleans?" He punctuated the question with a couple quick jabs.

"I don't know," I punched the bag as I conjectured, "but maybe what separates the dimensions is like a membrane. Chaos, such as in natural disasters like Katrina and other big releases of energy make holes, so it's permeable in places."

"So would there have been ghosts seen after other disasters, or the bombing of Nagasaki and Hiroshima?" Lowell asked. He gave a ridge-hand and elbow combination.

"I've read about ghost sightings after earthquakes, battles, and, yes, the atomic bombs," Mouse said.

"Really? Or is that an urban legend?"

Mouse shrugged and kicked the bag. "Don't know."

"Katrina was over a year ago. Why would there still be holes?" Connor kicked.

I gave a pair of elbow strikes to the bag.

"Think of it this way. Right now, houses—whole neighborhoods—are being torn down, and people are coming and going. New Orleans is a chaotic place, even when it's not recovering from a hurricane. Look at how we party—we get over half a million people here in one big celebration that goes on for days. Hell, think of something as simple as a funeral. Around here you get jazz bands, dancers, professional mourners who will weep as they dance, it's anything but orderly. And now so much of it is being torn down and other parts are being built up. It's still chaotic." I paused and threw a couple ridge hands to the backside of the bag. "Admittedly, I'm getting the idea of chaos being a factor in the dimensional breakdown from science fiction stories, but it's the only thing I've been able to come up with so far.

"Now the ghosts you're seeing, and what Connor and I saw, that's easier to figure out. There are creatures from that other dimension. We can't see them, so we fill in the blanks with something from our subconscious."

"And your subconscious image is a flaw in a piece of glass, while Connor's is a humanoid-shaped tunnel," Mouse said. He kicked the bag to me. I struck.

"I think their nature is so alien to us, since they're from another dimension, that we can't conceptualize them at all, so we go to some template we have in our subconscious for things we can't perceptually deal with. Being from another dimension could make them exist in a way our minds can't process, so we fall back on whatever we can."

"And when you had too much to drink, you got in touch with your subconscious easier," Joe said, giving a side snap kick. "Y'know, I've never seen you drunk, Sensei. I wonder what that would be like."

"Boring," I said. "I get really tired and fall asleep."

Lowell stepped up and delivered a front kick. "I got an idea. Maybe the speed of light is different there. That would make everything—from atoms to everything made of atoms, which make up everything, of course—just so different. We've adapted to seeing certain spectra, so how could we see light that came at a different rate? And if their matter is going at a different rate, and we see because light reflects off the objects we see, the light coming from these other dimensional beings, or any other objects from that dimension for that matter, would be altered, too." Lowell took a deep breath after that—he had been kicking and hitting as he spoke.

"That might explain why the time dilation technique works to help us see them," Mouse said, starting his own attack on the bag.

I nodded.

"What do you think they're after, then?" Lowell asked.

I had no idea. I hit the bag a couple times; it swung away from me and I gave it a slapping hook kick. I still had no idea.

"I don't know," I admitted. "Any theories?"

"It's an invasion force?" Mouse said. He did a one-inch punch, but not well. He didn't put his formidable weight behind it.

"I think they're predators." Joe's one-inch punch was well executed.

"Could be," I said.

"And they've been getting stronger. I think we have to defend ourselves from them, and the best defense is a good offense," Joe finished, punctuating the claim with a front snap kick.

"I forgot about one thing Hemlock said to me," I said. "He saw an old homeless guy who also saw them and had scars on his arms. He said they were trying to take him with them."

"They were trying to take Hemlock or the homeless guy?" Lowell hit the bag.

I stepped up to it. My turn. "I don't remember exactly, but I think the implication was that the ghosts were trying to take people with them to wherever they came from." The bag swung from my forearm strike.

"And they've been getting easier to see since Hemlock," Lowell said.

"I wonder about that. Since we can see them, maybe Hemlock wasn't so special. He lucked into it, so he appeared on their radar. Then they got a taste of him and they wanted more. That's why they killed him."

"Maybe it's just the way they say hello, and we're just too weak to handle their greetings," Connor said and kicked the bag.

"If that were the case, we wouldn't be able to beat them up," Joe said.

"Good point," Connor admitted. He added a pretty good palm-heel strike.

"What about when we kill them? They just disappear. Do they go back to their dimension? Do they fade away? What happens?" Mouse asked.

"Good question," I said. "If they're all energy, then they'd fade away. Maybe they're coherent energy."

"Which is how they manifest in this reality," Lowell said.

"In that case, maybe they dissipate in this dimension. Like the energy of a fire when it's put out," I suggested. I gave the bag one last punch.

"And don't forget the ghost idea. They could still be ghosts," Connor said.

At that, the bell over the door rang and the first of the day's real students entered. It was the Fairstein kids, Mordechai and Aviva and their mother, Rachel. The mother would sit and read while the kids went through their motions. I went over and greeted them.

Chapter 9

There was too much talk for Joe. He wanted to hunt the things again.

He spent the two hours doing the same workout he'd do the day before a mixed martial arts competition. He focused on power and speed, but didn't push it. He didn't want to be tired or sore that night when he went out.

Would the ghosts look different now that he knew what the guys thought they were? And why did they only come out at night? Did they only come out at night?

It didn't matter. They were bullies. The things were coming to our reality and hurting humans. Joe wasn't going to stand for that.

He had another reason he wanted to try the things again. When he fought the ghosts, he could hit full force and not have to pull his punches. It was liberating. He couldn't train that way against anyone in the dojo—he didn't want to injure or even kill his training partners. Training at full power would be more like what he needed to do when in real combat. It would give him a fantastic edge in the MMA contests he entered.

After practice, he ate a light meal of fish, vegetables, and rice. That was always his training meal. Then he meditated and napped until dark.

Dressed in a tight fitting t-shirt and a loose sweatshirt, he went into the night. He elected to leave his car behind and walk out into the night. There had been only a little flooding in the Bywater area, but buildings were torn to shreds of brick and framework by the fierce winds, and there had evacuation, crime, and all the chaos that would be needed for rifts between dimensions to open. At least he hoped there was an opening.

He didn't have to worry very long. A few blocks from his home were three ghosts. Three of them. When it had been two of them, he was sorely pressed. He had done well against one, but when there were two and they were after his blood, he needed help.

Did he need the help, though? Layton took on three of them at one time. If the old man could, so could Joe.

He rolled his shoulders to loosen up and stepped toward the things. It was important, he knew from training in multiple-person scenarios in class, to not let one get behind him. He knew it wouldn't be like the movies, where the evil ninjas or the henchmen of the warlord attacked one by one. Multiple attackers used their numbers. They attacked from behind; one would hit high while the other would hit low; they never took turns. The trick was to keep them in each other's way and make the fight one by one. He wouldn't throw any through solid walls, so they wouldn't have a chance to sneak up behind him like the night before.

His forward movement caught the attention of the ghosts. They approached him and he saw his strategy. The first one to him reached out with its two claws. Joe sidestepped him, grabbed the nearer arm, and used that as a lever to control the thing as he spun in a full circle, pushing the thing around and then into the second one, which was within range. The two of them went down. The third raised both arms and silently snarled. Joe kicked it in the middle, where the solar plexus should be. It staggered backwards. One of the ghosts was pushing itself up from the sidewalk. Joe stomped on its neck and it disappeared. The other one had half risen and Joe drove a heel hard into its face. He didn't see it evaporate into nothingness, but felt it go intangible. He was already doing an about face to the one that was now recovered from the kick. Joe blocked, struck a couple times, then did what he had come to do.

He hit with full force, as hard as he could ever pound the heavy bag—much too hard to hit another person. It stumbled and a succession of hard punches took it out for good.

Joe breathed hard for a few seconds. He assessed his environment—no other ghosts were coming out of nowhere to attack him.

"That wasn't too hard at all," he lied. He looked around again. More self-conscious for talking to himself than he was for fighting invisible ghosts. No one would have seen the ghosts, if they'd been watching, and he hadn't been concerned about that.

For a moment, he stood there. He was all wound up and had no place to go. The fight still has his adrenaline going. Maybe he'd celebrate, he thought.

*   *   *

Even Sunday night in the French Quarter has its parties. He knew just the girl to find for a little party. She worked in a shop there and was into ghosts and vampires and all that stuff.

Her name was Gina, and although she was into the goth lifestyle, she kept her name instead of calling herself Belladonna, or Mistress Nightshade or Citronella or whatever. Her co-worker at the souvenir shop on Bourbon Street said that Gina was probably off with her friend who did readings at Marie Laveau's Voodoo Shop. Joe backtracked up the half-crowded street to the landmark store. A knot of drunken college guys blocked his path, but they parted as Joe walked through them. They didn't challenge him, and he didn't try to instigate anything. Maybe some other time he would have pushed it with them, but he didn't need to. Karate taught him to hold his temper, but sometimes it was fun to get tough.

At the back of Marie Laveau's, Gina was leaning on the counter talking to her friend, who looked hopefully at Joe for a reading.

"Hey Gina," he said. She turned and cracked a quarter-smile.

"Well, if it isn't Spiderman Joe. How's the superhero racket?"

"Mixed martial arts, actually." He had told her his nickname at the dojo, and she teased him with it when she could.

She was a small girl. Not as tiny as Bruiser, probably about five foot four and one ten, most of it in her chest. Her arms and legs were thin, almost anorexic-thin. Joe was a little over six feet tall and about one eighty. He had no body fat to speak of and his wide shoulders and muscled arms were a good match for her impressive chest.

"I'd rather think of you as a superhero," she said. Her hair this week was platinum blond, except for jet black bangs.

"I like it when you think that."

"Rose, this is Joe."

Rose nodded and Joe nodded back.

"Mind if I steal your friend for a little while?" Joe asked.

Rose shrugged.

"Who says I want to go anywhere with you?" Gina asked.

"C'mon, I got something I want you to see."

She rolled her eyes. "I probably won't be long," she told her friend, who said nothing.

She followed Joe down to Chartres and away from Downtown. He didn't know if there would be any ghosts, but last night they had found them by just randomly roaming.

"So you like the idea that I'm a superhero?"

She giggled, a little shyer once she was away from her friend.

"You believe in ghosts?" Joe.

"Uh huh. I've seen them," Gina said.

"Really? Here in New Orleans?"

"Promise you won't laugh?"

"I promise."

"Back home, in Calgary. I was thirteen. It was right after my grandmother died. We were having a blizzard and I got lost in it. It wasn't snowing when I went out, but the weather forecast said the storm was heading toward us. I was rounding up the cows and then it hit. It was white all over and I was lost. I couldn't see ten feet in front of me. Then I saw my grandmother. She was glowing. She led me to the barn. After that, I was able to get back to the house."

Joe said nothing. If these creatures were all evil invaders from other dimensions, how did that jibe with Gina's ghost sighting? Maybe she had just hallucinated her grandmother being there, or maybe there were ghosts in addition to these things. He'd have to suggest that to Layton and the guys. He was proud of himself for this idea. On the other hand, blizzards are chaotic. Maybe one of the things had come through, and, by coincidence, she had found her way to the barn.

"Any here in New Orleans?"

She nodded. "I've seen some things. That's why I believe. I saw some hazy shapes, like people, but you could see through them."

"Cool," he said.

"I was high each time, though," she said and laughed. "I was high when I saw my grandmother, too."

"At thirteen?"

"My parents grew the stuff, c'mon."

"I've been seeing ghosts," Joe said. "And I've been able to touch them, too."

"You're not making fun of me, are you?" she said suspiciously.

"No. I believe you. I can show you how to see the ghosts, too. If we can find any, that is."

"Really?"

"You wanted a superhero?"

"I don't know. I just like teasing you, Spiderman."

"They're hurting people. They've killed people, in fact," Joe said. To her wide-eyed gaze, he filled her in on what had been going on. He told her about Dirk Hemlock coming to the dojo, and teaching Layton how to see them and make them solid. Then how Hemlock was killed by the things and how Joe himself learned to fight them and how he killed some of them. He left out the brainstorming session and Layton's tortured explanation of them. He never said they were extradimensional invaders. He kept it about ghosts.

"So you're hunting them?"

"Yeah."

"And we're going after some tonight?"

"Yep."

"Cool. How can I see them? Do I have to get high now?"

"I think we can do it without getting high. I don't want to try fighting that way, anyway."

They wandered for about twenty minutes, with Joe coaching Gina about how to see the ghosts. She said she used to do Zen meditation, so extending her chi and trying to tune in on them might be something she could do.

On Ursulines, near the site of the encounter the night before, when Lowell and Mouse helped him out, he saw another knot of ghosts. He grabbed Gina's hand and stopped her. They were almost a block away, which was good. There were five of them.

"There they are," he whispered. He pointed. "Extend out and try to see them."

Gina squinted. She was quiet. "I don't see anything."

"Try to see past them. Hold our breath and look right in front of the burnt out street lamp. Then breath out and look past that spot."

"Oh my god. Look at them."

"Keep your voice down," Joe whispered, although she hadn't be any louder than his whisper. "I don't want them to see us."

"I thought you were going to fight them."

He was quiet for a few seconds. "I fought with three of them a couple hours ago. But I don't know about five of them."

"I see six now," she said.

"Let's get out of here," he said and pulled her back with him.

"OK." They got around the corner and hustled away.

Minutes later they were down by the French Market. "Did you see that sixth one at first?"

"No, I think there were five, then there was a sixth."

"What did they look like?"

She looked up at him. "You saw them, same's as I did."

"Go ahead and tell me anyway," he urged.

"They were wearing old-fashioned clothes. That's all I saw, really. We were pretty far away to make out features. A bunch of men in, like, those old jackets and hats, like in *Interview With The Vampire*. Kinda hazy, too. You could see through them."

Joe nodded. "Yeah, that's them." The ghosts he saw were nothing like hers, but he knew that already. This was good information for Layton and the guys to talk about. The sudden appearance of a sixth one was also probably important. He knew it was important to him. Six of them was too much to mess with.

"Let's walk along the river," he suggested.

The cold water that had poured down from the upper Midwest hit the warm, humid air of New Orleans and brought fog with it. When the December weather was right, the fog would creep over the city, but usually it stuck closer to the river. This night wasn't too humid, so the fog barely spilled over the banks of the Mississippi. Some trick of the light made the fog look white—as if they were in one of the blizzards from Gina's childhood. The air temperature dropped ten degrees as they got close to the river, and they huddled together.

The lighting was eerie—and the fog lent a claustrophobic atmosphere. A shape materialized ahead of them, it lurched toward them for a couple steps, then twisted. A cry came from it and two more shapes appeared. There was laughter and two more drunk kids caught up with their friends. They passed close to Joe and Gina; one of the girls held up a forty ounce beer bottle in a toast to Joe. The girl slurred something Joe didn't catch. The others kept their forties to themselves.

"I remember my first beer," Joe joked. The kids didn't hear, or they weren't paying attention. They were soon absorbed by the fog.

"This is weird. Everything looks so spooky," Gina observed. "It's spookier here than when we saw those ghosts."

"Yeah, the fog is pretty cool."

"Are we going to see any ghosts here?"

"I don't know. We might." He didn't really want to encounter ghosts in this fog. They could be on him before he had a chance to react.

"That would be awesome."

They walked farther, but only saw a few tourists and a couple homeless people. They turned back to the French Quarter and left the fog behind.

"That was the coolest thing. It was so surreal. First ghosts, then the fog by the river. I really thought that first guy we thought was a ghost, although the way he walked was like a zombie or something," she chattered excitedly. Joe let her ramble on. He was keeping an eye out for further threats, but nothing came. They were getting to the populated areas. Loud music blared from the open doors of clubs on and near Bourbon. Hard rock came from one place, karaoke from another, jazz from yet another—there was a whirlwind of sounds, light, and drunken, reeling people. This was chaos.

Gina pulled him past all the same old cheap thrills of Bourbon Street and two more blocks to her Burgundy Street apartment. Before they were upstairs of the abandoned storefront and in her place, she was tearing off his clothes.

Chapter 10

The spongy suspension of The Lady, the thirty-year-old Cadillac that he loved, bounced and rocked as Mouse pulled into the parking lot. Joe's truck was there.

Mouse had been spending his evening working on his novel or playing World of Warcraft. Ever since Katrina, he spent most evenings on his computer instead of going out. He used to have a pretty good social life. He sang in a choir, was a regular at a karaoke bar, and had his gaming group. Now Karate was his only social outlet, and he didn't attend too often. This recent business, however, was getting him excited about getting out again.

"What's this about?" he asked as he squeezed into the booth. The waitress stopped by the table and Mouse ordered a Diet Coke and a fried oyster po'boy. He wasn't really hungry, but Momma Khatukaryan didn't raise her baby boy Bobby to be rude. Mouse ate for many reasons, but finishing all the food on his plate was a central tenet.

"I went out last night and killed some of those things," Joe said.

"Cool. What happened?"

Joe summed it up pretty quickly.

"There were more when you came back?"

"Yeah, that's why I didn't fuck with them."

"It's cool that you took out three of them."

"It was just like the multiple-opponent training we do. Keep them in each other's way, hurt them hard and fast, and don't kick them through walls so they can come at you from behind."

"Nice."

"That's why I called you. I want to try them again, but I need someone to cover my back. If there are more than I can handle, I want someone there to jump in."

Mouse felt a thrill of pride for being asked. "Yeah, I can do that."

"I tried calling Lowell. He wasn't answering, so I thought I'd call you."

"Thanks," Mouse said. His smile disappeared. He grabbed the drink from the waitress as she returned to the table.

"After all, you killed that one. I need someone who can see them. I'd ask Mr. P., but I don't think he'd be into it."

"It's nice to be asked." He drank half his soda in one suck through the straw. "Why are you going after them?"

"It's great training," Joe said. "I can hit them as hard as I can. It's not like sparring with you guys. If I hit as hard as I can, I'd be breaking bones and probably kill some of you guys."

"I can take a punch."

"How hard did you hit that one?"

"It was a stomp—I really got it hard, too."

"That's how hard I get to hit these things." He lowered his voice as Mouse's po'boy arrived. "You can hit them hard enough to kill. You never get a chance to do that in class. What d'ya think?"

"Yeah, that would be cool." He raised his glass for more Diet Coke when his meal came. He opened the po'boy and added some of the horseradish sauce that came with it and took a big bite. Crisp French bread crackled as he bit and crumbs fell onto his shirt. The first bite awakened his appetite. He was hungry after all.

"When you're done, let's go find some of those suckers," Joe said.

In five more bites and the rest of his second Coke, Mouse was ready. They settled up and climbed in Joe's truck, leaving The Lady behind. Before he got in the truck, he looked longingly and lovingly at the car.

The Lady was Mouse's only connection to his father. His father, Stosh Khatukaryan, worked for General Motors. Like many of his co-workers, every year he traded in his old one and bought the newest model Cadillac. Mouse, or Baby Bobby at that time, never knew old Stosh. He died of a heart attack when Mouse was six months old. His mother put the car away under a tarp in their garage for Mouse to have when he turned twenty-one. It took three years before a neighbor, who heard the story from his wife, removed the battery, drained the gas tank, put the car on blocks, and otherwise readied it for a long hibernation. The neighbor thoughtfully left a note detailing what to do to get the car going again. When Bobby was twenty-one, he struggled through the illegible writing and the tortured grammar and got the car back into shape. Since then, he kept it in the best shape he could manage.

As they drove off, Mouse looked back to the brown 1977 Sedan DeVille. In some ways, it was a security blanket. He felt some fear, going after ghosts or, if Layton was right extradimensional beings, but he also felt some excitement. Joe was a serious fighter. He had been with the dojo for a year before Katrina and the six or seven months since Sensei reopened the place. He came to the dojo with a black belt in Ju-Jitsu and a brown in Shotokan and got his black belt the May before Katrina. He said he was training for Mixed Martial Arts competition. Mouse sometimes felt intimidated when practicing with him. Joe was a lot more serious than Mouse was, and maybe this was why. He couldn't wait to fight full force against those things again.

Mouse was excited about fighting them, but not as confident as Joe seemed to be.

They drove by where they had crushed the things the other night, where Joe had seen them the night before, but there weren't any they could see.

"There were some in my neighborhood," Joe said. He took a right and headed out of the Quarter.

"If we can't find any, maybe there'll be some in the Lower Ninth."

"Why?"

"More chaos there. At least that's the theory."

"Let's go see." He gunned the engine and they took off to the area of the city that had been most destroyed by the hurricane.

"We can't get in, can we?"

"Sure, why not?"

The Lower Ninth Ward was still somewhat closed off because of the devastation, but it wasn't totally quarantined. For most of a year, people were coming back and trying to fix their houses. At first, returnees had to show proof that they lived there, but after more than a year, one could come and go.

In some neighborhoods of the district, there was no electricity, no house lights, no streetlights. The quarter moon and the headlights of the Chevy painted a strange landscape of destruction. It had been a year and a quarter, yet the houses were still in ruin. Roofs were torn off. Vehicles were still leaning on their sides, some had drifted up to roofs when the water was high, and when it receded, the car or SUV wound up propped against the building. Piles of debris, rubble, waste, still lined some of the streets. Joe mumbled something.

"What?"

"I hope I don't get a flat. There's so much crap on the street."

"I didn't think of that," Mouse paused. "But I was right. Look at them, they're all over here."

Joe looked, squinted, then turned off the headlights and continued with the running lights.

"Look at them," he said.

The truck passed two ghosts standing together on top of a small house that had the windows boarded up, but it had a hole chopped in the roof—probably where the inhabitants had escaped from the floodwaters. The house was probably abandoned for good. It didn't have the ubiquitous blue tarp over the hole. A few more ghosts floated ahead of them and as they drove through the neighborhoods. Mouse wasn't reminded as much of *Nosferatu* as of The Gentlemen, from the "Hush" episode of *Buffy the Vampire Slayer,* just wearing long coats, like dusters or cassocks. They looked like his nightmares.

They drove around randomly, counting over thirty ghosts haunting the streets.

"There's a good spot," Joe said. He parked on the street, with the engine still running. Two ghosts were ahead of them, glowing in the running lights of the truck.

"Here's the plan. I'm going to hit them, you back me up. Then we'll bolt back here and go find a few for you."

"OK," Mouse said excitedly. "Go for it."

Joe jumped out. Mouse climbed out of his side and kept an eye on Joe, scanning the area to see if more were trying to sneak up on them. Joe jumped into the first one with a flying side kick, spun, and drove a knee into the lower back of the second one. The first one was on its feet and he caught its arm, twisted behind the creature, and broke its neck. The second one staggered in a half circle to face him. Joe elbowed it repeatedly in the face and head before it could raise its hands to block the attacks.

Joe jogged back to the truck, panting heavily. Mouse climbed aboard.

"Damn, that was cool. I can hit them really hard, it's awesome."

Mouse grinned. "Let's find me one."

They drove around. Joe wanted to stop at the first group he saw, but Mouse didn't want to fight against five of them, even side-by-side with Joe.

"There's two of them," Joe said.

"And another two just down the street," Mouse observed.

They took a right, then a left. Mouse refused with a group of four.

"C'mon man," Joe said. "Grow some balls."

"Fuck you," Mouse said. "Find me one or two."

A few minutes later, a single ghost crossed the street in front of the truck. Joe hit the brakes and Mouse bounded out. He hurried up to the thing. It turned to him and he hit it—he passed right through the thing.

"Damn," he said. He tried to center himself and feel past it, to extend his chi. He felt sharp claws rake his chest. He stumbled back a few steps. The claws snatched at his eyes, but he ducked. He swung at it again and whiffed right through it. Cold fear clutched at him. Why wasn't Joe here to help him out?

"Make it solid," Joe yelled. "Remember?"

He had forgotten to try slowing the things down. He did the same things as the night before. He could see the thing, but couldn't touch it. What had he done before? He breathed deeply. He had to slow them down by slowing himself down. He dropped into a deeper stance and centered himself. He imagined the slow-motion sparring they did in class.

An arm came up at him and he blocked it. Excitement replaced the fear he was feeling. He could touch them now.

Block, strike. Block, block, kick. They stood and sparred for a few exchanges. It raked its talons across his chest, cutting through his shirt and scratching his chest. Wincing, Mouse leaned back and sent a side snap kick into its groin. The thing paused and bent. He did a spin kick to its head, crushing down. It disappeared.

"Damn," he said. He walked back to the truck.

"Have a hard time connecting to it?" Joe stated the obvious.

"I forgot how to make them solid for a minute," Mouse wheezed.

Joe nodded. "I'm going to try a few more."

"I want to try again," Mouse said.

They drove around and found a group of three. "Let's get those," Joe said. He stopped the truck and got out. Mouse was still getting down from the passenger side when Joe said, "Both of us. In and out real fast."

Mouse hurried after him. Joe sent the lead attacker, and they did attack as soon as they saw that Joe and Mouse could see them, to Mouse with a swift *irimi*. Mouse met him with a palm-heel to the face and followed with an elbow. He felt claws rake along his forearm, but the thing was disappearing by then.

Joe was working on the second one, keeping it between himself and third one. Mouse circled around Joe and his ghost and engaged the third one. It lunged at him, snapping with teeth and grabbed at him with those sharp claws. Although he was taller than the thing, he went low. He kicked its knee and it dropped down. He slid to the side and took out the other knee. It dropped and he kneed it under the chin. It was gone.

Joe was still working with his. It was a better fighter than its friends. It was pressing Joe back. Mouse kicked it from behind, snapping its spine.

"Damn," Joe gasped. "That was a strong one. Let's go."

They got in the truck and hit the headlights. Joe sped from the Lower Ninth Ward.

"Mouse, man." Joe stuck out his fist. "You killed three of them."

Mouse rapped Joe's knuckles with his own and grinned.

The next night Mouse and Joe found Lowell and Connor. Four ghosts were on Ursulines, near the same spot from the night before. They each killed one apiece. Joe had no problem with his, neither did Mouse. They were getting better at not holding back. The brothers took a little longer with theirs, and Connor took a few big punches before using an *irimi* to get behind the ghost and breaking its back with a side kick.

They backtracked into the Quarter a little ways and had fried chicken at Fiorello's. Mouse suggested the place and they had a good meal of fried chicken. Joe had gumbo instead. The waitress, the cute young girl with glasses who always treated Mouse well when he came in, kept their drinks topped off. She flashed him a grin and he thought he saw a wink as she put down his second order of fries.

"We are the ghost butt-kickers." Joe held up his water and they toasted.

"Oh. That's such a good name for a team," Connor said.

"I don't think we need a name," Joe said. "We're not the X-men."

"Mess with me and you'll be an ex-man," Connor said.

"Tough guy now that you're killing ghosts, eh?"

Connor grinned. "I'm feeling my oats." He put his hand at his crotch, pretending to cup himself. "Damn big oats."

"Now now, guys," Lowell said. "Save the tough stuff for the ghosts."

Joe and Connor slapped each other's palms and laughed.

Mouse slurped down the last of his Diet Coke. "So what now?"

"Only four ghosts. We could go get more."

"Lower Ninth?"

"Definitely."

In the Lower Ninth, they fought more groups of ghosts. Joe drove and the other three sat in the truck bed. When they saw ghosts in small numbers, they'd jump out and fight them. Lowell took out two, so did Mouse, and Connor took on one. Joe jumped into a group of four of them and didn't need help. The guys were ready to back him up, but he didn't call them in.

"Tomorrow night?" Mouse asked. He'd been playing World of Warcraft on line for a couple years, but that was nothing like the real thing. He had gotten into Karate just to lose weight, but it was pretty hard to stick with it. When he started five years ago, he was gung ho, but he got busy somewhere in his second year and progress hadn't been as quick as he had wanted. He barely made brown belt before Katrina, and hadn't done anything since—except gain twenty pounds.

Fighting these things was a hell of a workout. Like Joe said, it was a chance to go at full power. It got the adrenaline pumping and the heart racing. He was going to start going to the dojo more and working out. He wanted to trim down to fight these things. He also resolved to cut down on the food. His usual habit was to have a bag of chips in the evening while on his computer. He would start his diet by giving that up. Hunting ghosts were a chance to get his life in shape again.

Chapter 11

Two weeks passed without incident—except for getting a good look down Diamond's gi when we were stretching. She wasn't wearing a bra, just a loose tank-top under her uniform, so I got a good look. I knew that I could have gone to the strip joint where she worked at any time and that she'd be fine with it, but it wouldn't be professional. She had said that we could come by, but I don't think any of the students at my school had taken her up on the offer. I know I would have been self-conscious about working out with her if I saw her at work.

Diamond and Rufus were the only upper level students who came to classes regularly over the week. Bruiser skipped the classes, so did Mouse. Lowell, Connor, and Joe made it erratically.

I tried getting a date with Brianne on Saturday, a week after our first date, but she didn't have anyone to watch her daughter. I think she wasn't happy with me for not going to her place with her to see her etchings. The phone call was friendly, though, so there was hope for the future. Other than that, I worked hard at the dojo and my teaching. The semester had ended. All I had left were my final grades for a few papers. With my extra time over the winter break, I was planning on finally finishing the renovation of the back room. Very few of the kids would be coming to Karate class when it got close to the holidays, although I could expect about half of them and most of my advanced students.

On Friday, during the class of the smallest children, Bouchard skulked in. I had thirteen five to eight year olds doing floor exercises. They'd do a Karate exercise, then a game based on the exercise. I was planning on a standardized drill and then the Red Light/Green Light game with the same punches, blocks, and kicks.

I saw Bouchard waiting, but I didn't interrupt my class. We had ten minutes left, and most of the parents were in the waiting area. Mothers sat gossiping or watching their children. If the phone rang, they would answer and take messages. They were wonderful women, and if I ever thought them bored housewives killing time while their kids did an activity they'd never follow through on, that was before Katrina. Now I saw their courage to come back and start over. Some were rebuilding houses, some were looking for work in a city that still had no economy to speak of, some had lost loved ones. None had any real reason to take their children to karate, but they did it because they wanted their kids to have a normal life after being uprooted by the worst nature could throw at them. They were heroes who would always be overlooked.

Ms Brown—the mother of George and Brandii, five and eight years old towheads—was talking to the detective. She was probably telling him to wait and that class would soon be over.

I ended the floor exercise, and got the game going. After that, I knelt on one knee and held a kicking shield. Each student hit the foam pad as hard as he or she wanted. A few of the older students, Brandii Brown among them, hit pretty hard. I was proud of them.

"I have ten minutes until I have to teach a bunch of teenagers. What can I do for you, Detective?"

"I'm gonna cut to the chase, Layton. Where were you last night?"

"I was here until nine. Went home, graded, went to sleep around midnight. I caught the beginning of Letterman."

"Anyone see you after you went home?"

"Last night? Maybe about ten, ten-fifteen I helped my neighbors carry a sofa bed upstairs."

"Why so late?"

I shrugged. "They work late."

"And why you?"

"I'm a helpful guy. You know that."

He looked at me scornfully. "What are their names?"

I told him. I didn't know Cissy's, Diane's, or Latrice's numbers, but I gave him their address. "What's this about?"

"When's the last time you were in the Quarter?"

I'd been working pretty hard with the end of the semester and the dojo, so it had been almost two weeks since I'd been there, that Saturday morning for breakfast with Joe and that evening when Bri and I had wandered around there.

"Can you prove that?"

I made a wry face. How could one prove a negative like that—didn't the man know basic logic? I almost laughed at that though. Of course he wouldn't. That would be contrary to his job. "Sure, I had every moment of my life videotaped since last week because I thought you'd come asking. Want to sit through a week of my life?"

"Don't be a smart ass."

"What do you want, Bouchard?"

"If your alibi holds up, you got nothing to worry about."

"What would I need an alibi for?"

He shrugged and his too tight suit jacket rode up to his ears. "Be seeing you, Gillian."

I bit back a reply...and a roundhouse kick. He started to leave.

"One more thing," he said.

"What's that?"

"What's 'pwned' mean?'

"What?"

"I don't know...pooned? Pwinned? P-w-n-e-d."

"That's not English," I said. "I don't know what it is."

"It's on your video," he said and went to the door. "That's the video you told me to look up. I found it. It says you 'pwned' the guy."

It was my turn to shrug. I still felt like giving him a roundhouse kick. Instead, I went to the steel plate I had mounted on a wall and punched it for my Iron Fist training. The ringing of knuckles against metal covered up Bouchard's exit. I hit it two hundred times, then got ready for the next class.

I was lucky; I knew that. Usually I was home alone. I could go days without seeing my roommate or neighbors. I hadn't resented helping the girls next door move the sofa bed upstairs. The three of them took the top end and I took the bottom end as we hauled it up the stairs. We laughed a lot. It was an unusual night, but I was glad now that I had witnesses as to my whereabouts the night before. I didn't know what Bouchard was fishing for, but I could guess that he wasn't on the Citizen of the Year Selection Committee.

Kids were coming in for the next class, and I had one after that. It would be a while before I could find a television.

I didn't have to find one. Mouse came in with a copy of the *Times-Picayune*. I almost slapped my forehead. I could have gone a few doors down to the machine on the corner and picked up a paper.

"Have you seen this?"

I took the paper. On the front page, under the fold, I saw the headline, "Three Killed in the French Quarter." I scanned the article for the important information. Three people, two girls and a guy, were killed on Ursulines. They died from dozens of puncture wounds. One of the girls had her face ripped off.

"Those were the same wounds that Dirk Hemlock died from, right?"

"Shit," I said. "They're attacking more people."

"That is how Hemlock died, right?

"Yeah. They have claws."

"They ripped off that girl's face."

"I know. I saw that."

"Did we do that?"

"I don't know."

I read the article more closely, and turned to page A-3 to read the rest of it. They were killed around eleven. The bodies were reported by a man with a Spanish accent who had left the scene of the crime by the time the police arrived, and the paper conjectured that he was one of the thousands of Mexican workers, many in the country illegally. The police didn't have any clues, but thought it might be gang related. They refused to speculate about the nature of the many wounds.

"Joe's going to be upset," Mouse said. "I'm pretty sure he knew the girl."

"Oh no."

"Yeah. A big 'Oh no.'"

"No, I mean Joe just walked in," I said.

"Oh crap."

Joe entered the dojo. He bowed before stepping onto the practice floor from the lobby. I stepped over to him and handed him the paper. He looked at it for a few minutes. When he looked up, his eyes were watery.

"I—I gotta go," he choked.

"Why don't you have a seat?"

"No," he said and walked out of the dojo.

I tried calling him on his cell and Mouse watched the dojo when I drove around the neighborhood hoping to spot Joe or his truck.

When Lowell and Connor came by, we filled them in.

"These extradimensional creatures, or whatever, are getting more aggressive," Lowell observed.

"We should just call them ghosts," Connor said. "I mean, we don't really know what they are, y'know? It's as good a name as any."

"Good point," Lowell said.

"Might as well," Mouse agreed. "So do you think these ghosts are going to start attacking innocent bystanders?"

"I hope not. But it looks like it."

"If they do, we're all in trouble. We may be able to fight them, but most people in town will be sitting ducks. The ghosts behave like ghosts. They can't be touched, but they can make themselves solid if they want to. That was always their advantage."

"And until Hemlock showed me how to make them corporeal, they had nothing to fear."

"There might have been others who could do it," Lowell suggested.

"But they weren't a threat. We are."

The guys nodded at that.

"We've been hunting them," Mouse said.

"You what?"

"The other week, I think, Joe took me out to fight some of them. He told me he had fought some the night before. He was using them to practicing full-contact fighting."

"And you went with him?"

"Yeah, he wanted me to back him up. I'd killed that one on Saturday night, so he knew I could make contact with them."

"And the next night, we joined him," Lowell said, indicating his brother.

"We've been going almost every night. We've been finding more and more of them. Sometimes twenty in a night. Some on Ursulines, some in the Lower Ninth," Mouse said

"The Lower Ninth Ward? Why did you go there?"

"I figured it was a place that was still chaotic. It's been through a lot," Mouse explained.

I nodded. I had helped with some of the clean-up there. I always felt guilty for not doing more, but I was juggling so much, including cleaning up my dojo.

"There's a ton of them there. They really look like ghosts in all that rubble."

"It was for training," Connor said. "We didn't have to hold back. And we had to keep our cool."

"I get that," I said. "But you guys could have gotten hurt. We don't really know what these things are capable of or what they want, for that matter."

Mouse shrugged. "I don't know. But they're nasty and aggressive. They've been trying to kill us. We're just returning the favor."

I didn't like it and grumbled something to that effect. He had a point. The things had started it by attacking Hemlock. I got caught up in it and defended myself, but then they killed the boy. Since then, they had gotten more aggressive. We were defending ourselves. And with these guys going after them, I could still justify that. We were fighting off an invasion of a sort.

After two hours, Joe returned. He looked angry.

"You OK?" I asked. I half-sat on my desk with a cup of coffee in my hand. Joe stood in front of the door, arms crossed.

"I killed her," he said. "At least I might as well have."

The guys came up from the back room to the lobby and sat in the folding chairs that the parents usually used.

"Do you want to tell us what happened?"

"I taught that girl Gina how to see those things," he said. "The night after the guys and I first went out to fight some. Gina and I went out and I showed her. She'd seen them before, but only when high, so I showed her how to do it. I didn't teach her how to make them solid, though."

I couldn't make eye contact with him. I saw the other guys looking away, too.

"I took her to where we fought those two of them on Ursulines. There were more of them—too many to fight, so we took off."

"How many were there?" I asked.

"Five at first. Then another appeared out of nowhere. We both saw it just appear."

"I'm sorry," I said. I didn't know what else to say. I was sure he was kicking himself for letting the girl in on the method to see ghosts. She obviously took some of her friends and told them how. Now she was dead and Joe felt like it was his fault. I was feeling guilty, too. We all were, I guessed.

"Don't go saying you killed her," I said.

"Yeah, those things did," Mouse said.

"She wouldn't have seen them without me. She wouldn't have taken her friends. They'd still be alive."

"After Hemlock died, a detective from the NOPD came by asking if I had anything to do with it. He's been bugging me, and he came by this afternoon, asking where I was last night."

"He thinks you killed Hemlock?" Mouse said.

"He knows there's a link between Hemlock and," I looked at Joe, "the people last night."

"Oh man," Connor said.

"They all had the same wounds." I looked at Joe. I could see he didn't want to think about how his friend died. "Don't be surprised if he starts asking you guys things."

"What's his name?" Mouse asked.

"Bouchard. He's an annoying fucker. Gets one idea in his mind and he won't let it go. For him the first idea is the only idea."

"Typical cop," muttered Joe.

"Douche-Hard," Connor said.

I laughed, but there wasn't much humor in it. Joe was hurting, and it wasn't the time for fun. Still, I wished I had come up with the name. I'd had a week to think about the sleazy cop.

"So what should we do? If he asks us anything?"

"Say you don't know anything. Tell him the truth as much as you can, but not about ghosts or having any theories about what's going on," I paused. I felt like was starting some sort of criminal conspiracy. "And alibi each other if you can."

"What do we do about those the ghosts?" Mouse said.

"I'm going to kill them," Joe stated.

"I don't think that's a good idea."

He didn't say anything. He turned and went out the door into the night.

"What do we do?" Mouse asked after a moment's pause.

"We go help him. Right?" Connor asked his brother.

"Yeah." Lowell stood up.

"We should stop him," I said. "He could get hurt."

Joe's truck roared to a start outside.

"Think he's going back to Ursulines?" Lowell said. He went out to the parking lot. Connor and Mouse followed.

I looked around. I had to close up, but I could just get the lights and lock the door. The coffee machine was off and I could clean it in the morning. Most of the pads and equipment were in the right place.

"I'll catch up," I said.

They scrambled out the front door. I locked it behind them and ran to the back. The coffee had been working on me, though, so I stopped in the bathroom. I didn't want the guys to have to wait while I urinated, so that's one reason I sent them on their way behind Joe. When I finished, I hit the lights, got my bike and helmet, and left through the back door.

I had never tried it, but there was a chance I could beat them by bike. They'd have to stop for for a bunch of lights, then the parking in the French Quarter would be difficult on a Friday night. If it had been Carnival—before Katrina that is—I could have walked, stopped for drinks, and still made it there in time. The parades would have blocked most of the roads and they would have had to go way around the Quarter and come in from the east. Parking would have been impossible. Things had changed since Katrina, though. There were fewer parades and the crowds were smaller.

I sped out, pedaling furiously. To avoid traffic, I went down to South Front, which becomes Convention Center Boulevard and through Woldenberg park along the Mississippi. Some fog was coming in, but the going was clear. I got up to Decatur and zipped through intersections and passed stopped traffic. Tourists stepped out in front of me and I weaved around them like a New York bike messenger. At the right intersection, I took a left and coasted up the street for a block. I didn't see my students, but I stopped by the convent. Ahead of me there was a knot of ghosts—six or seven of them. I went around the corner and locked my bike to a post.

I was a little out of breath. I didn't want to alert them so they would come after me. I wanted to talk Joe out of doing anything rash. The five of us could probably take ten ghosts, but if someone made a mistake, or couldn't concentrate, he could get killed.

I waited ten minutes and the guys didn't show up. I ransacked my pockets, but I had left my cell phone at the dojo in my haste. I could have called the guys. I'm still not used to having a cell phone, but I bought it for work and try to keep it with me. By now, they should have made it there. As fast as I had been, they could easily have driven in that time. I saw some open parking spaces, too, so that wasn't the problem.

They had gone to the Lower Ninth Ward. The idea finally became the obvious answer. I mentally kicked myself. I had never biked there, but I had biked into Faubourg Marigny and even Bywater, which was the neighborhood next to the Lower Ninth Ward. It was a mile or so to the Lower Ninth, and the roads out there were still littered with broken glass, bits of metal, and other rubble that would shred my tires. The Lower Ninth was also a big area. I could roam around all night and not find the guys. My best bet was to bike back to the dojo, get my phone, and then go home for my car and meet them there. I was looking at as much as an hour before I'd get back to them.

I started to unlock my bike when I heard voices. One was speaking in a confident, assured tone. That sounded like it could be Joe, but after a second I realized it wasn't his voice.

Fifteen people or so were walking up Chartres toward me. A long-haired man dressed in a white ruffled shirt, leather pants, a long leather coat, and a black top hat was leading a crowd of tourists. He was telling them about the fires that had wiped out the city. Apparently, they had just come from Lafitte's Blacksmith Shop, which was one of the two remaining structures that hadn't burned. The Ursulines Convent was the other. Both had ghost stories associated with them. They were on the Ghost Tour, the Vampire Tour, the Haunted History Tour, and I think the Voodoo Tour also.

He led them in front of the convent and started his story.

"New Orleans was just a swamp, a bayou with alligators, snakes, and Indians. You could go forty miles out there," he gestured vaguely in an outward direction. "Even now and you'll be in the middle of bayous that are just as dangerous now as they were then.

"Back then, to clear the land, they needed labor. Do you know where they got the labor?"

"Slaves?"

"That's what you'd think, but no." He paused. "Do you know why they didn't want to use slaves?"

No one answered.

"Slaves cost money. So they used prisoners. They gave men who were convicted of the worst crimes—murder, rape, kidnapping—a choice. They could clear out a swamp in the New World. If they survived, they would be free. If they didn't want that, they'd be hanged by their neck until dead."

"Not a guillotine?" an older man asked.

"No, Monsieur Guillotine," he pronounced it correctly, "had not been born then. That came along during the French Revolution."

He indicated the complex of buildings behind him. "The prisoners were under the watchful eye of the priests."

The tour guide went on, educating visitors to my town about its dark history. I got on my bike and was about to head back when I saw a light hovering behind the young couple who were last in the tour group. He was skinny, with a buzz cut and an olive green t-shirt. He looked like he was in the Army. She was plain and plump, and they held each other closely. I hoped I was just seeing some glare from a street lamp reflecting off a store window, but I cleared my mind and saw what I was afraid of. The crowd had attracted one of the ghosts, and more were coming.

I was straddling my bicycle, about to put on my helmet, when I saw a few more come along, stalking the lagging couple.

I swung my leg over the bike. I was going to have to fight some ghosts to defend those kids—with another few not a block away. And what about the crowd? They couldn't see the ghosts.

"Hey!" the young soldier snapped, turning his head behind him. He pushed the girl away from himself with his jerk of surprise. It wasn't surprise, though. It must have been pain. There was a red dot on his shoulder that was growing in diameter. His skin had been punctured.

The tour guide stopped his ghost story. He looked in horror at the damage to the young soldier. The crowd looked at the young man as he was picked up onto his toes and dragged backward. He flailed, but his hands met no resistance. Blood was soaking the shoulders of his t-shirt and running down his arms.

I rushed forth, shouting, "Get out of here! All of you!"

The first ghost I found by grabbing where I thought its neck should be. This one was much taller than I had guessed. I felt a muscular back. Quickly I struck higher. The soldier fell down as the thing turned on me. I snapped my knee against its elbow. I got cut down my forearm, but used that to get inside its reach and I kneed it until it disappeared, all the while trying to gouge eyes and twist its head off. A second ghost grabbed me, but from the front. I wrenched its arms apart and kicked in both knees before twisting its head so far its neck broke. It felt like a regular, human head.

"Oh my God, they're real ghosts," the guide said in a quavering voice.

"You can see them?" I snapped. "Get out of here." At my feet the young soldier was trying to get to his feet.

"Someone call the police," a woman in the crowd yelled.

The tour guide already has his cell phone out.

I looked around. The girl wasn't where she had been standing. A shriek came from beyond me.

We all looked. She was floating, carried shoulder high, facing up and struggling, by three of the ghosts.

"Oh my God," someone said. "Do you see that?"

"Fuck!" the tour guide said. Others started speaking, but I was in motion.

The group had started following the floating girl. I pushed past the couple who were in my way and hit the two ghosts in the rear with a jumping scissors kick. They flew to the left and the right. I fell on my side. The girl tumbled down, landing on top of me and quickly scrambling away. She was big—generously proportioned—and had knocked the breath out of me.

Painfully, I rose to my feet. I kicked toward the only floating light I saw, but missed. I didn't know if it was the pain from my fall getting in the way of my concentration, or if I was just missing it because I still couldn't see the damn things. I didn't know where the two I had caught with the jump kick had gone, but I didn't think I had killed them. I kicked again and felt contact. I pressed that attack and felt a blow from behind. Something hit me below the ribs in my left side, where I had landed from my jump kick.

I closed my eyes. I couldn't see them anyway. In class we trained with our eyes closed every day. I was able to settle myself and get back to something I had done a million times. Block, kick, twist, throw, punch, palm heel, and more. I felt their joints snap, their bodies disappear as I beat them, and I kept going. When I felt all three go, I opened my eyes. I was in the middle of the street. Behind me stood the tour group, looking at me like I was crazy.

Ahead of me there were a few more ghosts. I had earlier counted seven, and I had just destroyed five of them. I saw two flaws floating.

Behind me I heard the girl crying and the guy's ragged breathing. I backed toward the group.

"If you want to see real ghosts," I heard the tour guide saying to his crowd. "Clear your mind. Relax and think past the point where they are. They're about halfway down the block on the right. Try to push. Breathe in deeply and let it out in their direction, like you're going to breathe on them."

I suppose I should have expected the guide of a ghost tour to know how to see these things, but it was unexpected.

"I see something. Jesus Christ, there are ghosts over there," a man's voice said exultantly.

A woman spoke up. "Two of them. Right there. They just appeared." Others saw them, there was an excited buzz.

I approached the guide. "You should get these people out of here. Go back up to Royal or Bourbon."

"But everyone's seeing them," he protested.

"And they'll kill you," I said. "Move it."

"Uh...should I call the police?"

"Why don't you get that kid some medical help."

He turned to the group. "OK everyone. Let's walk away. Down this way." He started off down Chartres. "No lagging behind."

I kept an eye on the two floating flaws as the group followed the guide. A gray-haired woman with gold-rimmed glasses stopped next to me and touched my arm.

"I see them. I don't know what they are, but I can see them, too."

"Just keep away from them, ma'am."

She hurried to her husband, a short, fit looking man with thick white hair. When she caught up with him, he grabbed her hand and pulled her with him.

"OK now," I said. I was alone with them. It was time to fight again.

I didn't have a plan for my attack. How could I? I still couldn't see them. They were just glints of light floating in front of me. I would do my best, trying to use one against the other to keep them from double-teaming me, surrounding me, or using their numbers against me.

Neither ghost was closer than of the other, so I couldn't take out one before the other could reach me. I led with one of my favorite attacks, the skipping front kick. With that, could cover fifteen feet and when I connected, it would be all my weight and the power of my kick hitting the target. My two hundred pounds and the strength behind my kick knocked over the middle ghost. I continued with my forward momentum and turned to see the other coming at me. I kicked, felt an arm, twisted it, and drove the thing down onto the first one, which I had knocked down, but not killed. I kicked until its back broke. The other one was still on the ground when I found its center and stomped as hard as I could. The resistance disappeared and the flaw was gone.

I scanned the area for more ghosts. None were around.

I heard sirens. I ran back to my bike, picked my helmet up from the ground and took off. I was flying by the French Market by the time I had gotten my helmet secure on my head. I zipped home as quickly as possible.

Samir wasn't in, so I couldn't use him as an alibi, should the cops show up. I ran upstairs and took a quick shower. I slipped on some old jeans and a sweatshirt. Then I fired up my laptop, turned on the TV to the local news, and brewed a pot of half-decaf, half regular.

When Bouchard did come knocking on my door, I greeted him with a smile and a cup of coffee in my hand.

"I looked it up," I said.

"What?"

"P w n e d." I pointed to my computer. "You looked up that video of me and those punk kids who were bothering that girl. The title of it, 'Frat Boys Get Pwned.' That's what you were asking about today."

"So what if I was?"

"I looked it up. It's a misspelling of 'owned'. It became an expression on the Internet. People on the Internet can't spell very well. Like those T-shirts you can get at the souvenir shops in the Quarter that say 'Psyche', but spell it 'S-I-K-E'."

"What are you talking about?"

"Nothing. The expression is 'owned'."

"Owned?"

"Meaning beaten up, knocked down, humiliated."

"Oh. OK."

"And since you looked at it, you can see I didn't have anything to do with the girl. I bookmarked it, in fact, so we can look at it if you'd like."

"No. That's not what I'm here about."

"Oh yeah. You were going to ask my neighbors if I helped them move their sofa. They're next door right now. I heard them come in."

"I talked to them already," he said, panting a bit. He was getting impatient and he was very out of shape. He took a chair.

"Social call, then?"

"What were you doing tonight?"

"Tonight? It's only nine o'clock. I haven't even decided if I was going out."

"Can you account for your whereabouts today?"

"I was at the dojo—the Karate school—since noon. The last class was over at seven-thirty, then a few of the upper level students and I B.S-ed for a while. They left. I straightened things up a bit, then came back here. I've been here for maybe twenty minutes."

I could see him adding up times in his head. "Were you on the corner of Ursulines and Chartres this evening?"

I shook my head. "Nope. Why?"

"Got some reports 'bout someone who might be you."

"Me? C'mon Bouchard, there are lots of guys who fit my description. Middle height, burly, brown hair, mid-forties. That could be you," I lied—one of the biggest lies I've ever told. He was about five eight or nine, weighed about two-forty, most of it around his middle. What hair he had was brown, but it was in a comb over. He looked a lot older than I did.

"I'm thirty-nine," he said.

"Sorry, but you can see my point." Either he was lying about his age or he had aged very poorly. I was proud I was forty-six.

"Hmph."

"Anyway, I was at the dojo, then came home. So it had to be someone else."

"We'll see about that," he grumbled.

"So what did this guy do?" I asked. I was actually curious what the police were called about. I hadn't hurt the guy, and I saved the girl. Enough people saw it to be clear about that point.

"I don't know. We got some weird calls about ghosts and some ninja guy."

I looked at him like he was crazy. "You're kidding, right?"

He shook his head. His jowls wobbled.

"I just know there was a disturbance and some guy who fits your description scared off a tour group with some of that Kung Fu shit."

"What kind of tour group?"

He reddened. "The Ghost Tour."

I laughed. "And you don't think that the ghosts and stuff were just just some drunks seeing things? Some tourists had a few drinks before they got started, then loaded up on a few more somewhere on the way. I bet you get all sorts of weirdos in a town like this."

He sighed heavily. "You don't know the half of it. We get every sort of freak here."

"You want a cup of coffee? You look like you need one."

He smiled. I think, with the complaints about how hard the job was and the offer of coffee, he was warming up to me. I didn't like him, but I'd rather have him think of me as someone he could complain to than as someone he wanted to pin every crime in the city on.

The phone rang before he could accept. I grabbed it. "Hello."

"Sensei," Connor said. "Just checking to see if you were at home."

"Yep, I'm here."

"We tried your cell."

"Oh yeah. I guess I left it at the dojo," I said, aware that Bouchard had dropped the bonhomie and now looked at me through narrow slits. Any good will that was starting to develop had gone back to his disdain for me.

"Can we come by?"

"Hang on," I said. I spoke to Bouchard without covering up the receiver with my palm, so Connor could hear. "Well Detective, I guess I do have plans for my Friday night. Are you going to arrest me for something or can I have a life?"

He wheezed to his feet. "I'm not taking you in now. Tomorrow I want you to come by the station for a line-up."

"A line-up? What, now you think I witnessed something?"

"Jesus. I want to put you in the line-up, *Perfessor*."

"Oh, yeah." I shook my head.

I put the phone back to my ear. "Yeah, come on by."

"Is that Douche-Hard?"

I laughed. "Yeah."

Bouchard went to the door. "Noon. Downtown. Don't miss it or I'll haul you in myself," he called over his shoulder and left.

"Did you find Joe?"

"For a while. Hey, Lowell says we'll we'll be there in ten minutes."

Chapter 12

"Think he's going back to Ursulines?" Lowell said. He went out to the parking lot. Connor and Mouse followed.

The three of them jumped in the SUV to chase after Joe as he sped off in his truck. Connor called shotgun and Mouse took the back. They zipped up Melponeme instead of going down to Tchoupitoulas or along the river.

"He's going to the Lower Ninth," Mouse said.

"More of them in the Lower Ninth," Lowell said.

"This feels weird," Connor said. "Going after Joe." He was always Lowell's younger brother. People always expected the younger Stuart brother to be just like the older one, but other than Karate, they weren't too much alike.

He got into Karate when he was fourteen because his brother had been at it for over a year, since he was a junior in college. His own black belt test was coming up in in the spring, and he had been worried that he wouldn't be able to pass. He remembered Lowell's grueling three-hour test and couldn't imagine himself being that strong—until that week.

Fighting and killing ghosts had taught him he could center himself and react with appropriate power. He was able to hit hard enough to kill. His blocks were hard, causing damage in themselves, and he was keeping from being hurt while causing damage with his reflexive reactions. All he had been learning was coming together and he felt he was truly a martial artist now. He wasn't in Lowell's shadow now. He was a valuable member of the team with almost as many kills as his brother. Like Joe said, they were superheroes.

"What are we going to do if we catch up to him?" Mouse asked.

"Mr. P. said to stop him," Connor said.

"And we said we were going to back him up," his brother reminded them.

"He's getting on Ninety," Mouse said.

They followed up the twisting ramp to I-90 and soon to I-10 East. Lowell had to speed to catch up. Fortunately, Lowell was a fast driver. Whenever they'd go out, Connor would always grip the handle above the window until his knuckles were white. The only time he drove at a reasonable speed was when their mother was in the car with them.

"You should call Mr. P. and let him know to head to the Lower Ninth," Lowell suggested. Connor got out his phone and tried calling.

"Voice mail," Connor said. "Hi Sensei. We're on I-10 heading to the Lower Ninth. Um, I guess that's where Joe's going."

Soon they followed Joe off the highway onto Claiborne and into the neighborhoods that had been the hardest hit by the flooding. Although it was dark, they could see the destruction.

Joe went in to the Ward. Soon they saw ghosts in small groups. More were ahead, and that was where Joe screeched his truck to a halt.

He jumped out and waded into the group of ghosts, extinguishing them from this planet as he attacked. Soon, however, they surrounded him. Lowell and Connor attacked those from behind. Mouse followed up a moment later, using his mass to bull his way through to Joe's side.

"Back to back. Circle up!" Mouse shouted. The brothers followed in his wake and worked their way to the middle of the circle. There they stood in a small ring, facing the swarm of ghosts.

"What are you doing here?" Joe yelled.

"We came to make sure you don't die," Mouse said. Then they things closed in on them.

Training together for years and the past few nights of fighting against the ghosts had whipped them into a team. The four of them dispatched more than a dozen ghosts

"What's your fuckin' problem?" Joe snapped. "Who asked you to come here?"

"Layton," Lowell said. "But we would have come on our own."

"Well I didn't ask you to come."

"And what would you have done?" Mouse asked. He stepped in front of Joe. "Were you thinking of killing yourself there? Going down fighting?"

"You don't understand."

Mouse shrugged. "No, I probably don't. But I'll tell you something. We don't leave a teammate behind. Don't you get it?"

Joe said nothing.

Connor looked from one friend to another. His brother didn't seem to have an answer, either. Joe was really hurting.

"Now let's get out of here, man," Mouse said.

Joe shook his head. "I'm not going anywhere. I'm going to kill every last one of those things."

"Then we'll back you up," Mouse said. Connor looked at his brother who was nodding. "Yeah."

Joe shook his head. "No. I've got to do it on my own."

"We'll just follow you."

Joe put up his hands, as if holding a large ball. He shook them, unable to express his feelings.

"You can't."

"C'mon Joe. You can't do it yourself."

"No Mouse," Lowell said. "We'll back off." Joe turned to face him. "You really need to do this?"

"Yeah."

"Then don't do anything stupid."

Mouse laughed humorlessly. "This is all stupid."

"Don't do anything too stupid," Lowell amended. "Don't go into large groups of those things. Pick them off, one by one. Make sure you have a way out."

"And don't get yourself killed," Connor contributed, happy to say something.

Joe walked to his truck. He half waved to the guys and took off. The other three got into the SUV.

"What do we do now?" Connor asked.

Lowell started the vehicle rolling in the way Joe went. "I'm going to follow him for a bit."

He drove slowly, with his lights off. They saw more ghosts. Down one street they saw Joe returning to his truck. He looked winded. Lowell went down another block, then turned around and started backtracking.

"I think he'll be more careful now."

"I hope so," Mouse said.

*   * *

They tried calling Layton again on their way back. There was no answer on his cell phone and they tried his home phone.

"That detective's there," Connor reported after his conversation with the sensei. "He wants Sensei Layton to be in a police line-up tomorrow."

Lowell sped up. They pulled up in front of Layton's house in the ten minutes that Connor had promised.

"Smells like coffee," Mouse said as they entered. "You drink too much of the stuff, you know that?"

"I worship at the altar of caffeine," Layton said. "Anyone want some?"

"I'll have a cup," Connor said. "What?" he said as his brother looked at him, "I'm tired."

"It's half decaf, if that's OK?"

"That's OK. I'm going to add enough sugar to wake me up from a coma, anyway," Connor said.

"I'll have a beer if you got one," Mouse said. The group went to the kitchen and Layton served drinks.

"Did you catch up with Joe?"

"Yeah, we helped him out. But he's still out there." Lowell started filling Layton in and the other two supplemented the story.

"There were, like, a dozen of those things," Connor said proudly.

"I made him promise that he'd be more careful and not to do anything really stupid. I thought he needed the catharsis," Lowell said. "He was in a bad state."

"I hope he's OK," Layton said.

"What about you?"

"Yeah, where were you?"

"And what's that detective want?"

"I went to Ursulines, not the Lower Ninth, I was mixed up. A tour group was there and the tour guide saw the ghosts. He told the group how to see them and some of them actually did."

"They saw the ghosts?" Mouse said.

"Yeah, which is a good thing. Otherwise I was a crazy guy pretending to fight something in the street."

"Weird."

"Yeah. And they tried to take a girl with them. Two of them attacked the guy she was with, and three of them started carrying her off while I came to his aid. Then I killed two more who were watching."

"What happened to the girl?"

"I got her away from them."

"You killed seven of them?" Connor said. And he thought they were super-heroic with four versus a dozen or more.

"I didn't really have a choice."

"Jesus."

"These were just people who couldn't see them. So far, we know they were attacking people like Dirk Hemlock, us, and that girl Joe showed the trick to."

"The tour guide saw them," Connor pointed out.

"Good point. But they weren't attacking him. He didn't say anything about seeing them until they attacked the couple."

"Weird. Here's another thing," Lowell said. "There's more and more of 'em."

"Really?"

"We saw two on Ursulines the first time we went after them. Then Joe fought three of them the next day. Later that night there were six of them at that same place. And you got seven of them. And in the Lower Ninth, they're all over. Tonight we ran into the largest group I've ever seen. If we weren't there, they would have killed Joe."

Layton nodded. He didn't look too happy. "This is bad. Look, I don't want any of us to go out alone. We all need back-up. These things are very dangerous. Don't go out at night. And if you have to, do it with a partner. Don't try to kill them, just get away from them."

"Are you sure they can't attack in the daytime?"

Layton shrugged his broad shoulders. "No idea. All I know is that they haven't been attacking in the daytime. Also, they haven't come indoors to well-lit places. I think they avoid light, but like I said, I'm not sure."

They were all silent for a while.

"What about the detective?" Connor asked.

"That's the other thing. Stay with each other so you can have alibis. Also, if anyone asks, we were at the dojo until around eight-fifteen instead of seven-thirty."

"Are the police going to start coming after us?"

Layton shrugged again. "I think Douche Hard is just after me. You guys keep your noses clean."

"I'd like to see him try something," Mouse said. "He should be afraid of us."

"Yeah, right," Connor said.

Chapter 13

I spent the night worrying about Joe. The next morning, I woke up late, put on a dress shirt, tie, and my most professorial tweed jacket. It was all I could think of to look different from how had the night before.

The desk officer was expecting me. He was a heavy-set black man who looked long past retirement age for a cop. I wondered what kept him working

"Hi, I'm Dr. G. Paul Layton. Detective Bouchard wanted me to come down today."

He scratched his head, looking at a list. "I don't have a Doctor anything on my list. I got a Jillian Layton."

"My name is Guillaume Paul Layton, Ph.D.. I'm a professor. Bouchard knows that. He asked me to come here. I'm only doing this out of courtesy."

"Bouchard ain't here. He has Saturdays off."

I fumed. Bouchard had the day off yet he threatened me to make me show up. What did he think I was? A gentleman of leisure? I had work...Bruiser was covering my early classes, the youngest children, then Lowell and Connor were going to take the next level of students. I could trust them, sure, but I didn't like delegating responsibility.

"So I'm just wasting my time coming here, then. Right?"

"No," the man grinned. He pressed a button and a door buzzed. "Go down that hall and ask for Detective Lucas. He caught the disturbance last night."

He called over his shoulder, "Mary, how about a visitor's pass for this gentleman." He chuckled. "This doctor professor Layton."

I entered and a heavy woman in civilian dress gave me a visitor's pass. She guided me to Detective Lucas's desk. Finally, someone on the NOPD who wasn't fifty or more pounds overweight. Lucas looked about thirty, light-skinned African American, and slim. He wore jeans, a blue button-down Oxford shirt with no tie, and a navy blazer. He dressed like I did when I was junior faculty.

"So you're the guy Bouchard has a bug up his ass about."

I shrugged. I didn't want to go into any assessment of Bouchard's personality or integrity at that moment.

"You don't look like a superhero ninja to me," Lucas said.

"I'm a retired English professor," I stated.

"And you teach Karate?"

I nodded.

"We got a few people from the tour group last night. Bouchard wanted you to stand in a line-up, so let's go."

I followed.

"And take off that tie. What were you thinking?"

"It's my first line-up," I mumbled. I removed the tie but left the jacket.

"OK. Here's what you do. Don't say anything and do what we tell you over the speaker," Lucas said. "Get in line with those guys." He pointed to four men. None of them looked anything like me. One guy was about six-eight, was bald, and had muscles on his muscles. Two were average height and on the fat side, one with black hair and one with blond. The last one was a short, thin Hispanic. I was put in the number two spot.

We stood there, in front of a one-way mirror. I looked at the guys reflected back at me. The Hispanic guy was probably about a hundred and fifty pounds, the other three were in the two-fifty to two-eighty range with the bald giant on the heavy end of the spectrum.

"Turn to your left."

We all turned.

"Turn to your right."

"Number one, step forward." A pause. "Step back."

"Number two, step forward." I stepped out. "Step back."

"Number three."

"Number four." The bald giant stomped forward.

"Number five." The Hispanic guy stepped up.

For a while, we stood there, not moving. Then number four was asked to step forward, then back. I was asked to step forward, to turn to the side, then to return. Number four was asked to step forward again.

"Thank you," came the voice.

We filed out. I put on my jacket and stuffed the tie in its breast pocket. A uniformed officer led me to Lucas's desk. She was a cute blond woman with only an extra twenty pounds to lose, so she was not at the level of most of the cops I'd seen, but not quite as thin as Lucas. She smiled at me.

"Can I get you some coffee?"

"Umm, thanks, but everything I've heard about the coffee at police stations has been negative."

She giggled. "You got that right."

Lucas returned to his desk. "Thanks 'Lissi," he smiled at her. She gave him a fingertip wave and bounced out of the room.

"Officer DuBois. Very dedicated to her work," he said with a smile. "Well Mr. Layton. You're free to go. People couldn't tell you from Sergeant Franzetti."

"Which one was he?"

"Bald. Muscles. Gigantic."

"Oh yeah, the resemblance is amazing. It was like looking at my long lost identical twin."

He laughed dryly.

"Who selected the members of the line up?"

"Detective Bouchard called them in."

I sighed. "Detective Lucas, you seem like a sensible guy. Maybe you can tell me why Bouchard keeps bothering me?"

"Honestly, I looked at your file and I can't see anything wrong. He has nothing on you. I don't know what it is. You must just rub him the wrong way."

"Isn't there anything you can do about it?"

Lucas shook his head. "He outranks me. Nothing I can do."

"I see." We were both silent for a moment. He looked embarrassed.

"Anyway, you can go. Drop your visitor pass off at the desk on the way out."

I thanked him and left. At least one cop on the NOPD was decent.

Outside the police station, as I walked to my car, I saw a familiar couple. It was the woman who had talked to me the night before and her husband. She had seen the ghosts.

"Hi," I said.

"There you are," she said. "We were afraid we missed you."

"Oh. Were you in there?" I pointed my thumb at the police headquarters.

"We saw you in the line-up."

"Thanks for not saying anything."

She laughed, showing a slight overbite. "They had Nicholas, he's the tour guide, and two other people from the group. We all said different things. Nicholas kept saying it was the big guy. So did the girl you saved. Dave and I were the ones who said it was the Latino gentleman—just to screw with them. It was the other young man who said it might be you."

"Her husband? The soldier?"

Her husband shook his head. "No. He's in the hospital with a punctured lung. Apparently, the lungs go above the collarbone and can be damaged from above."

I nodded. I had seen that in anatomical drawings. I didn't realize he had been so seriously injured.

"It was another young man. He wasn't very persuasive, though," the woman said. "He had a fidgety quality about him. And he didn't see the ghosts."

"I didn't see any ghosts, but something must have been there," the man said. "And if Jan here tells me that I saw ghosts, that's what I saw."

"Thank you."

"Are they really ghosts?" the woman asked.

I shook my head. "I don't really think so. This may sound like science fiction, but I think they're creatures from another dimension. They're invading here and have been hurting people." I expected them to look at me dubiously, but she nodded and he only squinted.

"That's a relief," she laughed. "I don't know what this old atheist would have done if ghosts were the only explanation."

"Maybe you'd start coming to church with me," her husband said.

"Oh Dave," she said. She kissed him on the cheek.

"If I may," I said. "New Orleans is dangerous right now. If you can go out of town, please do so."

"We've got a flight out at four. We have to go back to the hotel and gather our bags," the man said. "Do you know of any good place to eat on the way to the airport?"

"What hotel?"

"Hotel Monteleone, in the French Quarter."

"You should just get something in the Quarter and then head out. What are you looking for?"

We discussed fine dining for a couple minutes—he wanted gumbo—so I recommended the Gumbo Shop.

"Thanks again," I said and we parted ways. I hurried to the dojo.

*　　　　　*　　*

"I need to talk to you," Bruiser said when I came in to the dojo. On the main floor, Lowell had one group of kids and Connor had another. I could let them teach for a while.

"What's up?" I asked.

"Not here," she said. Several mothers and some smaller siblings awaited their junior *karateka.*

"I've got to change. Let's go to the back," I said.

She followed me to the back. Outside of the men's changing room, she filled me in.

"I was attacked last night. One of those demons followed me home from church. I got away, luckily."

"Did you try to fight it?"

"No. I just did an irimi and got out of there."

"That's the best thing to do. Where were you?"

"I was coming back from downtown. I went there for dinner."

"The first ones I saw were downtown," I said.

"Why are they coming after me?"

"I don't know, but they're more active lately."

"And why can I see them more easily now? I saw it out of the corner of my eye, then I focused in. I don't think I could have seen it so easily last week."

"I think part of it's just practice."

"Part of it?"

Other students were entering the dojo. It was time for the three o'clock class, a small one, and the older, more advanced students could work out on their own.

"I think we'll have to talk about it more later. Lowell and Connor can fill you in while you practice, though."

The bell over the door opened. Rufus and Diamond entered, him holding the door and bowing as he made a sweeping motion for her to enter.

"But don't tell them. I think it's better if they don't get involved. It's too crazy as it is."

"Rufus knows. He just doesn't want any part of it. I don't think Diamond knows anything."

"That's good, at least."

I changed and went to the main floor and greeted the middle and high school students. Most were intermediates—green and blue belts—but several lower belts too. Before Katrina, I had three classes of students in that age range; one of intermediates and two of beginners.

"Hi Diamond, Rufus." I said as they came from the changing rooms. "How were your weeks?"

"Good," Diamond said. She had once told me she was born in Beijing and moved to the U.S. when she was young, but she had worked hard on eliminating any traces of accent.

"The usual," Rufus said. He looked at me suspiciously. Knowing that he was aware of the ghost activities, I figured he was trying to read something about it on my face. Or maybe I was just imagining things.

The went to the other senior students and started working out. I lost myself in the class I was teaching, so I didn't hear what they talked about.

The senior's class started at four. Two of the teens stayed a little late, like they had the week before. When their ride arrived, I went to the adult students.

"Anyone see Mouse?"

Heads shook.

Mouse didn't make it to practice. I suppose that was typical of him, but I had been seeing so much of him lately, I expected him to start working out regularly. The nocturnal battles against the ghosts must have been his workout.

"Oh well. What have you guys been working on?" I asked.

We spent some time working on katas, then we did some wrestling. Bruiser and Diamond worked out together, despite the height difference. It was hard to find a partner for Bruiser, since Diamond was almost six feet tall. Bruiser claimed to be four feet, ten inches, but I think she might have exaggerated. Lowell and Connor worked out together and Rufus beat me three out of five times.

When Rufus and Diamond left at five, I finally had a chance to update everyone on my trip to the police station. I had to back up to explain things to Bruiser, and Lowell and Connor had to fill her in the rest of the way.

"And you saw one yesterday."

Lowell and Connor's eyes widened. She told them about the one she saw.

"That's just not fair. You never touched any of them," Connor said.

"And they're easier to see," I added.

"So what are you thinking? Just more data?" Lowell asked.

"That's about it."

We had no new ideas, but I warned the group about not going out alone and to keep to well-lit and populated areas. I was concerned about possible ghost attacks, but Connor pointed out the need for alibis in case of good ol' Douche-Hard.

"What are you guys up to tonight?"

"We're just going home and helping Mom put up Christmas stuff," Lowell said. "Our Aunt Dottie is coming tomorrow."

Connor rolled his eyes. "She still thinks the city's under water."

"What about you?" I asked Bruiser.

"I was going to go to church again, but after that one followed me, I don't know."

"If you want, we can take you home. In fact," I looked at the clock. It would soon be dark. "I can take you to church and pick you up afterwards. We can hang out before then, too."

"I…I don't know."

"When's church?"

"Seven."

"When does it end?"

"Eight."

"Did you have plans for later in the evening?"

"No, I was going to go home."

"That'll work. I have a date at ten, so I can get you to and from church with no problem. Want to get some dinner before then?"

She breathed in deeply. "I don't know if I need a chaperone."

"I'd feel better if you had someone with you." She started to say something. I held up a hand. "I know you're an excellent martial artist, but these things are ganging up on us. And you haven't fought them yet."

"That's fair." She grinned. "Did you really take on ten at once?"

"Only seven."

"You'll be good protection. You can come to church if you'd like."

"Not me, but thanks."

We had dinner at the Juan's Flying Burrito on Magazine. She'd never been to one and I thought it was a good little restaurant chain. It wasn't the typical Cajun or Creole food I loved so much, but true to the city, it was good food and that's what I liked. It was also in the direction of her house. She lived in Uptown, in a neighborhood that was like mine, full of students and locals. The common theme is cheap housing.

We discussed the demons, as she saw them. I told her my theory about how our subconscious minds filled in the dimensional dissonance with images that make more sense. She insisted they were demons, though. She wanted a religious explanation, I wanted a logical one.

I got her to church about twenty minutes early. We didn't see any ghosts, but it was still early. While she worshiped, I went home and showered. No ghosts there either, but there hadn't been much devastation in my neighborhood. There was some trash—the ubiquitous refrigerators that had to be thrown out because of months of rotting food—but that had all been cleared up by now.

That morning I called a woman I had dated a few times when I first moved to New Orleans, and we still saw each other once or twice a year. Michelle was a nurse. She had been here for the hurricane and its aftermath. She was one of the select few who hadn't evacuated, although she could have. Two months after Katrina she moved in with her grown daughter in Lubbock, Texas. Eight months later she returned. She was a serious, no-nonsense woman, but she said she was trying to lighten up after all she'd been through.

I was going out with her that Saturday so I'd have alibis for Bouchard if something else should happen. I had dates for the next five nights. Bri and I were having dinner Sunday night. The rest were women I had dated before. Mary, a chef I met on line, was on Monday. Keisha, an administrator at a Catholic school whom I met when at a club on Bourbon Street, was Tuesday. Lorna was a wealthy socialite whose son took Karate from me for a month, was Wednesday. And Dawna Rae, who worked at a shop in the Quarter that sold sex toys and who I met in the shop when I ducked in there for cover from a sudden downpour, was Thursday. If Bouchard tried to check me out for anything, I would be covered.

Chapter 14

Joe spent all of Saturday in bed. The night before he had gone out and killed as many of those things as he could. He kept his promise to Lowell and the guys to avoid the big crowds of them, but it had been hard. He wanted to kill them all for what they did to Gina.

They weren't close, Joe and Gina. He had only discovered she was from Calgary that Sunday night, and that had only been the second time they slept together. But she was a friend and he had led her to her death.

Over the week Joe had gone out every night to fight the things. He even went out without the guys to back him up on the nights they couldn't make it. He was out hunting ghosts in his own neighborhood the night Gina was killed just a mile away.

Hunting ghosts was the most incredible thing Joe had done in his life. He had done every extreme sport he could, from rock climbing to hang gliding to skateboarding to BMX, to a dozen others. Mixed Martial Arts let him really let loose, but he still had to hold back. Against these ghosts, he could go all out. When he was fighting them, he was exorcising his own demons.

Childhood for Joe wasn't easy. They were poor. Joe was teased. His father left. His mother drank. Different men moved in, sometimes for a night, sometimes for months. There was a lot of fighting. Joe learned to cook for himself, to clean the house, to do laundry, to fight the kids who teased him, and even to fight the men who were his mother's friends.

He kept up good grades until high school, but it got difficult after that. He had too much to do to keep it all together. His mother had stopped having strange men over and stopped drinking. She married a much older man, Sandy, who was very sweet to her and accepting of Joe. But although Sandy bailed Joe out of many scrapes and was a good, gentle man, Joe still felt the anger of the bad years. Sandy had suggested Joe take martial arts for the Attention Deficit Disorder he had been diagnosed with and found him a school that taught Ju-Jitsu and Karate. That was in tenth grade. It did wonders for his ADD, improved his grades, and channeled his fighting. Sandy only lived two more years and then things got harder again. Joe resented Sandy coming along and then leaving them when things got good again.

Activity made the frustrated, lost, and lonely feelings go away, at least while the adrenaline was running, and often through the aches and pains afterwards.

But fighting ghosts all Friday night—literally until the predawn light drove the things away—hadn't worked this time. Every time he hit them, he thought of Gina. The fact that he had to calm and center himself to be able to make the things tangible probably didn't help. If he were only fighting, he wouldn't be able to think of how he betrayed Gina. Exhausted, he lay in bed not sleeping.

Finally, past noon, he slept. He would go out that night, he knew that, and get more revenge.

It was dark by the time Joe woke. He woke up sore. His muscles ached and his fists throbbed. In the living room his roommate, Diane, lay on the couch under an old afghan, her back to him.

Joe showered. The hot water heater had gone out and the water was cold. It didn't help his sore muscles, but he didn't want to dress, go downstairs, reset the thing, and wait until it warmed up. He sluiced off the dried sweat, the soap not foaming very much in the hard, cold water as he quickly washed. He stepped out of the small bathroom in just the towel, goosebumps on his skin.

"Hey guy, how ya doing?" a man's voice said. Mouse was sitting on the couch. Diane was nowhere around.

"Shit. I thought you were my roommate," Joe said.

"She let me in. I've been here since about four. It's seven now."

"What are you doing here?"

"Lowell and I talked about it. You had your night of revenge. I'm supposed to watch you tonight."

"You're babysitting me?"

"Lowell and Connor are coming by later. If you're going out, we're going with you."

Joe said nothing. He went to the kitchen and started some coffee. In the fridge he found some stale bread, put some peanut butter on one side and some honey on the other, and took two bites to have something in his stomach, then took a few ibuprofens. When he had his coffee, he walked out of the kitchen, taking more bites of his breakfast.

"I don't need you guys. I don't need backup."

"I know," Mouse said.

"Even if you guys tried to stop me, you couldn't."

"I agree."

"So I'm gonna let you back me up."

"Got enough coffee for me?"

"Taking after Mr. P.?"

"You've got a cup."

"I slept all day."

"I just got up from a nap. Besides, I'm going to be up as late as you are tonight."

"It's in the kitchen."

"Some host."

"That's how it is when you break and enter."

Mouse lumbered to his feet and went to the dark kitchen.

"Jeeeesus. That's your coffee maker? It only makes two cups."

"Some of us aren't addicted," Joe called from the other room.

"No sugar or half and half?"

"Please," Joe dismissed the comment.

"You're a Philistine. You know that?" Mouse called after him.

Three hours later, Lowell and Connor arrived.

"Sorry, we had to help Mom clean up. Our aunt is coming by tomorrow," Connor rolled his eyes.

"So what's the plan?" Lowell asked.

"We were playing X-Box, not really planning," Joe admitted.

Connor sat down to a controller and started playing against Mouse. Pretty soon, everyone was involved in the game—playing, giving advice, joking, arguing. At eleven, Mouse ordered two pizzas. They talked and played video games into the night. By one, Connor was asleep in his chair. Half an hour later, Mouse dozed off. Joe kept nodding off.

"You should go lie down," Lowell said.

"I'm awake."

"Just for a bit. When these guys wake up, we'll wake you up, too."

"Just an hour. OK?" Joe stumbled to bed.

Mouse opened an eye. Lowell gave him a thumbs up.

Joe woke up even sorer than the day before. Mouse was still asleep under the afghan on the couch. Diane's door was closed, so she must have come in some time after Joe dozed off.

"Good morning," Mouse said, not moving from the sofa where he lay with his back to Joe. Lowell and Connor were gone.

"Fuck you," Joe said.

"You've got to admit, it's morning and you're not dead." His voice was muffled.

"You guys planned it, right?"

"And we have a winner. Layton wanted someone to check on you. Lowell thought you should take a day off, and I came up with the idea of how."

"What did Connor say?"

"He thought we should go out and fight some more. Frankly, I wanted to go out and fight them some more, too. But a day of rest sounded like a good idea. You can get more vengeance tomorrow."

"Hmph," Joe said.

"Lowell said you can talk to him if you want," Mouse said, twisting to his back and looking up. "I'd be your sounding board, but I'm not good at that stuff. I'm better with computers, not people—not that you're especially human most of the time."

"Then why'd you stick around?"

"They didn't want you to sneak out; I'm a light sleeper."

Chapter 15

Layton insisted he escort her to dinner, church, then home, where he left her with instructions to lock up and be careful. For two hours she sat around, watching TV, then trying to read, but at eleven, she put her hair up in a ponytail, pulled a baseball cap far down on her forehead, put on her brown leather bomber jacket and drove to the Central Business District, where she parked on Union Street. She walked the two blocks to the French Quarter and found herself on Bourbon Street.

When Layton asked her what she was doing that evening, she had almost panicked. She thought he was going to ask her out, and she couldn't bear to have another guy interested in her. She knew herself. If he asked, she might go out with him, or she might not, but she'd agonize over the need to find a guy and why she still hadn't. Layton wouldn't be good husband material. Her family wouldn't accept him, since he wasn't a Christian. But each time a guy showed interest, all those problems came to surface.

She needed a break, especially after the close call with the demon. Bourbon Street was full of sin, but she could be anonymous there. She'd look at women and avoid the men. She might even go down past Oz, where Bourbon had the gay clubs—no, she'd resist that.

She just wanted to be around people who weren't involved with such deathly serious situations. At work, they were trying to assess the future of New Orleans. At church they were trying to save the souls of the parishioners, and also to raise money for people who needed to build new houses. Her family was worried about the next generation, and now the guys she released stress with were going to war with demons.

In front of a balcony between Bienville and Conti, two bleach-blond girls were angling for beads. It wasn't Mardi Gras, but that didn't stop the flashing on Bourbon Street. Heather stood on the sidewalk as a dozen men swarmed with their digital cameras. The girls weren't going to show anything. They negotiated for beads, but either the beads offered weren't any good, or they were just the type who would never show. Heather started to go further down the street when the crowd applauded. She spun to see the two girls kissing each other. Immediately, Heather felt her insides go warm.

The girls broke their kiss and Heather flushed red. She put her head down and walked down the crowded street. Here it was, a week and a half before Christmas, and people were partying like that. She had heard that Bourbon Street was wilder before Katrina and that it would get worse as it got closer to Mardi Gras. She was planning on going home for Mardi Gras weekend, though.

She tried to keep vigilant but also to be unnoticed. She didn't want guys to ask her to flash them, so she tried to keep to herself. It wasn't easy, though. Out of towners, drunk and with their inhibitions mostly absent, blocked her path on the sidewalk and she ducked into loud shops that sold all manner of

New Orleans-based junk. When she first moved to town, she had sent some of the souvenirs back home, but after living there for a while, she found it all too tacky.

She meandered down Bourbon, the noise, the laughter, the freedom—all lightening her mood. Two more girls were flashing outside of the Cat's Meow, but Heather only saw their backs. Still, it felt good to be out on the town. She bought a hurricane at one of the bars that had a window right on the street. The Bible warned against strong drink, but one or two wasn't bad. Proverbs 30; verse 6-7 said, "Give strong drink to him who is perishing and wine to those who are bitter of heart. Let him drink and forget his poverty and remember his misery no more." She was bitter of heart. Of course, right after it, the same chapter warned against leaders drinking too much. Also, and she learned this from Layton and not her father, Judges 9:14 said that wine cheereth God and man.

On the next corner she saw the preacher. In the middle of the street a man stood with a large sign reading, "Jesus will judge you!" and "Fornicator's will go to Hell!" He was shouting into a megaphone, condemning passers-by for their clothes, their drinking, and their sexual preferences. Layton would probably have pointed out the apostrophe error. Instead, Heather felt another flush on her cheeks, this time from shame. She ducked down Orleans to Royal, continued for a block, and then came back to Bourbon on St. Ann.

She was there. To her right, gay clubs; the loud ones the men went to, the smaller clubs women went to, the Clover Grill, which was the city's top gay diner, according to the guide books, but everyone ate there.

A short block to her left stood the evangelist. To her right, women were meeting women and there was no judgment, shame, or guilt. She stood in the road until a car started crossing Bourbon and she had to get out of the way. She skittered to her right—away from the evangelist.

Suddenly she felt guilty. She walked a little further down the street, the crowd was thinner here, but she felt the pull to look behind her. All she was going to do was to go to the Clover Grill and get a coke and some fries. That's all. Still, like Lot's wife, she felt the need to look back.

Between her and the evangelist, four demons stalked along, filling the road. Two had black bat wings flared, two were wingless. They were heading to the crowds of people. It was chaotic, that was Bourbon Street. But it was well-lit. It was well-policed. She couldn't believe how unfair this was to her. She was just going to go to the Clover Grill—and now she saw demons.

Why weren't the demons were coming after her? That would be justice. Were they going after the street preacher because of her? They should chase her, not an innocent man. She could fight them; she evaded the one the night before. She was trained and had been training in Tae Kwon Do since she was eleven and they started offering the classes at her church's rec center. Those classes only lasted two years, but she learned a lot and was never picked on more than once during middle school and high school, despite always being the smallest person in her grade. When she started again in college, she was at the top of the class right away.

The demons were a sign. They were heading toward the evangelist and the rest of the crowds. Heather would have to protect them. The choice was obvious—and a lesson to her for her own sins.

She started toward the demons and stopped as a car crossed the street. They were close to the evangelist when the car passed and Heather started to run. She wouldn't make it in time—they were upon him.

And they just passed through him.

As they went to the brighter lights down Bourbon, the demons faded even more. They passed through more and more people, not seeming to notice them, and no one noticed the demons. Soon they faded away. There wasn't going to be a bloody repeat of the tour group on Ursulines that she had been told about.

Heather followed them, but they were gone. She couldn't see them. She turned and he was standing right behind her.

"Have you heard the word of the Lord, young sinner?" an angry voice said. He held a pamphlet out to her with one hand while the other held the big sign steady. The sign was on a long pole so he didn't need to pick it up, except for when he moved. The megaphone was on a lanyard around his neck.

She looked at him. He was a big man, a prodigious potbelly, dressed in work clothes and with a few days of beard stubble on his face. He was nothing like her father, who was her idea of a real minister. His eyes were cold. She took a step backwards, more afraid of this man than the demons. She turned and ran.

She would never tell anyone about what had happened. Layton would probably want to know that they disappeared as they walked into the lights and crowds of Bourbon Street, but she couldn't tell him she was there. There was no way she could explain what she was doing there.

She prayed for guidance and spend her Sunday in church. At night, she didn't go out. She prayed. By Monday morning, she felt the Lord had answered her.

Chapter 16

"Have a nice night?" Cicely asked with a flirtatious smirk. She was a tall, thin, light-skinned black woman who went by the diminutive of Cissy. Diane, the one white roommate in the other half of the duplex, giggled.

I blushed. Michelle was a screamer. For such a straight-laced woman, she really let go when she was in bed. We got together at ten, had dinner and drinks, and were in bed by midnight. She was loud for over an hour, then we slept a little, and about four, we went again, a little less loudly. She left about eight in the morning.

"Sorry about that," I blushed. It might have been a bit embarrassing, but I certainly had an alibi if Bouchard had it in his head that I did the ninja-superhero thing, pimp-slapped anyone, robbed the US Mint, or assassinated the President.

I hoped Bri would be just as loud. My neighbors might wind up thinking I'm a player, but it was the best way to cover my ass. Besides, Bri was very attractive. I thought she was hot when she was a punk waitress years before, and her being a young mother hadn't changed my opinion of her.

Of course I was counting my chickens before they hatched. The week before, she made herself available, but I rejected her. It was because I was worried about the ghosts, but now I had a better idea about them. I thought I could defend her, and she would be a good alibi, too. I felt guilty for using her as an alibi, but I wasn't going to put her in harm's way.

On the way to the dojo, I picked up a copy of the TP. The *Times-Picayune* had an article about the deaths. The reporter had connected Hemlock's death with Joe's friend, which he probably got from the police, but the interesting thing was the headline. "Wild Pigs Blamed for Unexplained Deaths." I read the article before I started my usual routine for opening the dojo.

> Police have been baffled as to the cause of a total of four unexplained deaths. Last week, three French Quarter residents, Gina Griffin, Kelly Baylor, and Jonathan Dvorak were killed. Three weeks earlier, another man, Eugene Helman, was killed in similar circumstances. All four individuals were stabbed to death with an unknown weapon. Each victim had between ten and fifty-five unusual puncture wounds with secondary injuries.

Former New Orleans Parish Medical Examiner, Andre Lecroix, proposed an unusual solution to the problem of what exactly killed the victims. "They were not knife wounds," a police spokesperson stated in both incidences. Lecroix blames the deaths on the wild pigs that taken up residence in City Park. "It's likely that feral pigs wandered from their territory in City Park. The diameter and depth of the puncture wounds as well as the force of the puncture and resultant ancillary injuries are consistent with the goring attack of a wild boar. That would also explain the extreme blood loss, which the pigs may have developed an appetite for. The victims may have surprised the pig or pigs. Most people don't realize how dangerous pigs can be."

> Representatives from the NOPD would not comment on Dr. Lecroix's hypothesis. Beauregard Gaston, who has been contracted by the city to trap the wild pigs since October, confirmed that an adult wild boar can weigh over two hundred pounds and easily kill a man. "I've trapped twenty pigs in the past three months, but there are more out there," he said.

I rolled my eyes. I thought the TP had more integrity than that, but I guess I was wrong. Lecroix, although a former Medical Examiner, was probably old and senile, or otherwise incompetent. On the other hand, I knew the cause of the deaths and the police were still guessing. It was typical that someone would come up with some outlandish explanation. No other account of the more recent murders mentioned blood loss, though. Perhaps the police were sitting on that detail. I wondered if the things were sucking blood. At least there weren't vampire theories going around yet.

Sunday passed like a typical Sunday—fewer classes, fewer students, and less structure. Mouse called and said that Joe had stayed at home all night and was feeling better. They had gone to a late breakfast and were still hanging out. Lowell was going to stop by later and talk to him. Joe's mental health seemed to be OK, from what Mouse could tell me.

Rufus and Diamond were the only upper level students who showed up that Sunday. The rest were probably exhausted or otherwise busy. I got in a good workout and Diamond taught Rufus and me a Wu Shu exercise.

When Diamond was changing, Rufus lagged back.

"Sensei, I was wondering about something."

"Sure."

"The other week, Joe was talking about fighting ghosts. I told him that it was very bad medicine to get involved with something like that."

"I agree."

"He said you showed him how."

I nodded.

"Are you still fighting with them?"

"Yeah. It's been getting worse."

He looked down at me sternly. "I told my grandmother about what was happening—that Joe and Bruiser and you had seen ghosts and touched them.

She said she knew about it. She knows people who are into voodoo, like she is. They say that there's more of the walking dead. They're getting dangerous. The spirits are discontent and striking back. You must back off—leave them to find peace."

"Your grandmother is a wise woman."

He nodded, looking at his feet.

"If it's any help, I don' think they're ghosts. I think they're something else."

He didn't seem to be listening. His eyes snaked to the back, where Diamond hadn't returned from the changing room.

"I've been seeing a lot of Diamond," he said shyly. His deep voice was almost a whisper.

I smiled. "Nice. I mean, I'm happy for you." I immediately felt guilty for stealing a peek down the top of Diamond's gi.

"I'm just worried about those things. What if they attack her? How can I protect her?"

"Now you want to learn to fight them? What about your grandmother; what would she say?"

I could see the conflict on his face.

The door opened and Diamond came out. "I'll tell you how to fight them," I said in a low voice. I'll call you later. OK?"

He nodded and went off to change. Diamond and I made small talk. The two of them left soon after. They weren't touching, but they were looking at each other affectionately.

Rufus worked with troubled kids. He was from Chicago and had been in and out of juvenile detention homes from childhood to his late teens. His mother tired of him and the problems he caused and sent him to live with his grandmother in Algiers, which is right across the river from New Orleans itself. He started taking Kempo, finished his G.E.D., took some courses at a community college, and started work as a tax preparer. That wasn't very satisfactory, nor was it year-round, so he started counseling kids through his church during the off season and soon was hired full-time for that. He went back to school again got his degree in social work.

I didn't know much more about the big man. He was in his mid-thirties. He liked the Bears and the Bulls and Chicago deep dish pizza. We had just had our deepest discussion. He would defy his grandmother's wishes in order to protect Diamond. I was hoping he wouldn't need to.

Another thought crossed my mind. Diamond was incredibly hot, but professionally so. She was an exotic dancer. I wondered how Rufus would deal with that. Maybe she'd give it up for him, but I knew how good the money was. A stripper I dated told me she was making in the area of thousand dollars a night before Katrina. She had evacuated and was plying her trade in Miami now, but she told me that her old friends were complaining of only getting three or four hundred a night since then.

Diamond didn't seem to be suffering. I couldn't see how three or four hundred dollars a night was bad. Maybe she'd miss the money and lifestyle if she did quit. Maybe he could deal with dating a woman in that lifestyle, and I was judging him too harshly. It wasn't any of my business.

*   *   *

Before I met up with Bri, I gave Rufus a call and explained how to touch the ghosts. I cautioned him to not try unless I was there to back him up. He didn't want to actually try, though. He just wanted to know in case the situation arose. Thinking about it, I was confident that if anyone could center himself, extend his chi, and make the ghosts tangible, and successfully fight them, it would be Rufus. He had a calmness about him.

The phone call didn't last long. I was able to advise Rufus and get ready for my date with Bri in plenty of time.

"I'm so hungry," were the first words she said to me.

"How's Indian? I was thinking of Tandoori on Magazine."

"Mmm, tandoori chicken at Tandoori."

"Then we're agreed," I slipped my arm through hers and we went to my car. I had driven to her house in Uptown, where she met me on the front porch. It was similar to mine, a shotgun-style duplex with high ceilings. She shared her half with another single mother, who was watching Brianne's daughter, Annie that evening. They shared babysitting since both did evening shifts.

"You're looking nice," I said. "Like you should be in a ski lodge in New England. She was wearing tight jeans, a silvery blouse and a red sweater over it. She looked Christmas-y.

"You're looking pretty nice, too," she said.

I opened the passenger door to my car. I was wearing jeans and a navy blue turtleneck. It had been a sunny morning, but there was a chill in the air.

We drove down Magazine. When we got to Tandoori, the lights were off. A sign in the window said they were closed.

"Crap," she said.

"Plan B, then," I said. I took the next left and went up to Saint Charles. I found us parking right in front of the Voodoo Barbecue. They're open late and have some good dishes.

"I love this place!" she squealed.

"I didn't know. We didn't discuss it last week, and we talked about so many restaurants."

"I know. Whenever I say how good this one is, people always tell me I'm crazy."

"Me too. I've never had a bad meal or bad service here, but some of the reviews haven't been too good."

We ordered pulled pork, side dishes, and beer. She was very hungry. In minutes, she had finished half her pork and was forking in macaroni and cheese. I ate at a more sedate speed, enjoying my fries, which I doused with their Mojo Sauce, and their rattlesnake beans.

"Oh God, that was good," she said. "I skipped breakfast and then didn't have time for lunch. I think today I only had a bit of Annie's banana when I made her lunch."

"Busy day?"

"Typical Sunday. I took Annie out to the park this morning, then this afternoon I spend cleaning the house and doing laundry. I just had to hurry because I had a hot date tonight."

"Lucky guy."

"You might just very well be," she said, her eyes slitted.

"Sounds nice."

Then her seductive look disappeared. "As long as you don't chicken out like last week."

"Sorry, I had a lot on my mind then."

"The cop?"

"Partly. And the student who died, of course."

"Feeling better now?"

I shrugged. "I was in a police line-up yesterday."

"No way."

"There was some disturbance in the Quarter and someone thought they saw me," I stuck with my official story. "That same cop who keeps bugging me had me come in."

"Did anyone pick you?"

"One person did. There were four cops in the line-up and me. One of the guys was six foot, eight, bald, and had muscles on his muscles. He got three votes. Another person thought it was a little Latin guy. It was ridiculous."

She asked more questions about the line-up. I described the room, the police station, what it felt like to be called forward. We laughed over it, but then she got serious.

"And this cop is really only after you because you defended some girl in Ohio?"

"That's how it seems to me."

"And you swear you didn't have any part in the death of that guy? I read about him in the paper."

"I had nothing to do with it. I swear."

"You know, I found that video of you on Youtube. The one with the guys beating up the girl and you stepping in."

"So did that cop."

"What did he say about it?"

"Nothing, but he still made me go through a line-up."

"Well, I thought you were hot. You were a hero."

"Thank you," I said, flustered. I didn't know what to say. I ate the last bite of my dinner and washed it down with an Abita Turbodog. It's a rich, dark beer brewed across Lake Ponchartrain in Abita Springs. Or maybe they were brewing elsewhere since Katrina. I wasn't sure. I had learned my lesson, though. I was only having one beer.

"You're blushing," she said.

"Um," I said.

She laughed.

"Well, you're pretty hot, too," I said. It was the best I could think of at the moment.

"Thank you," she said. "But I'm not a superhero."

It was my turn to laugh. "Superhero. You have no idea," I said. Which was stupid. It's the type of loaded comment that ends a scene in a movie, but in real life it invited further inquiry.

When she asked, I had no real answer to why I said that.

"Really, what did you mean by that?" she asked.

I couldn't fall back on "Oh nothing," which was my first effort. Later I would think of several stories I could spin. But at that moment, I had nothing but the truth to fall back on.

"What would you say to the idea that there are ghosts?"

"What do you mean?"

"Some of my higher level students and I have been hunting ghosts." I winced. This was all wrong. She was looking at me like I was a lunatic. What had I been thinking?

"I mean, we've been joking about being superheroes, since we've been looking into the supernatural. You know, ghost tours and stuff like that," I added lamely. I finished my beer to cover up how inane I felt I was being.

"I could use another. You?"

She held up her Abita Amber. It was almost gone. "Sure."

When I came back from the counter with her beer and a glass of water for me, Bri looked at me with a serious expression.

"A friend of mine told me she's been seeing ghosts on her street."

"Oh?" I said, trying to make it sound light, but I could tell it was hollow. "Where does she live?"

"She's on Canal, up in Mid-city."

That was far from where we had been seeing them, but they were flooded about six feet up there, so that fit in with my chaos-making-holes-between-the-dimensions theory. I said nothing.

"And I've heard from other people that there are ghosts all over town. I also hear that there are some Karate guys going out and killing them. Like superheroes."

"Interesting rumors. Do you believe them?"

"I don't know. What do you know about it?"

I grimaced. What was the best thing to say? She just said she had heard of the ghosts and what we were doing to them. She might think I was a heroic figure as my team and I fought supernatural beings. On the other hand, perhaps she would think that we were all nuts. Visions of the article about Joe's friend and her buddies flashed into my mind. I couldn't tell Bri about the ghosts. She could wind up the same way.

"Sounds to me like how urban legends get started. People talking about ghosts because of Katrina, like your friend thinks she saw. Then some talk about martial artists fighting them. That could have even come from a bad

Kung Fu flick. And now that some members of my school and I have been looking into ghost legends and saying we're ghost hunting, people put the ideas together and suddenly New Orleans is haunted and there are—what did you say—Karate guys being superheroes?"

I was on familiar ground. One of the assignments I used in my freshman writing classes was to analyze an urban legend. I liked urban legends—the choking Doberman, the killer's phone call coming from same house the babysitter is in, getting straight 'A's if one's roommate dies, the kidney thieves, and so many more. They were a fun way to see how gullible people could be. Even after doing the research, many of the students would still believe the legend instead of the truth.

"I guess," she said, after a pause.

"It's easy to see how the rumor grew." I laughed. "I can't wait to tell the guys at the dojo that they're starring in an urban legend."

"That's too bad. I kinda like the idea that I was dating some superhero." She looked startled and blushed redder than I ever could have. "Not that we're dating, but you know, we went on a date." She paused again. "And now we're on another one."

"Sorry I'm no superhero," I said.

She smiled. "You were pretty heroic in that Youtube video."

"Yeah, but not super-heroic," I said with a fake sigh of disappointment.

"We'll see about that."

*   * *

After we ate, we chatted some more and finally went back to my place. Like her appetite at dinner, she couldn't wait to get to my place. I was still processing the fact that she had heard about us ghost-hunting, superhero, Karate guys. I hoped that I had done the right thing by claiming it was all an urban legend. I also hoped that I wasn't too quick with my answer. She might start to question my story after a while. I had decided that the worst thing for her to believe was that there were ghosts and regular people, like or me, could control their existence. I didn't want her to start looking for them and get killed.

"Sorry, I don't have any etchings to show you," I joked. I was admiring her as she looked at the bookshelves. She had a tight little body and smooth pale skin with just a few freckles. "Want anything to drink?"

"No. I had enough beer for tonight."

"I can make some coffee or get some water, if you change your mind."

"OK, maybe later." She kept looking around my shelves. She had been so eager, I wondered if I had said anything to turn her off. Perhaps the mention of etchings, since that was what she was talking about on our first date when I didn't follow through.

She pulled a DVD from the shelf. "Is this good?"

I looked at the title—*This is Spinal Tap*. "One of the funniest films ever."

"I love comedies," she said. "I keep hearing about this one."

We watched the movie and she obviously loved it. I laughed at all the familiar scenes that always had me laughing. I had probably seen it more than twenty times at this point in my life.

While we sat there, I put my arm around her. She didn't pull back, which was a good sign, and after a while she leaned against me. I started to stroke her hair as a segue into kissing her, but every time I started to move, she would rock forward with shrieks of laughter.

After the film we finally kissed a bit. When I had stroked her hair, I realized how small her head was. I was expecting her kisses to be little things. Instead, her mouth fit mine perfectly. It was when my hand got away from her back and started moving toward the front that she stopped.

"I can't stay tonight. I've got to get back to Annie. Next time, though," she said.

She left around one. I wanted her to stay, not only because I was still worried that Bouchard would bother me again, but also because she was fun. Michelle was fun, but she was my age. Her skin was loose, her breasts drooped a little. Bri was young—tight skinned, fresh, and the small breasts she had pushed against me when she leaned on me were firm. I wanted to do more than just hold her on the sofa. Too bad I didn't get to.

The next morning, though, Cicely and Diane teased me some more.

"Damn, boy, you a playah," Cicely said as I was leaving the house with my laptop computer in its case over my shoulder.

I grinned, then blushed. I wanted to tell them that nothing had happened. What they hear was probably Bri's high-pitched laughter. It came in short bursts, so maybe it sounded like she was having quite a different time than just watching Rob Reiner's hilarious *mockumentary*.

"We're living next to a pimp," Diane said.

That brought me up short. Hadn't that been what Bouchard had thought I was? All I needed were my neighbors, three attractive college girls, to tell the detective that a parade of women were coming though my bedroom. They may have joked that I was a pimp, but he wanted me to be one. He thought that if I were guilty of one thing, I must be guilty of any other crime that came to his one-track mind. He'd found himself a suspect, he just needed a crime.

I would call my other dates and reschedule. I could find something else to do in the evenings to keep my nose clean. I'd hang out with my roommate. I would get in touch with some friends in the area. I started reshuffling my social calendar.

"Um, just a friend visiting," I mumbled.

"Yeah, right," Diane said. "If I liked older men, I'd be interested in checking out what these girls see in you, Paul."

"Yeah, and if I were into white guys, I'd give you a shot, too," Cissy laughed.

I grinned. "Good thing I haven't turned on the charm, then."

They laughed. I wished them a good day and went back inside. I grabbed my cell phone and started making some phone calls. I broke dates and came up with something else to do.

Chapter 17

"So I've got a theory," Mouse said. It was Sunday night and Mouse, Joe, Lowell, and Connor were having dinner at Fiorello's on Decatur again. It was cheap, and the fried chicken was good. Mouse had suggested the place when they started calling each other when the sun went down a couple hours before.

"What's the theory?" Connor asked.

"I read this book by Dean Koontz, *Odd Thomas*. It was about a guy who sees dead people."

"Like the *Sixth Sense*," Connor said.

"Yeah. But in it, there are these creatures called bodachs. They're always around before there's a serious massacre, like when someone goes postal and shoots up a school or mall...What?"

Lowell and Connor were grinning. Joe also looked confused. He had a black eye from the night before. Saturday was their night of almost enforced rest, but they went out again Sunday. There were even more ghosts than before. They only made it to the edge of the Lower Ninth before seeing them in groups of ten or more.

"You want to tell him?" Connor said.

"You go ahead."

"Our mom used to tell us stories about bodachs. They're like boogeymen. They're Irish, of course."

"They're supposed to be old men, like imps," Lowell added. He knew more about bodachs. He had done a report on Irish mythologies in high school.

"Yeah, they tweak noses if you're bad," Connor finished.

"Oh yeah. I think I remember. It was in the book. They weren't really bodachs from the myth, but that's what someone called them, so he kept the name."

"Maybe they're boggarts," Connor said. "From Harry Potter. Y'know, they take the shape of things that you're afraid of."

Mouse held up a chicken leg. "It makes sense. Bodachs or boggarts. They take a form from the subconscious, like the boggarts. They're from some other dimension and they're attracted to chaos. Maybe these writers, Dean Koontz and J.K. Rowling, have connected with some primal force out there."

"Like an archetype. A genetic memory."

"Yeah, Mr. Psychology. I've read Jung, too."

"I'm not disputing that. Maybe there's something to it. Things like bodachs, devils, imps, and all that are part of a racial memory. Maybe they've been here before. And some writers have been able to get in touch with that memory."

"Makes sense."

"Yeah, but I'm not a Jungian."

"Maybe you should be," Mouse said.

"Nyaah. Not my style."

"At least you're not a Freudian, like Mr. P.," Connor said. "He helped me with a paper for eleventh grade English. Man, what a dirty mind."

"Mr. P.?" Mouse asked.

"Freud."

"What grade did you get?" Joe asked.

"I got an A. And I think Mr. P. got a date with my teacher."

"What was his name?" Joe asked.

They laughed.

"It was a woman, Miss Zimmer. And most of the guys had crushes on her. She was hot."

"So what's the plan for tonight?" Lowell said. He was unsure how to begin.

"We're walking distance to Ursulines," Mouse pointed out. "My feet hurt from so much kicking lately—that and walking around every night."

"That's where we started with all this," Connor said.

"I'm starting to have second thoughts," Lowell said. He took a deep breath. "They just keep coming and coming. Maybe it's best to avoid them."

"What, you're chickening out?" Joe said.

"No, I'm not chickening out. I don't know if we're going anywhere with this." He pointed at Joe. "Why did you start fighting them?"

"I don't know. First 'cause they beat me up. If Sensei wasn't there, I'd be dead."

"Then why?"

"I thought they'd be good to fight for serious full-contact fighting. Tell me it hasn't been great training for that."

"It is. I think we're all much better fighters than we were two weeks ago. Remember what Connor said when we were going out the first time with Bruiser?"

"What did I say?"

"Something about how it'd be funny if someone tried to mug us."

"Oh yeah."

"We're a lot better now. I wouldn't put any odds on the muggers. We've had our full-contact training. Do you think we're going to get any better at this point?"

"True," Mouse agreed. "We've been going through a serious training regimen. I've lost almost ten pounds."

"Yeah. You'd sound more believable if you didn't have food in both hands."

Mouse looked at his hands. One had a couple French fries and the other held the bone from the chicken leg. He had been using it as a pointer, but nibbling on the remaining meat and gristle. He put the food down and wiped grease from his fingers. The waitress put a new Diet Coke in front of him and took away his empty one. He smiled at her and she smiled back.

"Still, it's great training. And I really have lost eight or nine pounds."

"Ah, so that's why you wanted to go here," Connor said.

"What?"

"You like her."

"Hmph. I love any woman who brings me food and refills my coffee."

"Yeah, sure," Joe said.

"And you got that line from Layton. I heard him say it a few times," Connor said. "You didn't even have any coffee."

"It's the principle of the thing."

"So Lowell, what were you saying?" Joe asked again.

"It's been great training. I bet you could do a great job in a full-contact contest now."

"I know I could."

"But the more we kill them, the more show up."

"So?"

"Ah, I get it," Mouse said.

"Get what?" Joe said.

"They're like a hydra. Cut off one head, and seven more grow in its place."

"Right."

"So we're wasting our time?" Mouse said.

"That's what I've been thinking." Lowell was happy someone got it.

"It doesn't matter. I'm going to kill those things," Joe said.

"Me too," Mouse said.

"I'm in," Connor said. His brother looked at him.

Lowell raised his hands in a gesture of helplessness. "OK. But we should think about it."

*   *   *

There were no ghosts on Ursulines. Lowell found it odd there weren't any, since the numbers had been growing. Joe suggested they go up to Lakeside. His job had been doing some clean-up work there and thought it would be a good place for ghosts.

They took the SUV and Joe's truck. Mouse offered his car, but no one wanted to ride with him. The car smelled of old food and sweat. Lowell and Connor laughed as the truck rocked when Mouse climbed in to Joe's truck.

"Do you really think things are going to get worse with the ghosts?" Connor asked.

"That's what's been happening."

Connor was quiet for a bit. "I like hunting them," he admitted. "I want to take out seven of them at one time, like Sensei did. That would be awesome!"

"You're really into this, aren't you?"

"Yeah, it's great."

"Why?"

"When I'm fighting them, I'm not second best. I'm not just your little brother, or even a brown belt; I'm a superhero. I mean, that's what we're doing."

"You think we're heroes?"

Connor was quiet for a moment. "I don't think we're real heroes. We're being superheroes 'cause we're fighting these ghosts and they're not human, y'know? That's super. A hero is like someone who runs into a burning house to save a baby or jumps on a grenade. We're not that kind of hero."

"I see."

"But it's cool to be a superhero," Connor laughed.

"Yeah, it's addictive." Lowell steered around a pothole. The city was full of them and they would be there for years. With everything else, they were a lower priority.

"Do you really feel like you're in my shadow?"

"Can't help it. That's what happens to younger brothers. Mom always tells me I should be more like you. I want to take another year off before college and she keeps bugging me to apply. I don't even know what I want to study."

Lowell held off a comment he had heard their mother say many times. If only Connor would get a job while he was taking time off. Lowell knew that would only make her warn Connor that he'd never get back in school.

"You should just take general studies for your first year to two. Take classes in all different subjects—even sit in on classes you don't know anything about, then decide on a major. But even after you have a major, that doesn't mean you have to work in that field." That was the track Lowell took in his own education. He wasn't sure if he wanted to go into business or the humanities.

"Yeah, but it all seems so pointless. I don't even know if I want to go to college. I thought about joining the Army."

"Mom would go ballistic if you did that."

"I don't think I will now, though. It'd be a let down after this."

"Don't become an adrenaline junkie. What'll you do after they're gone?"

"Think they'll every be gone?"

"I hope so. If it's an invasion, we've got to stop it. Then there won't be any more of them. We'll be back to normal." He was worried about that. Would they be able to return to normal? Would some of them wind up with Post Traumatic Stress Syndrome, like soldiers who have returned home from war and weren't able to fit in? Imagine trying to explain ghost hunting to a therapist. If Lowell had gone into Clinical Psychology, he wouldn't believe someone who came to him saying he fought ghosts.

"Maybe then I'll join the Army. Or take up bungee jumping."

Lowell had no answer for that.

"I was also thinking that someone's going to have to stand guard in case they come back. Maybe I'll hunt for other supernatural things. I could be a ghost hunter or night stalker or something. If there are ghosts, there's got to be other things."

They were in Lakeside, but there were no ghosts. The vehicles circled around; a night view of Katrina damage surrounded them, but no ghosts were in sight.

"Want to call Mouse?"

Connor pressed the speed dial on his cell phone.

"Yeah," he said into the phone. "What do you want to do?" He listened. "OK, I'll tell Lowell."

"We're going back to the Lower Ninth."

"Are they sure they don't want to take a rest tonight?"

His answer was the truck taking a U-turn and speeding past them. Lowell turned around and followed.

The Lower Ninth was filled with ghosts. As many as any other night—perhaps more. Maybe the low number of ghosts elsewhere in the city was because they were all congregating in the Lower Ninth Ward.

The vehicles stopped by a group of six ghosts and they jumped out.

"They're mine," Joe called and jumped into them.

"That's not fair," Connor said.

"He's still pissed at them," Mouse said. "Let's just back him up this time. There will be more."

"Like those," Connor said. Another group was coming around the corner—a big group.

Chapter 18

I brought a couple bottles of wine to dinner. I had driven up to Hattiesburg, Mississippi to visit some friends. Nick Cicero was a former colleague of mine from my first teaching job as an adjunct in Virginia. Back then he was looking for a job at a real school and so was I. He made it, teaching Mathematics at the University of Southern Mississippi. His wife, Natalie Carter, taught chemistry—she was a few years older than he was and on the faculty at USM when he arrived. They made a nice couple. They were vegetarians, and both loved to cook and would try to on-up each other in the kitchen. When I'd visit, I would get a great meat-free meal. After all the Cajun food I ate in New Orleans, I hoped their food helped my arteries.

Although it was a year after Katrina, Hattiesburg, a hundred miles from New Orleans, still had blue tarps over roofs of houses. My friends were lucky; they had only lost the roof of their garage and their back fence to the tornadoes spawned from Katrina. Nick showed me the repairs they had made and the landscaping changes the loss of trees and the overgrowth had caused.

I wasn't their only guest that evening. I had asked Nick if he knew any theoretical physicists at the university, and he invited a grad student who he thought would fill the bill. He wasn't able to make it to dinner, but he was going to try to get there for dessert and coffee later. Nick and Natalie agreed that Marvin Feinstein was the most *out there* physicist on campus. They had asked some colleagues in the Physics department and all agreed. The kid was brilliant, but had strange ideas.

We had a good meal of curried eggplant, brown and wild rice with onions, and homemade spelt bread. We opened the bottle of red with it. Dinner conversation was just catching up—I inquired about how their clean-up had been going and how things were at the school. They, in turn, asked the same of me.

"I still can't believe you're down here," Nick said.

"Still teaching?" Natalie asked.

"A few courses to tide me over. I'm not working as a cook anymore, so that's good. Last semester I had three classes, and I'm signed up for four next semester. I hope to get more students in the dojo, so I won't have to keep running around."

"Dating anyone special?" Nick asked.

I shrugged. "I went out a couple times lately."

"Same woman or different ones?" Natalie asked.

"To be honest? Three dates with two different women in the past two weeks."

"Ever going to settle down?" she asked. I could feel that she was judging me. We were friendly because Nick liked me. I didn't delude myself that she and I could be real friends. She didn't dislike me, but I was Nick's friend.

"How about you guys? What have you been up to?"

"Natalie got a paper published in the *Journal of Polymer Research*," Nick said proudly. "And that's not even her primary field."

"That's wonderful."

"USM is a big school for polymer research. I co-wrote it with two other professors and two grad students."

"Natalie's being modest. She was primary author, and it was her idea originally."

We chatted a bit more—the specifics of Natalie's article were way beyond me, but I was able to hold my own when we talked about cooking. It's nice to be humbled sometimes. At least it should be. I felt pretty stupid when she talked about chemistry and polymers.

I helped with the dishes and got a pot of coffee going while Natalie got plates ready for dessert. She had made a pie and they had homemade ice cream. Not long after that, the grad student arrived. He looked like the typical science nerd of about twenty. He was tall, skinny, and wore an ill-fitting polo shirt. His hair was messy and his glasses were Coke bottle thick.

"I brought rugelach," he said, holding up a plastic container. "My mother said I should bring something." That was my first surprise about him. He had a thick southern accent. His voice was also unusually deep and rich—he sounded a little like the actor and singer, Jim Nabors. From the visual I had, and the preconceptions I had of a Jewish physicist, I thought the was joking with the voice, but it didn't waver. The accent was pure Mississippi.

"Thank you Marvin," Natalie said. She put the cookies on a plate and started to get the pie and ice cream out.

"I'm sorry I'm so late. I had a series running and I had to wait until it was finished before running the diagnostic. We're working on pairing weak force bonds between particles here and at the Oak Ridge Particle Accelerator in Tennessee." He held out a hand. "I'm Marvin."

"Paul."

"We don't have a particle accelerator here." He pronounced it 'hay-yuh', but I got the gist of it. "So we're using a supercooled quantum containment field to pair the particles."

"Interesting," Nick said. "I've heard of things like that. Two particles behaving the same despite distance under certain conditions."

"We're using the particle accelerator to artificially age the particles in Tennessee. The weak force properties in the particles here anticipate the conditions there. It's as if the particles here predict what's happening with the others. Maybe they just influence the faster particles, or maybe it's time travel."

"I get it," I said. "That's amazing."

"It's still early, though." He stopped and picked up his fork. "This pie looks really good, Doctor Carter."

"You can call me Natalie," she said.

"Thank you Miss Natalie."

She hid a smile behind her hand. She'd been in the South a long time, but I could see she still wasn't used to the formal manners.

We dug into the pie and had coffee to wash it down. Marvin didn't want coffee until I assured him it was decaf. That had been Natalie's idea, and I went along with it. When we finished the pie and ice cream, Nick, Marvin, and I went into the living room, taking the cookies and coffee with us. I sat in a rocking chair, Marvin sat on the love seat that matched the sofa. The furniture was bamboo, as was the cloth covering the cushions and the rug on the floor.

"So Marvin, Nick and Natalie told you why I was hoping to meet you, right"

"Oh yeah, your novel."

I had told my friends that I was writing a science fiction novel and wanted someone to help me with understanding dimensions.

I started telling him about the ghosts we had been encountering, but I changed everything I said. Instead of telling him that we were killing ghosts in real life, I told him I was starting a book about how Katrina tore holes in dimensions and creatures from the other dimensions were invading.

"So the story is set in New Orleans?"

"Post-Katrina."

"That makes sense."

"I wanted to talk to someone who could tell me about dimensional portals."

"Well, there are some theoretical ideas about dimensional portals, but it's all speculation. You could just make up anything you want."

"I know, but I want it to be internally consistent. I guess I want to know, if you posit that something like Katrina could cause a breakdown between the dimensions, what would the rules of that be?"

"Tell me what idea you have," he said. He was on his turf with physics. I was the student there.

I told him about the invaders and how they could be seen. Natalie came in during this time and curled up on the sofa next to Nick. I skipped over chi and time dilation, since it was my conviction that those were just tricks in martial arts that people thought were serious mysticism. I talked about the growing numbers of the invaders and asked him if it would make sense that the portals got bigger because of our intervention. Of course I said that it was the characters fighting the invaders instead of me and my students fighting so-called ghosts.

"I can't see how killing the invaders would open up the portals even more," he said. "Generally the natural state would be returned to. It may take a while, but the holes would probably close."

"Really?"

"Well, the theory of wormholes states they would be temporary. They may only exist for microseconds. Larger holes—I mean with a wider diameter—would collapse even faster. But you're talking about something different. Holes that aren't long, but between dimensions that were next to each other spatially. Even if that were possible, they'd be closing as time passed." He had a smirk that told me I was just another amateur science fiction writer.

"So we're not making it easier for them to come over?"

He didn't catch the slip. Nick might have, but he didn't say anything.

"I mean, in the book, we're not making it easier for the dimensions to be permeated? If the invaders are coming over in larger amounts, it's not because of the dimensional walls breaking down, then?"

"I can't see how. Unless the walls are breaking down between the dimensions in general."

"How would that happen?"

"Well, a hurricane releases a lot of energy, like dozens of nuclear bombs. If that's punched a hole between dimensions, then it would heal. If there's some other reason for the dimensions to merge, such as an erosion due to entropy, then nothing could heal them."

"Is that possible?"

"None of this is possible, but no one has ever seriously theorized that dimensional walls could just break down. That's just an idea I had for some fan fiction I've been writing." He blushed. "I'm not too good, but maybe you could look over some of the stuff I've been working on?"

"Sure," I said, "I'd love to."

"I never know how to end these things."

"Maybe I can help. Anyway, what about the increase in the," I paused, forgetting for a second that I wasn't to use the term 'ghosts', "the invaders? I need to have them increase in number for my conclusion."

"That sounds cool. I don't know, maybe you can just have them smelling blood, like sharks or something. I don't think the dimensional walls will break down more, or else that would be the end of everything."

"The end of everything?"

"Nyaaah. I'm exaggerating. But imagine the dimensions not being differentiated. Maybe nothing would happen. What if they were all in place at once?"

Nick finally spoke up. "It would be schizophrenic, to say the least. If there are further spatial dimensions, we couldn't see them if they existed. They would probably be partly visible, but we'd only see parts of the objects."

"I see," I said.

"I'd like to read it when you're done," Marvin said.

"Yeah, me too," Nick agreed.

"What's the story?" Natalie asked. "I get the idea behind it, the invaders in New Orleans. But who's the main character and what's the point?"

"Oh yeah," I laughed. I had thought about it on the way up. I blended fact and fantasy. "You know those ghost tours? One of the tour guides is the first ones to find out about the invaders...he thinks they're ghosts. Then it turns from him not being believed, to invaders from space scenario. I've been in the Lower Ninth Ward since Katrina, and it looks like a war zone. I want to show that in a different way."

"I see. I didn't know you wrote fiction."

"Well, every English professor has a novel hidden in a drawer somewhere. It's an intellectual exercise. I tried writing one at one time, but never finished." I laughed. "You know, something to do in my copious free time."

That got some laughs, and Natalie seemed satisfied. We chatted more, until about eleven, then Marvin had to get home. I didn't get any more ideas from them, but I felt better from what Marvin had told me.

I spent the night in Nick and Natalie's guest room. The semester was over for them too, so we hung out a bit in the morning, until Natalie had her Yoga class. I got back on the road and headed south after we said our goodbyes.

"You should come back up the week after next. My sister Melanie is visiting," Natalie said. "She's a museum administrator in San Francisco."

"So that's why you wanted to know if I'm seeing anyone," I teased her. "You're trying to hook me up with her."

"Paul, you know I wouldn't do that. I just thought you might like to meet her. She's a great person."

"I believe you. Oh golly, look at the time," I looked at my bare wrist, pretending a watch was there. I opened my eyes as wide as I could in feigned shock.

"Very funny," she chuckled. "You drive carefully. We'll call you when Mel comes to town."

"I'll come back up if I can," I promised. I looked at Nick. He was standing a few feet behind his wife and he held up his hands, as if cupping two melons—or large breasts. He winked.

"Thanks again," I said, and headed on my way.

I didn't have any classes until five that evening. The dojo's winter break schedule was Tuesday, Thursday and Saturday. I took my time getting back.

Chapter 19

A big group of ghosts, easily a hundred, rounded the corner. Another group, maybe forty or fifty of them, coming down the street from the direction the guys had come. It didn't look like they had set up an ambush, since they were moving slowly. Some of them noticed the martial artists and started rushing toward them.

"Oh shit," Lowell said. "Connor, you're going to get your chance to fight seven of them at once if we don't get out of here."

Joe was battling four of them. He didn't seem aware of the sudden swell in the number of ghosts.

"Joe!" Mouse called. "We gotta get going!"

"It's no use," Connor said. "C'mon!" He rushed forward. Lowell looked around and hurried after, with Mouse lumbering behind.

They plowed into the ghosts trying to circle Joe. He paused in his battle and snapped something to them. Lowell caved in the ribs of one of them and it disappeared. Only Mouse and Connor were fighting, the rest of Joe's foes had been destroyed.

"Look at what's coming!" Lowell said. He pointed up the street.

Joe turned his head and his mouth dropped open.

"And that way." Lowell pointed to the smaller group coming from the other direction.

"Shit," he said.

"To the cars!" Joe said. His partners were already starting on their way. They were surrounded. "The truck! Everyone in the truck!"

Joe sprinted around to the driver's side of the truck, shoving a ghost aside. It was their habit to keep the engines running, in case they had to get out quickly. The other three were climbing into the bed of the truck. Lowell jumped in and Connor scrambled after him. Mouse frantically threw himself to the side of the truck, but he couldn't get in before the ghosts were on him.

Connor kicked at them from over the side of the truck bed. He grabbed Mouse's collar and tried helping the big guy up, but a shadowy hand grabbed his and he was pulled out of the truck bed.

Before Lowell could jump out after his brother, the truck jerked forward.

"Stop, they've got Connor!" he yelled. He hit the window behind Joe's head. The truck slammed to a stop.

Lowell jumped into a sea of ghosts and started to fight his way to his brother. Joe backed the truck up. It went through ghosts. He jerked it around. "Get back to the truck!"

He opened the door, kicking out.

The four fought furiously, trying to get together into one group. Lowell fought his way over to his brother. Mouse used his strength and size to bull a path in the direction of the brothers, but he wasn't faring well. His gray sweatshirt was torn to shreds and blood flowed from dozens of wounds. Joe was on the other side of the truck from them and being pulled deeper into the ghosts.

Joe spun around headed back to the truck. He was hit from behind and went down to a knee. A back kick propelled him a bit forward, but the way back was hard. He felt a cut open on the back of his head.

On the other side of the truck, Mouse was pulled down. He called out, but Lowell and Connor were now close enough to fight back to back. They worked a few steps toward the truck. "We're coming!" Connor called.

"To the truck," Lowell said. "I'll help Mouse!"

Connor kicked one of the shadowed shapes aside. There was a brief path to Mouse, but it was filled in a second. They flailed, punched, blocked, kicked, and felled ghosts. Joe got to the cab of the truck and jumped in. Hands reached through the door and cut at him. He blocked. Putting it in gear, he pulled forward and then popped it into reverse, cutting the wheel to put the rear of the truck between Lowell and Connor on one side and Mouse on the other.

"Get in! Get in!" Joe yelled. He flung the passenger door open. Lowell pushed Connor in and climbed after him, kicking at ghosts. He slammed the door, but they reached through the metal and cut at him.

The truck bounced heavily. Joe looked up. Mouse's bulk filled the mirror. He was savagely wrestling with something. Joe floored it—Mouse fell, but used the momentum of his fall to send the ghost sailing.

They peeled away, but ghosts reached into the truck, slashing at the passengers. Joe swerved left and right, trying to evade them, but there were too many. The truck drove through them, but they could still touch the people in the truck. As the truck sped up, however, the contact stopped. Soon they were past the edge of the mass of ghosts. Joe increased speed even more. He tore out of the neighborhood with the tires barely touching the streets as he took the corners.

"Connor," Lowell said.

"Jesus," Connor said. "Oh my God, that was...." He stopped. "Lowell?" He grabbed his brother's shoulders. "Lowell!"

Lowell's eyes were wide open, his mouth open to continue whatever thought he started to say to his brother. There was blood on his teeth. Connor wrapped his arms around Lowell and howled.

Chapter 20

I returned to a tragedy. Mouse met me at the dojo. He sat on the sidewalk, his head buried in his hands. When he looked up at me, I could see he was extensively bandaged and bruised all over his arms and face.

"Jesus, Mouse. Are you OK? We got to get you to a hospital!" I said.

He shook his head. "Lowell's dead. They killed Lowell."

I felt like I had been hit in the forehead with a sandbag. The world swam in and out of focus for a moment. I was aware my eyes were open and I as looking at Mouse. He wasn't talking, he was holding back tears, but I could see he had been crying.

"We went out again last night. There were too many."

"Oh man," I said. "What happened?"

"First we went to Ursulines, where we saw them before, but there weren't any, then we went to Lakeview to see if any were there. There weren't any, but when we got to the Lower Ninth, we got out of the cars and there were like a hundred or two hundred." He paused and took a deep breath. "They were all over us. I got pulled down into them, but they came back for me. We were getting away, but one of them got Lowell through the door of the truck." Tears were running down his cheeks. "If they didn't come back for me, he'd still be alive. It's my fault."

"You can't think of it that way, Bob. I don't know all that happened, but I know coming back for you was their choice. Nothing was your fault."

He sniffled a bit.

"What happened then?"

"We went to a hospital and they patched us up. We told them it was gangs. We had to talk to the police."

"How's Connor?"

"He's in shock. Their mom's there, but she's in bad shape, too."

"Where's Joe?"

"He went to get their car. I said I'd drive him, but he wanted to be alone."

"Is he OK?"

"He's not hurt, just some scratches."

"This is terrible," I couldn't believe it. Lowell was the smart one, the mature one. These guys had been going out when I had warned them not to, and it had stopped being a game. I had failed them.

I was standing there, facing Mouse who still sat on the sidewalk, for minutes. The same thought kept going over and over in my mind—that Lowell had died. A car door slammed.

"Mr. Layton," came a familiar voice.

I turned. It was Bouchard. He had four uniformed officers with him in two patrol cars.

"Layton, you're under arrest. You have the right to remain silent. Anything you say can and will be used against you in a court of law. You have the right to an attorney. If you can't afford one..." he continued with the Miranda warning. I had heard it a million times on television and in movies. It felt weird to have it said to me. It was sinking in. I was being arrested. They spun me around and put handcuffs on me.

"Hey, what are you doing?" Mouse struggled to his feet but one of the uniformed cops pushed down on his shoulder.

"Don't, Bob," I warned him.

Bouchard frisked me roughly. He slapped my legs apart and patted me up my legs, slapping me hard in the nuts. I jerked forward, almost stumbling to my knees, but two of the uniforms pulled me upright by my shoulders and Bouchard hit me there again.

"Stop moving around," he ordered. "What are you trying to hide, asshole?"

After a few more abuses they put me in the back of a squad car and we drove off. Bouchard wasn't in the car with me, which was the only good part of the episode.

"Any idea why I've been arrested?" I asked.

They didn't say anything. That's what I expected. I was left in the back seat with my shock and grief over Lowell's death. It kept running through my head. Lowell was dead and I had started all of the events that led to his death. I ignored what I told Mouse. They were my students. I was responsible.

I was fingerprinted, read my rights again, put in an interview room and left there for four hours with no water or food. At least when they fingerprinted me, they uncuffed me and put the cuffs back with my arms in the front. The chairs were uncomfortable, so I sat on the floor.

It was almost ten at night when Bouchard came in.

"I want a lawyer," I said. "And a bathroom."

"Yeah, yeah. Where were you last night around one in the morning?"

"I want a lawyer."

"Where were you last night?"

"I was in Hattiesburg, Mississippi from yesterday afternoon to this afternoon. I stayed with Dr. Nicholas Cicero and his wife, Dr. Natalie Carter. There was another guest, Marvin Feinstein, a graduate student. I don't know Mr. Feinstein's phone number, but Doctors Cicero and Carter's home phone is 601-52...."

"Save it, we'll get you a lawyer. Then you can tell us all the stories you want." He looked at his watch. "Aww, look. It's way past office hours for the Public Defender. I guess we'll have to call them tomorrow." He went to the door and it opened. "Take him to lock-up," he ordered an officer. Two of them escorted me down a long hallway. I talked them into letting me relieve myself. They took me to a tiny bathroom with no windows—it didn't matter, I wasn't about to try to escape, I just needed to piss. When I had finished, they took me to an elevator, then another hallway, and finally to a cell.

"What about the cuffs?" I asked one of the cops as they closed the door and started walking away. They ignored me. Bouchard must had given them orders.

There were five other men with me. Six of us and four beds. The men looked at me curiously. None of them were in cuffs.

I decided I'd try to break my shackles. I once read an autobiography of a carnival strongman who told his secrets about breaking handcuffs. I'd never had a chance to try the technique, though. I inspected the cuffs. They looked new and solid. Older locks could spring loose with a very sharp rap against a hard surface, but this pair didn't look like they'd just pop open. The chain was too short to use one cuff to pry the other cuff at the hinge. I needed something to use as a wedge. The frames of the beds were round—so no help there. I looked around. There was a flat ridge of metal around the lock in the heavy, barred door.

I slid the cuffs along the ridge of metal. Taking a deep breath, I got leverage and pushed. The metal of the handcuffs dug into me. Veins bulged in my arms. My breathing came in short pants. The hinge snapped.

With one handcuff broken, the other one was easier. I used the first cuff to pry the second. I would have bruises, but at least my arms were free.

A huge guy waddled up to me. He was a little shorter than me, black, and built like a keg of beer on Human Growth Hormone. I've seen refrigerators that were smaller. My hands were free, so I was ready. I was also ready to throw the metal cuffs into his face to distract him while I kicked his knee in.

"Man, how you do that?" He smiled, showing lots of gold teeth.

I grinned back at him. "It's all about leverage." I held up the remains of the handcuffs and started to show him the weak points and how to use torque to break the hinge.

"We figure you some bad dude if they kept the cuffs on you in here. Either that or they want us to fuck you up. After seein' you bust those cuffs off you, we think you a serious bad dude."

He was called Ray Dog. Two of the other guys were members of his crew. The other two were independent drug dealers, from what I gathered, but they respected Ray Dog. By the morning, I had promises from all five of my cellmates that they'd stop by the dojo and look into lessons. I didn't sleep at all. I may have been friendly with these guys, but I certainly didn't trust them.

*   *   *

By ten in the morning my new friends had all been released on bail or off talking with lawyers. I was still waiting for a chance to call a lawyer. I tried to get the attention of the guards every time the door at the end of the row of cells opened, but they ignored me. Finally, I let my frustration take over. For a while I punched the metal plate around the lock to keep up with my Iron Fist training. After a thousand punches, I started kicking it in the same spot—sets of a hundred kicks with each leg. I didn't think I was going to break it, but it was cathartic. The cell row echoed with my repeated blows. Prisoners in the other cells raised their voices, some urging me on, some telling me to keep the noise down.

After a half hour of punching and kicking the lock, an outraged voice interrupted the noise I was making. From the closed door I heard shouting. The door slammed open and Bouchard skittered in backwards.

"Hey!" I yelled. "I need a lawyer. Bouchard! Hey!"

I could barely hear my own shouts in the din. Bouchard was babbling and a bass bullhorn of a human voice was surpassing all the other noise.

Following the backpedaling Bouchard strode a big man with caramel skin and a white walrus mustache, wearing a very expensive three-piece suit. He was Mouse's size, which I could tell because Mouse had followed him into the room, grinning to beat the band. I'd seen this guy on television.

"This is an outrage!" Councilman Clarence Smith yelled again at Bouchard. Every time Smith yelled, Bouchard jumped back a little.

"No lawyer! No probable cause! Have you even bothered to check his alibi?"

Bouchard sputtered something incomprehensible. Behind Councilman Smith, Mouse grinned. Another man was there, also glaring at Bouchard—I think it was the Police Commissioner. Behind him, Detective Lucas and Officer DuBois were holding back their own laughter. A few other officers crowded in through the door to see the spectacle.

"Release this man!" Smith thundered. Bouchard looked helplessly at the lock. His eyes searched around imploringly until he saw someone who had the keys.

"Well, unlock the cell!" Bouchard snapped at the guard.

"It's stuck," the guard said after a moment.

"Pry it open!" Bouchard glared at me. "What did you do to the door?"

The guard twisted the key again and pushed. He jerked the door and it rattled. Finally, it opened.

Immediately Smith barged in and took my hand in his massive paw. He shook my hand and put his other hand on my shoulder as if photographers were present and I was being handed the key to the city.

"Dr. Layton, I want to apologize on behalf of City of New Orleans and the New Orleans Police Department. Bouchard overstepped his authority in bringing you in and treating you so abominably." He glared at the detective. "Let him out."

"Now wait a second. You can't just free my prisoner."

"Bouchard!" the Police Commissioner snapped.

"But there's something fishy about this guy," he whined. "Hey," he said to me, all suspicion again. "What happened to the handcuffs?" He turned to the Commissioner. "He broke his handcuffs. Those are city property."

"Did you put him in a cell with dangerous felons while he was still handcuffed?" Smith thundered. I smiled and held up my red and bruised forearms to show that was exactly what the detective did.

"Bouchard! In my office. Now!" his boss ordered.

Bouchard looked around helplessly. His eyes rested on me, but with Smith draping his arm over my shoulders, his anger became a look of fear and he looked away. With his head down, he left.

"Detective Lucas," the Commissioner said. "Will you take this gentleman to your desk? Check his alibi, then let him go if it's all OK. Do not—and I repeat—do not delay in procuring a lawyer for this citizen. Do you understand me?"

"Of course, sir."

"I am this man's lawyer," Councilman Smith stated. I was surprised. I knew Smith was a minister, but I didn't know he was an attorney. Locally, he was very powerful. For some reason, he was championing me. Considering Mouse's grin, he was behind this.

"Thank you, sir," I said. "I'm honored to have you as my counsel."

We paraded to Lucas's desk. I gave him Nick and Natalie's number and he made the call. It was interesting to hear the police side of the dialogue. I would have liked to hear it on speaker, but the big room was noisy with all of the other detectives and others busy on the phone. Councilman Smith and the commissioner's presence had stifled some of the noise, though.

"Hello, is this Doctor Cicero?"

....

"My name is John Lucas. I'm a detective with the New Orleans Police Department, and I have a question or two for you about Doctor Paul Layton."

....

"No sir, he's quite alright. I was just checking to see if he was with you last night."

....

"Thank you, sir."

....

"No sir, he's not in trouble for anything. Just a misunderstanding we're trying to clear up. You've been very helpful."

After hanging up, he scanned the group of us. "His alibi holds. Doctor Cicero said his wife and a graduate student will all vouch for Doctor Layton's presence last night."

The Police Commissioner, whose name I couldn't recall, but I was sure I knew him from television, took my hand. "Doctor Layton, we're very sorry for the misunderstanding. I'll have someone drive you home, with our apologies, of course."

"I'll drive him," Mouse spoke up. A few minutes later I was shaking hands with the commissioner, the councilman, and Detective Lucas again. I climbed into the passenger side of The Lady and, rocking with every pulse of the engine or touch of the steering wheel, we drove off.

"Thanks," I said. "How did you do all that?"

"It was nothing. I knew Smith from when I was working on getting the city wireless. He was on the committee and I was the liaison. We got along pretty well then, and I joined his church's choir for a while, till Katrina. I called him last night, but it took him until this morning to get my message."

"Wow." I paused. "You sing?"

"Yeah, I sing. I sing like an angel. I have a lot of talents I haven't gotten around to showing off to y'all. I'm a superhero ninja rocket scientist rock star, after all."

"If you say so." I was more surprised that he used a Southern expression like "Y'all". Mouse rarely used Southern-isms. "Well, I'm glad you knew him. Bouchard would have kept me in there for the maximum he could before getting me a lawyer or checking my alibi. That's forty-eight hours, I think."

"Yeah," Mouse said. "That guy doesn't like you very much." He laughed. "I hope they demote him to meter maid."

"His expression was priceless," I said, with a chuckle.

"Not as nearly as good as yours. You looked like a cow that's been poleaxed. You stood there with our mouth open the whole time."

I grinned.

"I can't wait to tell the guys," he laughed.

After a few seconds, his laughter stopped. So did mine. We were both thinking about the guys, Lowell specifically. At that point, I almost missed jail. I had been distracted by the arrest, the bad treatment, the incarceration, my cellmates, and the circus of a release.

We drove silently. On Saint Charles, a man waved at us.

"Friend of yours?"

Mouse shook his head. "People think I'm a gypsy cab. There's a lot of old Caddies that do that. It took me a couple years to figure that out."

"Oh."

That was the extent of the conversation until Mouse dropped me off at my house.

"So now what, chief?" he asked.

"I don't know. We keep out of the Lower Ninth, though. And we stop messing with those things. I'm going to call everyone and tell them not to go out for revenge or cheap thrills or whatever. We're going to stop it, and that's it. Then we see what we can do to help Connor and his mom."

"OK. Did you want me to call anyone?"

"Think you can convince Joe to not go out any more?"

"I'll try."

"I'll call Bruiser. And Mrs. Stuart."

His eyes filled with tears again. "We really screwed up, didn't we?"

Chapter 21

"Hi Bruiser, it's me, Paul Layton."

There was nothing on the other end for a moment. "Hello Sensei," she said cautiously, formally. "How are you?"

"I have some really bad news. Lowell's been killed. It was those ghosts. There were too many and the guys didn't stand a chance. Lowell, Connor, Joe, and Mouse to go fight them. Lowell didn't make it."

"Oh my God," she said. Softly she mumbled something I took to be a prayer. I gave her a few seconds. "Bruiser...Heather, I want you to keep away from those ghosts. OK?"

"Sensei. I'm in Virginia. I quit my job and moved back home. I should have let you know."

I was stunned again. She had left us. But my logical side took over. "It's probably for the best. We got in too deep. You're safer away from here."

"I'm getting married."

"You what? I mean that's great."

"I know. It's sudden, but he was my first boyfriend from high school. He manages the local grain elevator, and he ran for City Council last year. He didn't win, but he has ambition."

"He sounds great," I lied, rolling my eyes. She was a Ph.D. and a third-degree black belt—she was an incredible woman—and she was going back to nowhere in Virginia to be with some guy who ran a grain elevator? She was running from something here—the ghosts, of course. What a can of worms I had opened. I could only hope that her choice was saving her life and that her life turned out well, with her new fiancée or whatever she decided on.

"Congratulations, Heather," I said. "I wish you happiness."

"It's my calling," she said. "I can't go to the funeral. I really can't. Is that OK? Will anyone mind?"

"I understand."

"And can you tell everyone I had to leave town?"

"Sure."

"Say good-bye to Diamond for me, OK?"

"I will," I said.

"Bye."

"Take care," I said.

I tried telling myself I was relieved that she wasn't around. She was an excellent martial artist, and very intelligent, but I didn't want her to get hurt. Her size and physical strength was more of a concern. While she could hold her own, just a few of the creatures could overwhelm her easier than they could stop a bigger opponent. Still, it felt like she was abandoning the team.

I called Rufus next. I told him what had happened to Lowell and to not get near the ghosts. If he saw them, he was to run. If he was with Diamond, he was to take her away.

The hardest part of the day was calling Mrs. Stuart.

"Peggy, this is Paul Layton," I said. After that, I didn't know what to say. She was silent.

"Thank you for calling."

"I'm really sorry. I...if there is anything I can do to help..."

"Thanks." There was silence again. She finally spoke up. "Paul, is there, I mean, was there something to do with the Karate school? Was it, I don't know, some feud? Something they were trying to prove? Connor won't say much."

"No, nothing like that. I heard it was a gang they stumbled upon. I guess they were in the wrong place. It's terrible."

"What were they doing there?"

"I don't know. I don't know."

She was quiet again. "Thank you. I was afraid it was something bigger. I don't want Connor to...." Her voice choked in a sob. "I can't lose him. He's all I have now."

"I'm sorry. Let me know what I can do."

"Maybe the Karate helped Connor. Maybe if he didn't know it, he'd be dead, too." She sniffled. "I want to thank you for that."

I felt like shit. I was most at fault, and she was thanking me. I was lying to her, and she was thanking me.

I walked to the dojo and put up a sign saying that it was closed. Then I went back home and slept, from four in the afternoon to two in the morning. My dreams were filled with images of Lowell and of the ghosts. For the first time, I was seeing ghosts, although they were nightmarish shapes in my mind, not just flaws between dimensions. These were dead people—freshly dead. And they were people I knew. In my dream, all my students were coming to me, and they were all dead and walking.

When I woke, I replayed everything that had gone on in the past few weeks, everything that led up to the death of Lowell. I lay in bed for an hour before finally making some coffee.

It was less than a week before Christmas. On television, there were non-stop commercials and stories on the early morning news about how locals were rebuilding and having a holiday despite the catastrophe. Starting Friday, the dojo would be closed for almost week, but open again before New Year's. I felt like closing it permanently. I also felt like keeping it open so I would be there non-stop every day. I wanted to lose myself in work, but I had no classes, no papers to grade, no students at the dojo. Maybe I'd get a temp job over the holidays. I could cook or something. The service industry was still short on people.

It was four-thirty when I climbed into my car—my sad little Saturn—with a big thermal mug of coffee. I went directly to the Lower Ninth Ward. It was more than two hours until sunrise.

I drove all over the Lower Ninth Ward. I saw the neighborhoods where the ghosts were. They weren't all over the district, but in concentrated areas. Hundreds of them. I marked them off on a map of the city. I was guessing that there were portals they stayed near, like the one on Ursulines. It was odd that they had stopped coming to that one, but maybe it was sealed up or broken or something. Or maybe I had something to do with it. After I had killed a good number of them, they had decided that they were safer coming through to where there were more of them. They were safer in the Lower Ninth Ward. Ursulines was too dangerous for them.

A thought hit me. Maybe they weren't avoiding Ursulines anymore. Maybe it was just that one night the they had avoided the place. They could be back there again. It was close to sun up, so I decided to go back the next night to look.

I was almost out of gas. I stopped at a gas station on the way back home and also used the restroom. The clerk looked at me strangely when I asked to get the key, but she gave it to me. In the bathroom mirror I saw the reason for her expression. Tears had stained tracks down my cheeks. I washed them off. The light was dim in the men's room, but I didn't look too horrible.

"Thanks," I said, as I returned the key.

"You have a Merry Christmas, hon," she said.

"You too," I said.

*   *   *

The funeral was that Sunday. The Stuarts lived in Metairie, which is a separate city from New Orleans, but right next door, one merging into the other. The funeral home was only a few streets away from the family's house. The Stuarts were originally from Colorado. When Peggy and the boys' father, Ian, divorced, she found a job in New Orleans. The boys went with her and Lowell was soon enrolled at the University of New Orleans. He started Karate at the end of his junior year, and after getting his B.A., he enrolled in the graduate program at Loyola. Katrina hadn't slowed his studies down very long, but had slowed him a bit for his belt progression. He was due to test for his nidan, his second degree black belt, some time in the upcoming year. He would have made an excellent psychologist, just as he was an excellent martial artist.

The funeral was quick. No one said much, just the minister. It was too soon and too sudden for anyone to say much without breaking up. Mouse sang "Amazing Grace" in an incredible tenor or countertenor or whatever. I was no expert on music—his voice was way up there. I thought he had started in a register that was too high, but it seemed that there was no note he couldn't hit with a voice as clear as a bell. He was right. He sang like an angel.

I gave his mother Lowell's second degree black belt diploma. It was posthumous, but the least I could do.

"He's being buried with his belt," she said. "Connor thought of that."

"It would have meant a lot to him. He earned it."

"I'll have them put this in there also," she said. She blinked rapidly at tears that threatened to overflow her eyelids. Her eyes were red from days of crying.

I said something about how sorry I was and excused myself.

Joe was also there. He was pale and listless. His eyes were red and he avoided looking at me. When I spoke with him, I didn't say, 'I told you so,' which I'm sure he expected. I only asked him how he was doing.

"Feeling pretty bad," he said.

"Me too."

Joe and Mouse kept in one corner. I think they were afraid to mix with the rest of the guests.

The boys' father was there. He was medium built man who resembled Connor more than Lowell. We shook hands and engaged in small talk for a short while. It took some time, but I eventually got Connor alone.

"How are you holding up?" I asked.

"I wish people would stop asking me that."

"Sorry. I thought 'How's it going?' was too happy, so it was all I could come up with."

"It's OK."

"I'm sorry about Lowell. I should never have started all this."

He shook his head. "You didn't start it. It was that Emo guy. Then it got out of hand. We were all really stupid."

"Well it's done. No more ghosts."

His eyes widened. "They're gone?"

"No, but we're going to keep away from them. Everyone's agreed—no more hunting ghosts."

"Yeah."

"No going out for vengeance or using them for training. We're done with them."

He nodded. "I couldn't go back to it, anyway."

"We're done with them, for good."

"So we lost, right?"

"I guess we did."

Chapter 22

Over the next week I made great progress on my back room. I got rid of the black mold, lined the pit with tires, lay down the plywood, put the carpet padding down with my trusty staple gun, and covered it all with the mats I had bought with the money from the insurance. I finished my work on Christmas morning and spend the rest of the day doing nothing.

During the week I did other things. At night I cruised around the city to see if I saw any ghosts. They were back on Ursulines, and there were hundreds in the parts of the Lower Ninth Ward I had mapped out.

I called Michelle to see how she was doing. She wanted to see me again, but said it would be a couple weeks. I felt bad about using her, so I didn't commit to anything specific. I talked to Nick and Natalie and assured them I was OK and that I hadn't been involved in anything serious. I explained about Lowell and the gang that had killed him and that a cop had his ideas mixed up.

When Nick reminded me that Natalie's sister was in town, I told him I was too busy to visit. Not only did I not want to meet the woman, I felt guilty for using my friends as an alibi.

My guilt and recriminations didn't stop there. I went out with Brianne again. We didn't go back to my place or to hers. We had breakfast at Mena's Palace and I told her about losing Lowell. I wanted to come clean with her.

"Remember how I told you we were hunting ghosts?"

She nodded, wide-eyed.

"And you said you had a friend who saw some, and you heard about a Karate school pretending to be superheroes and hunting ghosts?"

"I remember."

"I lied to you then. It's not an urban legend in the making. We're not just going on ghost tours and talking about being superheroes. We were fighting actual ghosts and things got out of hand. One of my students was killed last week."

"Oh my God," she said. I couldn't tell if she was responding to my news that we were actual ghost hunters or that Lowell had died. Or maybe she was responding to the idea that she had slept with a crazy man who believed in ghosts. I said nothing while those ideas raced around in my head.

"I know it sounds crazy," I said, but she cut me off.

"You lied to me?"

Of course that's what she was responding to. I had lied to her. I was about to say I was sorry, but decided to be honest.

"I did. And I should have kept lying to you. I don't know what I was thinking by telling you just now. People who know about the ghosts wind up dead. I don't want you to be at risk. Will you promise me to stay away from them?"

She looked like I had slapped her. She had expected me to apologize, but I had confused her for a moment. Then her righteous indignation came to the surface. "I can look after myself," she said. "And you can't tell me what to do."

"No, I'm not trying to. I'm asking you to think of your daughter. Will you keep clear of the ghosts for her sake?"

"Oh, that's low," she said, glaring at me.

"I'm sorry," I said. "I'm not trying to imply that you're not thinking about her needs first." I could tell from her reaction that she was thinking of herself before her daughter. I let it go. "I lied to you because I was worried about you. I'd hate to see you get hurt or killed. OK?"

She shook her head, clearing away the implied accusation. "What about the ghosts?"

"There's a lot to that question," I answered. "But I'll try."

I told her. I went into detail about the ghosts. I told her about how the guys started going out to fight them and how it all escalated. The only thing I didn't tell her about was the night Michelle and I spent together. And Cissy and Diane's running commentary on my sex life. So it was two things I omitted. Even omitting those two things, it was a long story. I finished my shrimp Creole and she had eggs and toast.

Since it was so close to Christmas, the place wasn't crowded with tourists or staff from the Marriott right across the street, and our waitress didn't seem to mind us just sitting there talking. She even got us an extra loaf of French bread when I asked. I pounded back the Community Coffee as I told her about everything that had happened.

When I had finished, I answered her questions. She asked what the ghosts were. I couldn't tell her what they really were, only our guesses.

"Do you feel anything about killing them?"

"No, I wondered about that at first—what to feel. If they're ghosts, we can't really kill them, can we? If they're the traditional idea of ghosts, that is. If they're alien invaders, which is the theory I favor, we're doing the right thing because they are the aggressive ones, and they started the killing. The third theory is that they're demons. And in that case, we're doing the right thing, too."

"Why do you think they're alien invaders?"

I told her my theory and threw in a bit of what Marvin Feinstein and I had discussed. I liked the idea of the creatures being like wolves or sharks, attracted to the blood and violence instead of our interference opening up the dimensional portals even more. I finished by telling her about the funeral.

"And that's it?" she asked.

"That's all of it."

"No, I mean is that it? Are you giving up?"

I looked into my coffee cup instead of answering.

"Shit, I thought I was dating a superhero, but I guess not when the going gets tough."

"Bri," I said.

She crossed her arms and glared at me.

"Well, I've been going out at nights to keep an eye on them," I said. "I think their numbers have evened out. Most of them are in the Lower Ninth Ward, but there are still some in the French Quarter."

"I know. I've seen them."

If I had been sipping my coffee when she said that, she would have been covered in it. It would have been a classic spit-take. Instead, I just coughed. "What? Since when have you been seeing them?"

"After you told me that you weren't hunting them, I called my girlfriend who said she saw a ghost. We went out and looked for them."

"What did you see? And where did you see them?"

"In the Quarter. We went up Canal where she saw them before, but there weren't any. We saw two of them by Jackson Square. On the side away from Canal, by the Cathedral, I don't remember what street that is."

"Saint Ann, I think," I said.

"Anyway, it was around one in the morning. They were definitely ghosts. Kinda see through, really stern looking. They were dressed all in black—cloaks or capes or something like that."

"Bri, listen to me. You shouldn't go after them—not even to get a look at them. They'll kill you. I don't want you to die."

She was silent for a while, mulling it over.

"I'm serious."

"I don't like being told what to do."

"Neither do I," I said. "So I know how you feel. But I'm afraid for your life. Really."

She scowled at me. She really didn't like to be told what to do.

We talked until the place started filling up for lunch. Our waitress politely asked if we'd go so the table would be open. She was sweet about it, and we had been there for two hours, so I left a very large tip.

As soon as we got outside, Bri stopped. "I should have used the bathroom. Maybe we should go back in."

"Can you hold it for a few minutes?"

"Why?" she asked suspiciously, drawing the word out.

"Would clean bathrooms in the French Quarter be reason enough?"

She smiled. "Do you have to be a superhero in everything?"

"C'mon." I led her to the Jax brewery building, which was now a little mall.

"Wow," she said as she left. "You are my superhero."

"These are actually the second best restrooms in the Quarter, but the place with the cleanest ones are closed—I saw a sign when I came in today. Too close to Christmas, I guess."

"And where is that?"

"That's my secret 'til next time," I laughed.

"Typical male," she snorted.

We walked toward Jackson Square, to where she saw the ghost. It was about three blocks over from the portal on Ursulines. She pointed out where they had stood and where the ghosts were.

"Could you tell if they saw you?"

"I don't think so."

"That's good."

She scowled again. "OK, I'm not going to look for them anymore."

"Huh? I mean, great. That's great. What made you say that?"

"I remembered how cool it was to see them. But it was scary, too."

Chapter 23

Joe woke up with Diane's arm on his chest. They had been sharing at bed together since the night after Lowell was killed. He needed the comfort of his roommate to help him sleep at night.

It was four in the morning. Joe hadn't gone to work for a week. Before that, he was doing a crappy job and had missed a few days. He figured he was probably fired by now. He spent too many nights fighting ghosts. His was using the ghosts to train for full-contact contests, but that was only an excuse. Fighting them night after night was a thrill. But that was all changed now.

He moved Diane's arm and eased out of bed. On the other side of his roommate her new girlfriend, Cindy slept. Cindy was a short plump half-Korean girl whom Diane had been seeing for almost four months now. The three were in one bed, but it wasn't sexual, it was just comfort. Cindy understood as well as Diane did, although at different times both women had made it clear that they would be open to a threesome with him. He had thought about it in the past, but he wasn't interested now. He just needed the warmth of someone there. He couldn't make it through a night without visions of Lowell being killed appearing in his dreams.

Quietly he went to the kitchen. He had slept for only four hours, but he knew he couldn't go back to sleep. He decided that making coffee might wake the girls, so he slipped on some clothes and threw his long coat over everything and slipped out of the apartment. Out of habit he checked the hot water heater before he left the building. The button was sticking out. He pushed it back in. The girls and the other tenants would have hot water when they woke up.

There was a definite chill in the air. He almost went in to put on another shirt, but figured he'd warm up as he got moving. Leaving his truck parked on the street, Joe walked to the French Quarter, where everyone went, but he knew of a place that would be open.

Although he walked through some dangerous neighborhoods, he was walking away from the Lower Ninth Ward. No one bothered him. He didn't see any ghosts. No ghosts, no gangs, no suspicious characters. No one or no thing to fight with. He didn't want to fight, though. At least he didn't want to fight back.

After coffee and some toast he didn't finish, he walked to the job site. The walk took him over an hour, but he was still the first person on the lot.

"Mr. Gomez," he called, when his old foreman showed up at 7:45am.

"Joe? What are you doing here?" the compact man said.

"I was hoping I could get my job back. I messed up pretty badly. A lot of really serious stuff has been happening."

"So you do listen to your messages."

"I'm sorry."

Gomez looked him up and down. "Funny day to come back. Tomorrow is Christmas Eve, so we're shut down for two days. There's only a few people working today, since it's Saturday."

"Then you can probably use another hand."

The foreman looked around. He and Joe were the only people there. "Hell, it's Christmas. Don't fuck up today and start coming in regularly and you'll be OK."

"Thanks."   Joe started toward the tool shed. He didn't have his work gloves, and he was wearing the wrong coat, but he'd get by.

Chapter 24

Since that awful night in the Lower Ninth Ward, Mouse had stopped going to the dojo and had given up his diet. The ten pounds came back pretty quickly, but at least his wounds were healing. And he was getting out a bit. He had started going back to Reverend Smith's church and singing with the choir. It was the least he could do for the city councilman, and it made him feel a bit better. He wasn't religious, but there was comfort in the ritual. The choir was preparing for a Christmas concert, and the carols and spirituals felt comforting.

"You should be singing a solo," Professor Johns said. She was a skinny elderly woman who dressed in long, brightly colored robes that emphasized her African heritage. She played bass guitar in the band that accompanied the choir and was a professor emeritus of musical performance at Xavier College.

"Thank you, ma'am," Mouse said.

"Really, I'll talk to Frances, if you want me to." Frances was the choir director, a large, imposing black woman who always seemed suspicious of Mouse because he was white. He was the only white male in the choir, although there were two white women—maybe one—he couldn't tell with one of them. They were new in the choir since he had stopped coming. Now they were the veterans and he was the newcomer.

"It's OK. I'm just happy to be singing again," he said. The statement made him feel warm and happy.

As a child, Robert Khatukaryan sang for his mother. They went to an Eastern Orthodox church, so he never experienced the thrills he had at the First Church of the Redeemer. It wasn't until college and a trip to a karaoke bar that he found he loved singing in front of audiences. He went from the fat guy who sat in the computer lab all night to being the friend everyone wanted to take to karaoke night. He joined a student choir in college, but the bickering, jealousies, and backstabbing made him quit. It wasn't until several years later when he was invited to join Reverend Smith's church that he sang with a group again.

Hurricane Katrina had stopped his participation in the choir. The church closed for months, and the choir had slowly restarted. Mouse hadn't returned to the choir, but asking a favor from Reverend Smith made him feel he owed the councilman a favor. Singing at Lowell's funeral cinched things. He was a singer. Once again he was the ninja superhero rocket scientist rock star from his running gag—it was how he described himself on-line. Of course, on all of those things, he was just a bit short of the extreme. He knew martial arts, but he wasn't a ninja, and he was just a singer in a choir and at karaoke bars, not a rock star, and he was a computer specialist, not a rocket scientist. The only thing on the list that he really had been was the superhero, and that was subjective. Besides, they'd balled it up royally.

"And Bobby, Dr. Smith wanted me to tell you to stop by his office when you can," Mrs. Johns said.

"I'll get right on that," Mouse said. He put his sheet music in his nylon book bag and went to Smith's office. A sign on the door gave his name and titles: Reverend Doctor Clarence Smith, D. Div., Ph.D., Ed. D., J.D., City Councilman. The door was open and Smith waved Mouse in. The walls of the small church office were covered in plaques, letters, certificates, photos, honorary diplomas, and possibly real diplomas. He said he loved the person on the other end and snapped closed his cell phone.

"Kids," he said, with a laugh. "Do you have any?"

"No sir. Not even a girlfriend at this point."

"That's a shame. You should settle down. The love of a good woman can make all the difference in the world, Robert."

Mouse said nothing. The subject was something he didn't like to think about. It had been years since he had a girlfriend. The closest he had been to one was the girl at Fiorello's. At least he thought it was her. He knew she played WoW. He was pretty sure he knew her character and they'd campaigned together, in fact. Maybe that's what he'd do—get a girlfriend, try to settle down and have a normal life.

"How is your friend who was wrongfully imprisoned?"

"Oh, Paul. He's OK. He was at the funeral. Haven't seen him since, though."

"You haven't seen him? That's odd, considering you went to bat for him. I would think you'd see more of him than once in over a week."

"Well, it's Christmas week, so the dojo hasn't been open much."

"Dojo?"

"The Karate school."

"Hmmm. If you happen to run into him, tell him I'd like to talk to him some time."

"Sure. I'll give him the message."

"It's nice to have you back in the fold."

Mouse laughed. "I'm just in the choir, Reverend Smith. I don't know about being in the fold."

"Close enough," he laughed.

*   *   *

He had two windows open and was chatting at the same time. He was looking at some adult content flash animation on Newgrounds and checking the local news. The girl he was chatting with, the one he thought worked at Fiorello's, still wouldn't tell him who she was.

Mungor: So what did you do today?

BladePryncess718: Just worked.

Mungor: Get many tips?

BladePryncess718: That's 4 me to know and U to find out

Mungor: You already told me you're a waitress

BladePryncess718: maybe I was lying

Mungor: maybe not

BladePryncess718: What did U do?

Mungor: Choir practice.

BladePryncess718: I didn't no you were a sinerg

BladePryncess718 : *singer*

Mungor: No body ever believes I can sing. I'll have to show you some time.

BladePryncess718: U can sarinade me. :-D

Mungor: I'd be happy to

BladePryncess718: Did U see there were some killings in the ¼?

Mungor: No, what happened?

BladePryncess718: 2 people killed last night. 2 more thursday

Mungor: That's terrible. Gangs?

BladePryncess718: No1 knows

Mungor: Were they tourists?

BladePryncess718: The 1s last night not the other 2

Mungor: I hope you're being careful when you get off work

BladePryncess718: maybe a superhero would help

Mungor: Yeah, right.

BladePryncess718: Don't you know some?

Mungor: Not anymore.

BladePryncess718: That's too bad

Mungor: brb

Mouse checked the archives of the *Times-Picayune* and left the Foamy and Germaine video to navigate to a local news station's page. Both sources had articles about the killings. Two tourists and two locals. The locals were a woman who sold art in Jackson Square and her friend who was helping her carry her paintings home. A bit more looking and he saw four more gang deaths in the Lower Ninth Ward. They all had stabbings in common.

Mungor: Sorry, I gotta go

BladePryncess718: Awww

Mungor: S orry, something came up.

BladePryncess718: Be careful, superhero

Mungor: Thanks, but I'm no superhero

BladePryncess718 : lol ;-) I know better

Mungor: No. No you don't.

BladePryncess718: I heard about U and your karate guys. U r ghost hunters

Mungor: I don't know what you heard, but no. That's over.

BladePryncess718: Awww :-(

Mungor: I can't really talk abou tit

Mungor: *about it*

BladePryncess718: ROTFL Now I know where your mind really is

Mungor: Hmmm....maybe that's where your mind is

BladePryncess718: I'm shocked

Mungor: I'm sure you are

BladePryncess718: But your not a superhero anymore?

Mungor: No. I never really was

BladePryncess718: Too bad

Blade Pryncess 718 wasn't a good speller, and she relied too much on cyberspeak, but Mouse enjoyed the flirting. She still wouldn't admit that she was the shy waitress at Fiorello's, but he wasn't a hundred percent sure, anyway. Some things added up, but she never admitted it on line, and in person, he couldn't ask her. For all he knew, he was chatting with the wrong waitress there, and the one who grinned at him all the time and treated him like he was a VIP was just being nice. Or maybe she was grinning because she knew that someone else there liked him. Maybe it was all in his mind. She had mentioned waiting tables, and something about fried chicken, but she could work in a different restaurant entirely.

"Sensei. It's me, Mouse."

"Good to hear from you. What's up?"

"Have you been keeping an eye on the news?"

There was silence on the cell phone. "No, I've been pretty busy," Layton said slowly.

"There've been more deaths. Eight that I could find." He told him about the four people in the French Quarter and the four in the Lower Ninth.

"Shit."

Mouse said nothing for a moment. "So now what?"

"I don't know. We're out of the ghost business, and that's final."

"I just thought you should know."

"OK. Thanks, I guess."

"Oh, and Reverend Smith wanted me to ask you if you'd come by to his office some time."

"Sure."

Mouse gave him Smith's office phone number and the location of the church. Layton said he'd call him after the holidays.

Chapter 25

The dojo was on its holiday schedule of being open three days per week. It closed the Saturday before Christmas and the day after Christmas. Two days later, that Thursday, I opened it again. I had worked the whole time on fixing the place up—even Christmas. My family wasn't close, not geographically or emotionally. And I didn't want to impose on friends during a holiday, so I worked.

Some of the mothers commented on the improvements. The double doors to The Pit were open and the kids jumped up and down on the mats over the padding and threw the big exercise balls around. They played on it like one of those inflatable castles kids jump around in at carnivals and birthday parties. Perhaps, I thought, I could start holding parties there for the kids. I could supply the cake, refreshments, and party favors and charge enough to get a profit. Before Katrina, I had held movie nights for the kids, with films like *Three Ninjas* and *Mulan*. It was fun and kept them coming back.

I was trying to ignore what Mouse had told me. New Years was coming up, then Twelfth Night, the beginning of Carnival season, which ended with Mardi Gras. I didn't want to think about what could happen.

In addition to working on the dojo, I was working out a lot. Whenever my mind would turn to Lowell's death, I would hit the bag or lift some weights. I still thought of him, but the activity gave me an outlet for the frustration. Since then, my only contact with any of the upper level students was the funeral and the one call from Mouse. I needed to concentrate on the young students, but I did miss the older ones. The kids ranged from six to fifteen that day. Eight students were there, which was a good number for a class.

I clapped my hands together for the children. "OK, let's do some Karate!" I shouted. They rushed to the main room and stood at attention. The older kids and a few of the little ones were toeing the line, but the youngest were still all over the place. They'd get better at it, though. They were all yellow and white belts, so they had a way to go.

We went through the usual games and routines. I asked the older kids, a fifteen-year-old boy and a twelve-year-old girl, to be my assistants, and the younger children had a great time pairing off into different groups. First it was boys against girls in our slow motion floor exercise race, then we did a couple rounds of zombie-tag.

Later in the class, for the sake of the older two, I talked about extension. I showed the unbendable arm trick and we practiced punching through the punching shield.

After the class, all I could think about were the ghosts. Maybe it was a mistake to teach about extension. I wasn't trying to prepare them to hunt ghosts, extension is important in all areas of the martial arts. I certainly wasn't trying to replace my senior students—especially Lowell.

Extension was important. One strikes through the target when breaking boards or bones for that matter. One extends when throwing or flipping an opponent to keep the weight off one's lower back. It's an important principle to learn, and I'm sure some of the younger children benefited from it. I presented the idea and the exercises to all the students, but only expected the older two to learn it.

*   * *

On January third I started more than the three classes per week schedule. The local schools started that week, so the kids were back and the parents wanted to have a break after spending all that time with them over the holidays. That was also the day I got a call from Reverend Smith's secretary. I had completely forgotten he wanted to see me. I made an appointment for the next morning.

"Thank you for coming, Dr. Layton," he said, extending his hand.

I took the big man's hand and shook it. He had a good grip but didn't try to crush my bones to a pulp. Some guys would try that, to prove they were stronger or more manly than me, but I should have known that wasn't Smith's style. He was a politician. He knew how to shake hands.

"Please, call me Paul. And it's my pleasure. I'm sorry I was too busy to get back to you. I did get Mouse's, I mean Bob's, message."

"I'm sure you were as busy as I was over the holiday."

I nodded.

"Here, have a seat," he said. He sat down heavily behind the desk. "I thought it would be good to get to know the man I got out of jail."

"I wanted to thank you again for that. And I assure you, I was..." I started, but he stopped me by raising a hand.

"I'm sure you're an innocent man. Bobby vouched for you, and you were in a different state at the time they were attacked. I can't see how you were any part of the gang who killed your poor student. No, Detective Bouchard had some vendetta against you. That's obvious."

"Yeah, he's been picking on me for a while."

"That's a terrible shame."

"He's dangerous. I don't think he should be on the force."

Smith shook his head. "During the flooding, Detective Bouchard saved quite a few people. For thirty-six hours straight, he was chopping holes in roofs and taking people to safety in his bass boat. He's a hero."

"Oh," I said.

"Before that, he had one of the highest arrest rates in the city."

I blushed. Maybe I had misjudged Bouchard.

"But that's neither here nor there," Smith said. "I trust that you are a good man. I'd like to know more about you."

I suddenly felt on the spot, as if I were on a job interview or a bad date. I never knew what to say in such situations to let someone know what I was like as a person. And what did one say to a minister who was a city councilman and who got one released from jail? None of my classes in graduate school prepared me for anything like that, and I'm sure there was no etiquette book that covered it either.

"I am sure you're a decent man. I was told many good things about you. I've looked up your work and professional background, too."

"What would you like to know about me?"

"I'd like to know if you're an honorable man, for starters."

I wondered where he was going with that. It was starting to sound like the cliché, that he was asking if my intentions toward his daughter were strictly honorable. For a second, I wondered if Bri were somehow his daughter, but I knew she wasn't.

"I like to think so. I'm not sure what you mean, though."

"Are you a faithful man?"

"Are you asking if I have faith? No, I don't. I'm an atheist."

"What I'm asking is if you're a man of your word."

"It's been my experience that you can't trust the word of most Christians."

"Then they are not true Christians."

I was about to tell him that I knew Jews, Hindus, Muslims, agnostics, atheists, and Wiccans whose word I'd trust, but I decided not to. I didn't want to start an argument. Still, the rebel in me had to take a parting shot.

"Tell it to those Christians, not to an atheist. I'm on the sidelines here."

He thought for a moment, then chuckled. "I've gone to bat for atheists before. We're all God's children, whether we believe it or not."

"That's very accepting and open-minded of you."

He brushed off my comment with a wave of his hand.

"Dr. Layton—Paul—may I tell you a story?"

"Sure."

"It's not one of those stories that has a happy ending or has any sort of ending. It's really just an account of the day to day problems of a man in my position."

I nodded.

"Bobby tells me you evacuated when Katrina hit."

"I did."

"What else could one do? I went to Baton Rouge for a short while." He paused and sipped water from a plastic bottle. "I came back as soon as I could, though. The floodwaters were still high. Refugees were still in the Superdome and the Convention Center. The city was polluted from the sewage that had mixed with the water that was everywhere. Corpses still floated in the waters. People starved and died of dehydration although there was water all around them. Buses to rescue refugees were turned away from the city because there was no place to take the poor people to, and no one wanted to take responsibility for where they went. The police from Jefferson Parish turned away their neighbors, with guns. FEMA was useless and only making matters worse. The New Orleans Police and the National Guard even drew weapons on each other in a stand-off outside the Superdome when buses did arrive.

"It was a terrible time. Since then, I've seen the city come back from ruin. We've got a long way to go, but we're recovering. We're rebuilding."

I knew all this. I had the survivor's guilt of someone who had evacuated for a long time. Over the months I had been away, I felt as if I had abandoned the city. I should have been there to help rebuild, and I knew it.

"As a Councilman for our great city, I have many functions. There is much more to the position than trying to get zoning ordinances passed. I mediate between the people of my district and the city government. In times like this, I also mediate between the people and the state and federal governments. The citizens of this city come to me with problems, and I do my best to solve them."

"I understand."

"Now I'm not the councilman for the Lower Ninth Ward, as you know, but in times like this, people from all over come to me. I'm visible, so people come to me. I admit, I am well-known around here. I am on television often, and there is even talk of me running for mayor." His eyes twinkled. "Not this election, of course, Ray and Mitch have that already made enough noise." He chuckled.

He grew serious again. "Because people know me, I may take complaints from someone in Uptown or East New Orleans or even across the river in Algiers and turn to the federal government for a solution." He paused. "For a few weeks, I have been hearing some odd things about happenings in the Lower Ninth Ward. I was able to confirm some of the stories I've heard. Bobby—your Mouse—said a few things too."

He leaned forward, dwarfing his desk. "Tell me son, are you conducting a war with ghosts?"

"What, is this published somewhere?"

"There's a lot of talk, Paul. It's a small town, especially now."

"I guess it would be."

He waited for my answer. "Well?" he finally said.

"It's a long story."

"I've got time." He looked at his watch. It was a cheap one. I could see the expensive suit, but for a man of the people and the church to wear a ten thousand dollar Rolex was more than a bit hypocritical. His looked to be an old Timex. My respect for him grew.

"This boy came to my dojo for self-defense lessons," I started. I went through the whole thing, filling in what I didn't know first-hand with what the guys had told me about their adventures. I saw him look at his watch a few times, but he made no effort to stop my tale.

With Smith, I was more open than with Bri. I didn't think he was going to try to hunt the ghosts himself or even to get his thrills by trying to see them. He didn't need to be protected from the things.

"You believe they aren't actual ghosts, but aliens, then."

"Even if I wasn't an atheist, that would be my assessment. Like I said, everyone sees them differently, and they don't seem to have a ghostly agenda. They aren't haunting, they're hunting."

"Do you think they're intelligent?"

"That's something that's been bugging me from day one. They seem to be somewhat intelligent, but if they are aliens, maybe their intelligence is not the same as ours. In that case, they may be very intelligent. On the other hand, they may just be like smart animals. They could be here to hunt. They seem to want to take people with them and they also try to kill them."

"They don't just try, they succeed."

"That's true."

"Do you think they are evil?"

"I don't know. What is evil?"

His hand went to a well-worn Bible on his desk, but he didn't start to lecture me on the Ten Commandments or Revelations or any of the other Sunday School staples that religions use to keep people in line.

"They may have their own idea of good and evil. Their actions may be good to them."

He slid the Bible of the desk and held it against his chest, as if to ward off what I was saying.

"Think of it this way, is a lion evil when it hunts? We don't know if they're like animals, like people, or totally different from anything we know."

He nodded, getting my point.

"Good or evil, though, it doesn't matter," I stated firmly. "Their actions hurt us. That's what counts."

"You and your students are the only ones who have fought back. True?"

I nodded. "They were hunting them. I don't know; maybe that made them more aggressive. Maybe killing the ghosts made it easier for others to enter this dimension."

He drummed his fingers on the book in his hands. Then he said it.

"And what are you going to do about them?"

Bri had started me thinking about that same question. With her, I had a chance to change the subject because she had been looking for them. With Smith, I was had not way to change the subject.

"I don't want more deaths. I told my students to not interact with them at all. I can't lose any more students."

"You feel that your students are your responsibility?"

"Of course."

"My people are my responsibility, whether they live in my district or not." He paused for effect. He was a good orator. "And my people are being killed."

"I'm sorry..." He cut me off.

"Do you know how many people have been killed?"

"I heard about a few recently," I said.

"There's more than the ones lost in the French Quarter. Those deaths, while tragic, are not my concern."

I was about to tell him that Mouse told me about four deaths in the Lower Ninth, but he continued on.

"The FBI is about to release its list of the cities with the highest homicide rates. Are you familiar with this list?"

I nodded. New Orleans had been on the list, so had Washington D.C. and others in the past.

"New Orleans will not be on that list this year."

"That's good. Isn't it?"

"No. The reason we are not on the list is not because our murder rate is so low. We are being left off because of Katrina. The FBI can't even estimate what our murder rate is because of the evacuations, the deaths from Katrina, and the fluctuating population. Finally, there has been an incredible increase in the past six weeks. It hasn't only been a few people in the French Quarter. The total has been over fifty, as far as I can tell."

"Fifty?"

"In poor neighborhoods, such as the Lower Ninth Ward, Bywater, St Bernard Parish, and all over in East New Orleans. Most have been attributed to gangs."

"It's not gangs?"

"Some have been. The gangs are returning, and bringing their wars with them. But gangs use guns, not knives. Since the end of November, these so-called gangs have turned to knives to kill each other—and not just each other. Anyone who is out at night is in danger."

"Knives that cause unusual puncture wounds and massive blood loss."

"Exactly. The claws you describe."

"I see."

"And there's more. Seven people are missing. Six of them are women."

"That's terrible."

"Exactly. My people are being killed, Dr. Layton—Paul. What are you going to do about it?"

"I—I don't know."

He looked at me. His eyes looked through me like my punches went through boards. He had extension down.

I said nothing for a moment. He looked at his watch. He was definitely late for something.

"My people are dying out there."

"I understand that, but I don't really know what I can do."

"You and your students are the only ones who have been fighting these aliens. You're our only hope."

I started to object but he cut me off.

"You're a responsible man. And a bright one. I'm sure you will come up with something."

"I'll try." I rose and we shook hands. "Thank you again for your help at the jail."

I was just outside of his door when a thought hit me. There were shuffling sounds through the doorway as Smith got ready for his next meeting. I turned around and entered the office again.

"Reverend Smith," I said. He was loading a few papers into a leather satchel

"Oh, yes?"

"I want you to understand something. I'm not going to lose any more students. I can't."

"And I don't want to lose any more of my people."

"Of course not. But my student, the one who died. He was a good young man with a lot of potential. He started off in school wanting to be a forensic psychologist to go hunt criminals. When he took his first course in Forensic Psychology, he got excited about Psychology as a field. He went into clinical psychology because he wanted to help people. He had a brother and a mother and friends."

"Each one of those people who were killed had a family. The ones who will be killed in days to come have families, too."

"I know that." I paused. "I know Mou—Bob is in your choir and, I guess, a friend of yours. But I don't want him to get hurt. I don't want any of my students put in a situation where they would be at risk."

He narrowed his eyes at me. "I'm not going to encourage Bobby to go after the ghosts."

"Good." I paused. "It's my responsibility. That's all."

He nodded, then lifted his satchel. "Now, I really must go. I have a meeting at City Hall."

Chapter 26

I paid close attention to the newspapers after that. Every day I picked up a copy of the *Times-Picayune* and closely examined the Metro section. Every unexplained death felt like my fault. Every death attributed to gang violence felt like my fault, too. In the week that followed my meeting with Reverend Smith, two more people were unexplainably killed. The year 2007 was starting off just as dangerously as 2006 had ended.

On the positive side of things, attendance at the dojo was up. I signed up two new students the first week I was back to normal schedule and two more the week afterwards. Joe, Mouse, and, of course Connor, had not returned. Diamond had come to a few classes and Rufus made it one Saturday—Twelfth Night, the beginning of Carnival.

The first parade of the season was the Phunny Phorty Phellows. It was the satirical streetcar parade that usually went along the St. Charles line. This year, like the year before, it was along Canal Street. It was smaller than usual, and not well attended, but bigger than the first post-Katrina parade. It was still a sign of the city's recovery.

I went to the parade alone. It was right after class, but Rufus couldn't go and Diamond hadn't attended practice that day. Rufus and I didn't speak of the ghosts, but that may have been because he was teaching a children's class while I took some teenagers and put them through their paces. I didn't teach the older kids because they were more advanced and I was of a higher rank, it was just that the little kids loved Rufus. He was big, muscular, and had a great way with them. Watching him with normal, happy kids showed me why he chose to work with children, even if the ones he worked with were from broken homes, had parents who were on drugs, or were on drugs or in gangs themselves.

Afterwards, we did some grappling with both classes watching us. We demonstrated some specific moves, then did some freestyle, which was good for me. I tend to use my strength instead of skill when I wrestled. Rufus was the only member of the dojo who was physically stronger than I was. I had to be nimble and clever instead of all about power. He still beat me the first two rounds out of three. By then I was really exhausted and had to rely on technique.

I showed up to watch the Phunny Phorty Phellows parade. It was a short event. It was more a party for those who were members of the krewe, but there were some spectators. I hung out until the streetcars started rolling, then got on my bike and went home.

Like usual, I got up in the wee hours of the morning and cruised around the French Quarter and the Lower Ninth. The numbers of ghosts hadn't increased that I could tell, but there were still several hundred of them. About thirty were in the Quarter, about half of them were milling about on Ursulines. As I drove, every time I saw a group of the ghosts, I would turn the corner or back up and go to another neighborhood. I had been doing this for a couple weeks, almost every night. I kept my movements random and come at different times so they wouldn't anticipate me. They were sort of predictable. They kept in certain areas and in groups. I had a hard time figuring out their motivation, though.

As usual when I drove around, I saw houses with the long-familiar grids with symbols on the door. They were from the people who went door to door after the waters went down. A number in one quadrant meant the amount of dead in the house.

The people who died in Katrina were not exclusively the poor or the black. It wasn't the white or the rich. It was people who lived in one-story slab houses with no roof access. The floodwaters didn't care about race or socioeconomic status. The water rose over night, and people slept through it. If they woke, they couldn't get to doors, so they went up, into little crawlspace attics which were stifling hot from the heat. Some had roof access, some were able to bring an ax or hatchet and cut through. Those who made it through their roofs could be rescued if the Coast Guard saw them in time. In the meantime, they could watch bodies float by.

The Coast Guard were the only ones who seemed to know what they were doing at the time. They rescued over thirty thousand people, the poorest of the poor, in their boats and helicopters. All this I saw on CNN and other news outfits from my safety in Ohio.

Every time I drove around these neighborhoods, I felt the survivor's guilt for not being here when the city was going through so much hell. Sixteen months before, refugees were denied food and help and ways out of the city. Aid efforts were slowed because no one would work together. Off in Ohio, I was unable to help. Now, with a new problem flooding the streets of this tragic district, I was still unable to help.

To cheer myself up, I stopped for coffee and a little chat at the gas station I was now frequenting.

"How's it going, Paul honey?" the clerk asked.

"Not bad, LaTonya. How's your night been so far?"

"Slow." She held up her textbook. "Why ain't you an accounting professor, 'stead of English?"

"Some things in this world must remain as mysteries, I'm afraid. Like why you're working here nights instead of spending them in a nice warm bed with a hot, middle aged, white guy."

She laughed, showing her bright white teeth. She was short and a little chunkier than I liked my women, but certainly attractive. We had been flirting for a while, although we both knew there was nothing to it. She had a live-in boyfriend and two kids at home. She was twenty-seven and her goal was to be a CPA.

"Anything weird going on out there?"

"Ain't seen anything," she answered.

"Well you just be careful. If anything seems weird, give me a call. You still have my number?"

"Yes, Paul. You ax me every time."

"It's because I care." I gave her a dollar fifty for the coffee and headed out, blowing her a kiss.

I never told her why I was concerned, I just told her every night that she should watch out for anything that seemed unusual. She probably suspected I was a lunatic, but she treated me as if I were a harmless one.

I went home and slept until it was time to get ready for going in to the dojo.

*　　　　　　　　　　*　*

Belt testing was coming up at the end of the month. About half my students were testing. Most for yellow and orange, but one boy was testing for his green. I was with a class of white, yellow, and orange belts that day, seven out of the ten were going to test.

I walked out in front of the class with two pairs of nunchaku and went into my routine. This was the routine that won me some regional titles and got me nationally ranked. I had variations on the routine, but after a few years of competing, it got boring and I started using other weapons.

"Some dojos don't start the students on weapons until they're pretty far along," I said. "I have a different philosophy about them, though." I went to one of the weapons cabinets and opened it. Padded weapons of every sort fell out. I had foam nunchaku, foam swords, staffs, and even tonfa. I also had the children's equivalent to the whip chain and a few other weapons. In the other cabinet I had the real versions of the same weapons, but the kids didn't get to play with those until they were much older and I was sure they were able to handle them with proficiency.

The kids rushed to the harmless weapons and started playing with them. Before the class, I had talked to the waiting mothers. They knew the weapons were soft, but when their kids started playing with them, I could see looks of concern.

"We start off by selecting a weapon we like. From there we're going to learn some basics that everyone can use."

The kids would have played with the toys all day, but I stopped them after ten minutes and we sat down in a circle.

"Everyone got a weapons you're happy with?"

There was a little last second trading and some nervous looks.

"Luis, do you know what the name of that weapon is?"

"No Sensei," he said.

"It's a tonfa. It's just like the police use. They call it the PR-24, but the tonfa goes back almost four hundred years. It started off being the handle of a grindstone, but was turned into a weapon."

"Aviva, do you know the name of the weapon you have?"

"No Sensei Paul," she said.

"It's a fan. Fans can be used as weapon and can be very beautiful. It's a very graceful weapon. Sensei Diamond will show you her kata with it."

She smiled shyly. She was going to grow up to be a beautiful woman, so the fan fit her well.

To be honest, I didn't expect the students to find a weapon that called to them. The kids picked up what appealed to them, played with the weapons, and eventually everyone would learn a few basic weapons.

"There are two kinds of weapons, flexible and fixed. 'Fixed' means that they stay in one shape, like the staff or the sword. Flexible is, well, who can tell me what a flexible weapon is?"

"Numchucks?" David Duchamp asked. He was nine, small for his age, and very shy. He held a pair of nunchaku proudly.

"Very good. Nunchaku are flexible. Any others?"

"Are fans?" asked Aviva.

"Yes, they are."

"What's this one?" Donnie Hebert, the only black boy in the group, said. He also was David Duchamp's best friend. He was holding a padded pole with a fake blade at the end.

"That's a naginata. There are other, similar weapons. They're used like a staff and like a blade. You can get past a sword or shield, or even fight against someone on a horse. Can you tell me if it's fixed or flexible?"

"Fixed."

"Very good."

We went over all the weapons. Then we got to our feet and I separated them in to two groups, the flexible weapons and the fixed. For the fixed group, I showed them the basic blocks and strikes. Donnie, who was bigger than the rest of the group, was the only one who learned the moves right off. Most got the first three blocks and one of the strikes.

"Remember when you practice, you're not supposed to hit each other," I said to two boys, Mordechai and Brandon, who were starting to have a sword fight.

"Sorry Sensei Paul," they said.

I went over the basics with the flexible weapon group. I got them spinning their weapons in circular movements and for some we moved to figure eights. Aviva's fans could be used in straight lines, but the circles worked better. She had the wrist flexibility for it. I hoped she stuck with the fans.

"As you get better with your weapons," I told the whole group, "you'll find they are an extension of yourself. They will make the movements without weapons more graceful, too."

They looked at me blankly, so I continued.

"You've heard me talk about extension. We extend to push through a target. When we use a weapon, we don't think of where our hands are, but—where—our—weapons—are." My speaking pace slowed down. Since weapons were my primary area, I always thought of them as an extension of myself. That's how I always taught them. I knew about weapons—I had won championships with them. That poor Emo kid, Dirk Hemlock, didn't know the first thing about them, yet I trusted his word about them.

"Are we going to do anything else, Sensei?" one of the children asked, breaking the silence.

"Oh," I said. I looked at the clock on the back of the dojo wall. They had almost ten more minutes. "Let's put the weapons back in the cabinet, then we'll do some power jumping jacks." I clapped my hands. We jumped into motion after that, but my mind was on something else.

Chapter 27

We were sitting around a table at the Louisiana Pizza Kitchen at the end of the French Market. I had called Joe, Mouse, and Rufus and they all agreed to meet me after I begged a little. I had considered calling Connor, but in the end it was just the four of us.

I had ordered pizzas and they were served when the guys showed up. All the waiter had to do was to get drinks, then we were left alone.

"It's good to see all of you," I said. "We've missed you around the dojo."

"I was going to go," Mouse said. His wounds were mostly healed. Joe, also looking fully recovered, nodded. Rufus looked impassive. He had made a few classes, so I figured he knew I wasn't talking to him.

"This is about the ghosts," I said. I could tell they knew that already. "I've been concerned. They're attracted to chaos and with Mardi Gras coming up, there's going to be a lot more chaos. It could be a bloodbath."

"You think the ghosts are going to hit then?" Joe asked.

"They've been attacking. Over fifty people have died since Thanksgiving from those unexplained stab wounds. They're blaming them on gangs, but what gangs use knives? Some people are missing, maybe abducted by the things."

"Abducted?"

"Hemlock said the ghosts were try to take him with them. And that girl from the ghost tour I rescued was being carried off."

"Think they're eating the people?" Mouse asked.

"There's no missing flesh."

"But there's a lot of blood loss. Maybe that's all they can digest. They could be taking the people back to their dimension for fresh food."

"Gross," Rufus said. I nodded. We were all silent for a bit, no one was eating their pizza.

"I thought of something today." They perked up, even Rufus.

"Remember the beginning of all this? That crazy Emo kid? Dirk Hemlock."

There were nods.

"He told me that the ghosts were getting worse. And he had come to us, to me, for self-defense so he could fight them." I paused. "After I found they were real, what do you think the first thing I told him was?"

"That he was crazy?" Mouse said.

"No, to use a weapon."

"Oh yeah. That would be my first advice to anyone also."

"Yep. For home defense, a hammer will even the odds more than a year of Karate lessons."

"Don't get him started," Joe said.

"Right," I said, happy to have him in the conversation. "Anyway, he told me he tried using all sorts of weapons—silver, cold iron, holy and magical things. They just all went through them."

"Yeah, I remember you told me," Joe said.

I lifted up the bag I had on the floor. It was a paper shopping bag with handles—the longest one I could find. From it I pulled out a machete.

"Earlier tonight, not two blocks from here, I killed twenty of those things with Mr. Machete here."

They all leaned forward.

"You killed twenty of them?" Joe asked.

"You're not saying it's magic, are you?" Mouse said. "Or blessed or holy. I can't believe that from you."

"No, I wouldn't believe that from me, either. It's from the kata I do with double machetes. I came in first at the mid-Atlantic championships about fifteen years ago with them. That's about as holy as it is."

"Sounds pretty holy to me," Mouse said.

"How'd you do it, then?" Joe asked.

"Remember your first lesson on using weapons." I said. It wasn't a question. I wanted them to think about it.

"Yeah?" Mouse said.

"You all remember?"

"I think we both trained with weapons before we joined your dojo," Joe said, indicating Rufus.

"OK. Remember the first lesson I give on weapons. Think of what I tell the kids about how to use the weapons and what they're good for."

"I get it," Mouse said.

"So do I," Rufus said.

Joe looked at them.

"Extension," Mouse said.

"Oh."

"That's what it's about. That's how we can touch them, after all," I said.

Joe picked up the machete and held it on his lap, looking at it. "Of course. You extend your chi when you use a weapon," he paused. "And you got twenty of them with this? Nice extension."

"When it started getting dark tonight, I went to Ursulines. I stood around waiting at the spot where they seem to come from. Once it got fully dark, they started coming out, one at a time. I took them out, one by one as they came through their portal."

"Cool," Mouse said.

"So that's my plan. We go to some of the portals and cut them to shreds as they come through. I'm pretty sure there are four portals in the Ninth Ward. We start off with one person at each portal with swords, machetes, or whatever."

"Slicing and dicing," Mouse said.

"Exactly," I said.

"How about nunchaku or other weapons?" Joe asked.

"I think a sharp sword is more likely to kill fast. Nunchaku will break bones, but won't kill as quickly. Sharp things are the way to go." I paused. "Maybe something heavier than 'chuks. A hammer or baseball bat would work," I conceded.

"OK. So the rest of your plan?"

"Simple, when the ghosts start coming out too quickly, we run to our cars—keep those running—and we all meet in the middle. We'll rest until the ghosts get there, then we fight them together."

"All night?"

"Until we get tired. "I've got an exit strategy figured out. We'll stagger our cars and go to the one that looks safest. Only the closest one will have the keys in it and be running, though. I don't want out cars stolen while we're otherwise engaged."

Mouse chuckled at the idea. "We can keep The Lady running. No one would steal her. Besides, she idles so smoothly and quietly, you can hardly tell she's running."

"OK. One car close by, your car a little farther, the other two farther, but not running.

"This would be tomorrow night?" Joe asked.

"Yeah."

"Will it stop them?" Rufus asked.

"I'm not sure. If we make this dimension too scary for them, I hope they decide that we're too dangerous. So far they've been trying to beat just the few of us by sheer numbers. When we stopped fighting they continued killing other people.

"I honestly don't know if this is the right course of action," I said. "There are many possibilities as to what they could be and what could be happening. It's possible that our fighting them made the dimensional walls more permeable. If one died, more seemed to come through. It could also be that they're like sharks and attracted to blood. Or they could be like looters who have found an abandoned Walmart after a flood."

"That's in bad taste," Rufus said.

"I don't mean it to be. But for that last analogy, would the looters come in if they knew they were going to get chopped to pieces? Sharks would. Wolves wouldn't. Humans wouldn't, either.

"If we're not just making more holes between dimensions, then we have to hope that their intelligence is above that of sharks."

"And you don't know if this will work," Mouse said. It wasn't a question.

"Nope."

The three of them were silent for a moment.

"Eh, I'm in," Mouse said.

"Me too," Joe said. He had lifted the machete above the level of the table and was fingering the its blade.

"You should probably put that away. The management might not like their customers carrying their own cutlery," I suggested. He sighed and put it in his bag.

"Rufus, how about you?" I asked.

He put his big hands on the table. "I don't know if I can fight them. That's been your thing."

It was my turn to pause. Joe and Mouse were known quantities in this war. Rufus was new to it.

"If you join us, you'll have to learn to see and kill the things all in one night. Did you ever try to see them after we talked about how to?"

"I did." He looked embarrassed. "I saw them a few times. I practiced after you told me how. One time, Diamond and I were out at dinner, and I saw them. I hustled her away from them. She thought that was messed up."

"I've got to ask, are you seeing her?" Mouse asked. Joe looked up, interested.

"We went out a few times. But we were too different," he said glumly. "We're just friends."

"Oh," Mouse said. "I was just wondering...," he trailed off.

"What did they look like?" I asked.

"They were fine," Rufus grinned. "I mean, don't ask me that!" His grinned disappeared and he looked confused.

"I meant the ghosts."

"Oh." He chuckled. "Sorry. I thought you were talking about Diamond."

Mouse laughed and the Joe smiled. Rufus plunged on ahead.

"The ghosts looked like, well, zombies. Skinny, skin all torn up and falling off."

"What color were they?"

He looked puzzled for a second. "Some were white, some were black. Why?"

"Just curious. Research."

"We all see them differently," Mouse said.

"Oh."

"Are you in?" I asked.

We looked at him. He shut his eyes, thinking it over. "My grandmother does that voodoo," he said.

I nodded. I noticed Mouse was looking away, as if he was embarrassed.

"I swore I wouldn't do anything when you all got started in this. I changed my mind, though. I was worried about someone I wanted to protect."

"Rufus, the city is under attack. It's an invasion and people are getting killed. It's not gangs, it's ghosts."

"I know."

"You'll be protecting Diamond, your family, the kids you work with, people you've never met."

He looked at me angrily, or at least resentfully. Finally, he nodded.

"If I can fight them tonight."

"Let's go see if you can touch them."

We finished the last of our pizza and went up Ursulines. I hadn't lied, I had killed around twenty of them. They had kept coming as I sliced away. I sort of got into a zone—like doing a kata really well. When they stopped coming through, I put my machetes away and started making my calls.

There were two of them on Uruslines, though. All I saw were a couple floating points. The guys saw them, though.

"What are they doing?" I asked Rufus. I could have asked the other two, but I wanted Rufus to get used to seeing them.

"Just wandering, it looks like."

"Aimlessly?"

"Seems like it."

"Good. They're probably looking for their buddies." I clapped him on his shoulder. "Time to go to war. Go after the closer one. Remember, keep calm and extend. Watch out for the claws."

He breathed deeply to center himself, then strode forward.

Although I could only see one side of his attack, it looked impressive. He got close to the flaw, then dropped to a low back stance. He kicked to around knee height, grabbed a hand or forearm, pulled down in a wide circle, and kneed forward. The light disappeared.

"Nice," Joe said.

"Yeah, good job, big guy," Mouse agreed.

I pulled the machete out of the bag. The other flaw was heading our way.

"Rufus, remember your wakizashi training?" I used the Japanese term for the short sword.

He held out his hand and I tossed the weapon to him, handle first. He caught it easily and took to steps to the zombie-form of the ghost as he saw it and pivoted. With the machete held in a reverse grip, he spun and the flaw was gone.

"Excellent," Mouse said. "This plan could really work."

"I've got to try that," Joe said. There was a gleam in his eye.

Rufus handed the machete back to me, and I slipped it in the bag. He wasn't breathing hard, which was good. He would have no problem with keeping calm in battle.

"What didn't I see?" I asked. This had been a burning question of mine for weeks now. All I could do was feel the damage I was doing or the damage the ghosts did on me. All I saw was a little glint of light. It wasn't even bright light. It certainly wasn't in any specific shape. For this whole time, I had been blind to them. I wanted to know how it looked to kill them.

"Rufus went up to the ghost, spun around and slashed. The machete cut diagonally across its chest. He brought it up and severed the thing's arm. Then it disappeared. There wasn't any blood or anything," Mouse said. He laughed, "It looked cooler than I made it sound, though."

"Is that what you two saw?"

"Yep," Joe said. Rufus nodded.

We started walking away from the bakery on Ursulines. Too bad they were closed. The looked like a nice little place, with coffee, tables, and probably more than doughnuts and beignets. I would have to go there some time in the daytime. I wondered what the staff at the bakery would think about ghosts appearing in front of their shop. Or what they would think of some self-styled Karate superheroes hanging out at night and fighting the good fight.

"So now what?" Mouse asked.

"We go home, practice with bladed weapons, remember to extend our chi, and tomorrow we'll meet before it gets dark and head to the Lower Ninth Ward."

"We should find some more and try it tonight."

I shook my head. "I don't know where any more are, unless we go to the Ninth Ward. And by now there will be way to many of them for the plan. Besides, if they communicate with each other, we don't want to tip our hand."

"If your plan works, do you think they'll stop coming?"

"No. I think it'll be like the Japanese in World War Two. Two atomic bombs were made because the experts thought the Japanese High Command wouldn't believe the bomb was possible, since it was so much more powerful than anything that had come before it. The second bomb was also so there would be no question that it wasn't a one-time deal."

"So we'll have to come back?"

"Tomorrow we'll kill as many as possible. The next night we'll do the same. I don't know about after that. It might take a while for them to learn."

"You want us to do this every night?" Rufus said. "For how long?"

"I'm not sure; a few days, I think."

"I hope they learn fast," he said.

"I'm in," Mouse said. "As many nights as needed."

"Me too," Joe said.

"I'll do what I can," Rufus said.

"Does everyone have weapons?"

"I've got a sword at home," Mouse said.

"Anyone else?"

The other two shook their heads.

"Then we go back to the dojo. Time to raid the weapons cabinet."

Chapter 28

Two short swords in the trunk of The Lady, Mouse went back to the
French Quarter, to Fiorello's. She was there. He still didn't know if she was
Blade Pryncess 718, since she had been very coy when chatting. Tonight he
was going to ask her.

She wasn't there when he found a table and sat down. To start with, he
ordered a Diet Coke from a waitress who had black, spiked hair, piercings, and
tattoos. While he sipped at it, he looked around. The girl he liked wasn't there.
No one was looking at him

He pulled out his new Blackberry mobile device and got into Yahoo
Messenger. She was on.

Mungor : Hey hey. Guess where I'm chatting from?

BladePryncess718: IDK

Mungor : Fiorello's. What should I order?

BladePryncess718: OMG, really?

Mungor : What should I order?

BladePryncess718: The gumbos good 2nite.

Mungor : You should join me

BladePryncess718: lol

Mungor : Seriously. We could go somewhere else if you'd like.

BladePryncess718: Why?

Mungor : Because tomorrow I'll be a superhero again.

BladePryncess718: Wow.

Mungor : And I'd like to meet you before I fight hundreds of ghosts

There was a pause.

Mungor : Still there?

BladePryncess718: B at coops place in fifteen mints.

Mouse's heart jumped. He got his bill and left. Coop's Place was just
around the corner. He could make it there in minutes, but he felt like running.

Inside it was loud. It was a weeknight, but no tables were to be had. He
found two stools at the bar and waited.

About twenty minutes later, she showed up. He was right, she was the girl
from Fiorello's. She saw him at the bar and made a beeline to him.

"Hi," he said.

"Hi."

"My name's Bob."

"I'm Megan."

"What?"

"Megan. My name is Megan."

"It's too loud in here. Want to go somewhere else?"

She nodded and they left. They walked along for a little while, silently.

"You're really fighting ghosts tomorrow night?"

"Yep. It's going to be the big battle."

"You know, I heard you guys talking about the ghosts. Then people started talking. It's all over the Quarter that there's something going on."

Mouse shrugged. "I guess we weren't too good at keeping secrets."

"Is it for real?"

"Yeah."

"I can't believe it," she said, yet Mouse could tell she wanted to believe. She had probably been the first one to start the rumors of ghosts invading the Big Easy and some crazy people fighting them. He could see how the stories would grow. Now she would get the whole story.

Chapter 29

"Hi Grandma Bess. It's me, Rufus," Rufus said. He was sitting on the new sofa in his small living room. It was one of the purchases he made with his insurance money. Before Katrina, his furniture was all used. It was easier to find new pieces than used with the state of the city. Although it looked nice, the new sofa wasn't as comfortable as the old one.

"Zat my Rufus?" she asked.

"Yes ma'am," he said.

"Rufus all time be my good little boy," she said.

"How are you doing, Grandma Bess?" When he talked on the phone with her had to remind her often who he was. Calling her "grandma" put him in a category of only him and his two cousins.

"Cain't complain. They treat me good here."

She didn't sound bad. When she answered the phone, her more colloquial greeting made him think she was going backwards again. When he was growing up in her house, she wouldn't let him talk like that. If he learned some slang or talked with an accent, she would correct him. If he did it again, she'd make him repeat the proper phrasing a hundred time. She had a little counter she'd click each time to make sure he said it exactly one hundred times.

Her Alzheimer's made her revert to how she spoke before she was a mother, herself. She had cleaned up her act, but her discipline was falling apart.

"Grandma Bess, remember those nights you took me out to the bayou? When there was all that dancing and those drum?"

"What you know 'bout that?"

"Sometimes I woke up and watched. I remember seeing you dance and lead the people."

She was silent.

"Grandma, I got a question about ghosts."

"No, little Rufus, you *have* a question about ghosts."

"Yes ma'am. I have a question. Have you been seeing any more ghosts?"

"Spirits talk to me, boy, you knows that."

"Can your voodoo help control ghosts?"

"Control ghosts?"

"Can it help you see them or touch them?"

"Ain't no such thing as voodoo. I don't know what you talkin' about," she said.

"Grandma Bess. You were into voodoo—I remember. I never asked you about it, but you even brought some of it home. Now I want to know what you know about ghosts."

"Ghosts be bad medicine, boy. You leave 'em alone."

"What can you tell me about them?" he persisted.

"Who dis?"

"It's me, Rufus."

"Rufus? He just a little boy. You cain't talk to him."

"Grandma Bess," he said. "It's me, Rufus."

"He ain't heah."

He tried a little more, but she put up a good front. He suspected she wasn't having an episode. It was just her way of avoiding the issue.

Calling Diamond crossed his mind, but he didn't go through with the idea. He went to bed. He had to work the next day anyway.

Chapter 30

We met at the dojo an hour before sundown. It was a chilly night, which was good. We wouldn't overheat, at least. Mouse and Rufus looked worried, but Joe looked happy.

"OK," I said. "Everyone ready?"

They nodded. Joe was looking too excited.

"Joe?"

"There's a little portal up in Mid City. Like the one on Ursulines, not like in the Lower Ninth. I went up there last night and killed twenty-tree of them. They were already out and just roaming up and down the street. I used my katana, and it went through them like butter. I didn't have to pick them off one at a time." He said this proudly. He was competing with me, that was it. I should have figured it. He wanted to kill more of them than I did.

"Way to go," Mouse said, encouraged.

"Hmmm, I hope they aren't in touch with each other," I said.

"You killed all those on Ursulines. I don't see how this is different."

"Good point," I forced a smile. Mine was a test case. It was unavoidable if I was going to find out if we could use weapons on them. I hoped that the ghosts didn't communicate that we were using weapons now. "That's a lot of them. I'm impressed," I said. Joe grinned, sheepishly.

"Weapons check. What do you all have?" I took out a whetstone to sharpen any blade that wasn't up to my standards. My machetes were honed to razor sharpness, and I had a Chinese *darn do* temple sword as a backup weapon.

Rufus had a naginata. In several tournaments he competed with a similar weapon, the kwan do, the horse leg-cutter which had a heavier blade. I gave him two machetes that I had bought that day. Joe had a katana and a wakizashi short sword. Mouse pulled his sword from the back of his car. It was an oversized Scottish claymore.

"Nice," I said. "Can I see it?"

He handed it over and I hefted it. It was heavier than even the naginata and a bit dull. I started sharpening it. "What do you have for a backup weapon?"

He crossed his arms and reached over his shoulders, pulling two short, straight ninja-style swords that were somewhere between the length of a katana and a wakizashi. Those were incredibly sharp.

After I finished with his claymore, I handed it back and then opened my gym bag.

"And I have some more," I said. I pulled out a box of miscellaneous weapons I had around the dojo.

"Dibs on the punch dagger," Joe said. A punch dagger is a short knife one fitted in the base of one's hand and the blade protruded between the middle and ring finger.

"Oh yeah," said Mouse holding up a scary-looking sickle with a heavier blade and a sharp wedge shaped blade where a hand guard would be on a normal sword or knife. "Buffy used one of these in the episode 'Anne'."

"Something like that," I said. "It's a Hunga Munga. I think it's from the Congo."

"Sweet."

"Don't you have something like that? A Gurkha headhunter knife?"

"A kukri—it's at home," he said.

"So you use my toys and not your own." I shook my head. "You're getting farther from that black belt every day."

He snorted.

"See anything you like, Rufus?" I held out the box. He poked through, then pulled out a collapsible baton—the kind the police use called the Asp. He flicked it open, then collapsed it.

"Good choice," I said. I pulled my own collapsible baton out of my back pocket. It was something I've had and kept on my person for years. Unlike the Asp, mine was made of telescoping springs. It snapped with more torque than the stiff baton favored by the police. I snapped it open, traced a figure eight in the air, then put it away.

"It's not an edged weapon," Mouse pointed out.

"It's a back-up to use if you happen to lose all your other weapons. Use them on knees or the face."

"And more presents," I said. I handed out walkie talkies. They had a two-mile range, although they looked like the toys we had when I was a kid. "Clip these to your belts and when you have to go to the rendezvous point, let us know. If you get into trouble, let us know."

"And if you feel lonely and just want to talk, let us know so we can laugh at you while we're saving the world," Mouse said. He was trying to put his second short sword away over his shoulder, but not getting it into the scabbard at the right angle.

"Shit," he said. He took off his coat and sheathed the sword with ease.

I gave them some bottled water. In the dojo, I was always on everyone's case to keep hydrated.

I went over the plan one more time, gave them maps that I printed up from Google with routes and the rendezvous point marked in green highlighter. Then we got in our cars and headed off.

*   *   *

"Anyone see anything yet?" Mouse asked over the walkie talkie. Darkness had fully fallen. I could see the glow of the city, but most of the power was still out in the Lower Ninth.

"Nothing here," I said.

"Nothing here," Rufus said.

"Same here," Joe said.

"When you see something, let us know," said to the group.

A few minutes passed. I thought about how nice it would be to get some coffee and flirt with LaTonya.

I had spent the day taking care of things, myself. I had gone to the bakery on Ursulines, the Croissant d'Or Pattisserie. When I left the bakery, I noticed that it was a couple doors down from a place called the Haunted Hotel. How had we missed that? Too bad it was in the opposite direction of the portal to the ghosts. They would have had quite the story to tell people with the ghosts emerging from their lobby.

At the Croissant d'Or I had some coffee and a small loaf of multi-grain bread. I spread butter on the warm bread that I had broken with my hands instead of cutting it. I was put in mind of the ending of "A Small, Good Thing," by Raymond Carver. I loved the endings of his stories, but this was my favorite. A simple baker easing the pain of a couple who had lost a child.

I didn't want to think about endings, though, so I pulled out my cell phone and called a few people. I wasn't saying good bye, but I did want to let a few people know I was thinking of them. The bakery had good coffee and excellent baked goods. If I survived the night, I'd be back.

"They're starting," Rufus's deep voice announced through the walkie talkie.

I looked. Two glints of light had appeared.

"Same here," Mouse said.

"I'm on them," Joe said. I added my agreement and went at the beings behind the flaws in the air.

The two of them were just the beginning. Two more were right behind them, then four of them. I kept up with them for a while, slicing them as they came in. More crowded through and I had to fight them in groups. I let them surround me, then I turned into a whirling dervish—blades flashing. Any time one got close, and they keep pushing toward me, it got a slash or a stab.

I was again in a zone. This was what katas should be, instead of punching or kicking the air. There should be resistance and threat.

"I'm going to have to head to the rendezvous," I heard Mouse say over the walkie-talkie. He was breathless.

"I'll meet you there," Rufus responded after a few seconds.

"I'm going to keep going here," I gasped. I was holding the *talk* button with one hand and fighting with the other.

"Me too," Joe said.

"Only for five minutes," I called. I didn't want Joe to try to be a hero or to compete with me. And the other two would need reinforcements if too many ghosts reached the guys.

Five minutes and probably another forty ghosts down and I fought my way to my car. I sped to the rendezvous point. The spot was city block that had been flooded into an empty field. It was close to where Lowell had been killed.

They had forgotten the plan about the cars. Rufus and Mouse had both parked on the same street. I stopped my car a block away, turning it around to face away from the lot. I had misgivings about turning off the engine and putting the keys in my pocket, but I did. I quickly walked to where Mouse and Rufus stood. I drank half a bottle of water on my way.

"Joe, how's it going?" I called over the walkie talkie. He didn't respond. I reached the other two.

"Any word from Joe?"

"Nothing," Rufus said. He was calm, but Mouse was still breathing heavily. He was sharpening his claymore. His coat was off and the straps to the sheaths of his two short swords made an X on his chest.

"Everything go OK?"

"Yeah," Mouse said. "I couldn't believe how many there were."

"Kill a lot of them?"

"Oh yeah. Too many, but more showed up. I had to leave."

"Me too," Rufus agreed. He didn't have his naginata with him, just the two machetes.

"Lights," Mouse said. I looked. A vehicle was coming. It parked a block beyond my car.

"Joe?" I called into the walkie talkie. There was no answer.

A couple minutes later, though, Joe approached us at a trot.

"Sorry, I dropped my walkie talkie and wakisashi. How's everyone?"

"We're good. See any on the way over?"

"A bunch were following me. I drove slowly so they could see where I was going. I saw bunch more coming from that direction," he pointed in the direction of his truck.

"Those are probably the ones who followed me," I said. I looked in the direction of the other two portals. "I think I see some." I pointed.

"What's the plan?" Joe asked. "Let them come to us or do we go to them?"

"The best defense," Mouse started.

We headed in the direction of the nearest group. It wasn't a large group, maybe thirty ghosts. Our blades went through them in no time at all. They hadn't surrounded us, we had surrounded them and fought in to the center. A few had squeezed out of the crush, but quick jabs and slashes got rid of them.

By then, the second group had made it to near where we had all met up. We went back and did the same thing to the larger group.

We kept at them for a while, until there weren't any ghosts left. By the end, we were all panting.

"Shit," Mouse gasped. "We did it."

"More may come through at the portals," I cautioned. "We should go back and get any stragglers."

"Ooh, you had to say it," Mouse said.

"Let's go back to the portals and see if more are coming through. If there are only a few, we fight them. If there are a lot of them, we try to lead them here again."

"Where do we meet if there aren't many?"

I looked at my watch. It was only nine-thirty. "Want to get some dinner? Let's hang out at the portals until ten and then meet up somewhere?"

"Sure. Where do you want to meet up?"

"Fiorello's?" Mouse suggested.

"Liuzzo's?" Joe said.

"How about something on Magazine?" I said, since that was closer to my house.

"I like the French Market Cafe," Rufus said, keeping to the French Quarter theme. "I used to work there."

Joe shrugged. "It's got clean restrooms."

"And it was one of the few restaurants open right after Katrina. I had some very good gumbo there when I came back."

We had gone from being ghost hunters to being New Orleanians and concerned about where we'd eat. I looked at my watch. "OK...we'll hang out at the portals until ten, then meet up at the French Market Cafe. I hope they're open."

"Yeah, they will be," Rufus said.

"OK. And Joe, still got your cell phone?"

"Yeah."

"If you get in any trouble, call one of us. The rest of you guys, keep your walkie talkies on."

*   * *

At my portal, I killed five more ghosts that had appeared while I was away. After half an hour, no more seemed to be coming out so I headed off. On the way I caught up to Mouse in The Lady. We were the first there. We got a table and ordered beer. Joe soon joined us, with Rufus coming in five minutes later.

The guys looked exhausted—I hadn't noticed their condition when we met in the field. It must have been too dark to tell. Joe was favoring his right arm. He had a small cut on his face. Mouse was pale and Rufus was limping. Both had puncture wounds, but they didn't look serious. I was the only one of the three who wasn't injured. I thought about pointing that out to Joe, but we weren't competing, although he seemed to think so. Most of them had lost a weapon or two. Mouse had his three swords, but the hunga munga was gone. Joe only had the katana left. Rufus was down to one machete and the Asp. I had everything I had started with. I never even used my collapsible baton or sword. It was all machetes for me.

I had a good appetite and the food was tasty and filling. There wasn't much conversation. We ate and went our separate ways. They all had work in the morning. It had been quite a night.

Afterwards, I walked to Ursulines. There weren't any ghosts roaming that street. My machetes and sword were in my car, but I had my baton.

Chapter 31

We went out the next night, but there were only about forty ghosts total. Either we had killed the whole population, or we had discouraged them. I think we scared them and only a few brave or foolish beings ventured to our world. After a couple hours, we split up. Mouse and Rufus went home and I checked out Ursulines. Joe went to the spot he had found in Mid-City.

Over the next few nights, I went to the Lower Ninth Ward early in the evening and a few hours before dawn. A few ghosts roamed the streets, and I took them out. I didn't want them to return to their world reporting that we were vulnerable again. I wanted the creatures from that dimension to decide once and for all that our dimension was too dangerous. I also found some of the weapons my team had left—a short sword, a machete, and a broken naginata.

Eventually, I went there only on random nights. After a couple months and only seeing and killing thirteen ghosts, none reappeared.

*   * *

The 2007 Mardi Gras had the typical problems of drunks fighting on Bourbon Street; a shooting near the parade route; and a tragic falling death at the Superdome during one of the balls following one of the super krewe parades. Before Mardi Gras, there was more of the same political bickering about what parades to allow, what parade routes to open, and if curfews were needed.

The crowds were about twice those of the year before, and since more people had returned to the city, there were more servers in restaurants and hotels were better staffed. There were complaints, but those were from people who were expecting the city to be back to normal. They were probably the same type of people who complained before Katrina.

Over Carnival and through Mardi Gras, I cruised the French Quarter to protect the revelers from the ghosts. A few roamed the streets, making it to near Lafitte's Blacksmith Shop, but I made sure they didn't hurt anyone. As far as I could tell, there were no deaths or even attacks that could have been caused by the ghosts. I kept the machetes in the car in case I saw a group of them. I was only fighting one at a time, not hundreds. I used my baton or bare hands.

I didn't know if they'd be back. But I knew one thing: Hurricanes, low enrollment at the dojo, too many part-time jobs to have a social life, it didn't matter. I was a New Orleanian. It was my town and I was going to protect it the best I could.